Billionaire Lumberjack's Baby

Gwyn McNamee

BILLIONAIRE LUMBERJACK's BABY

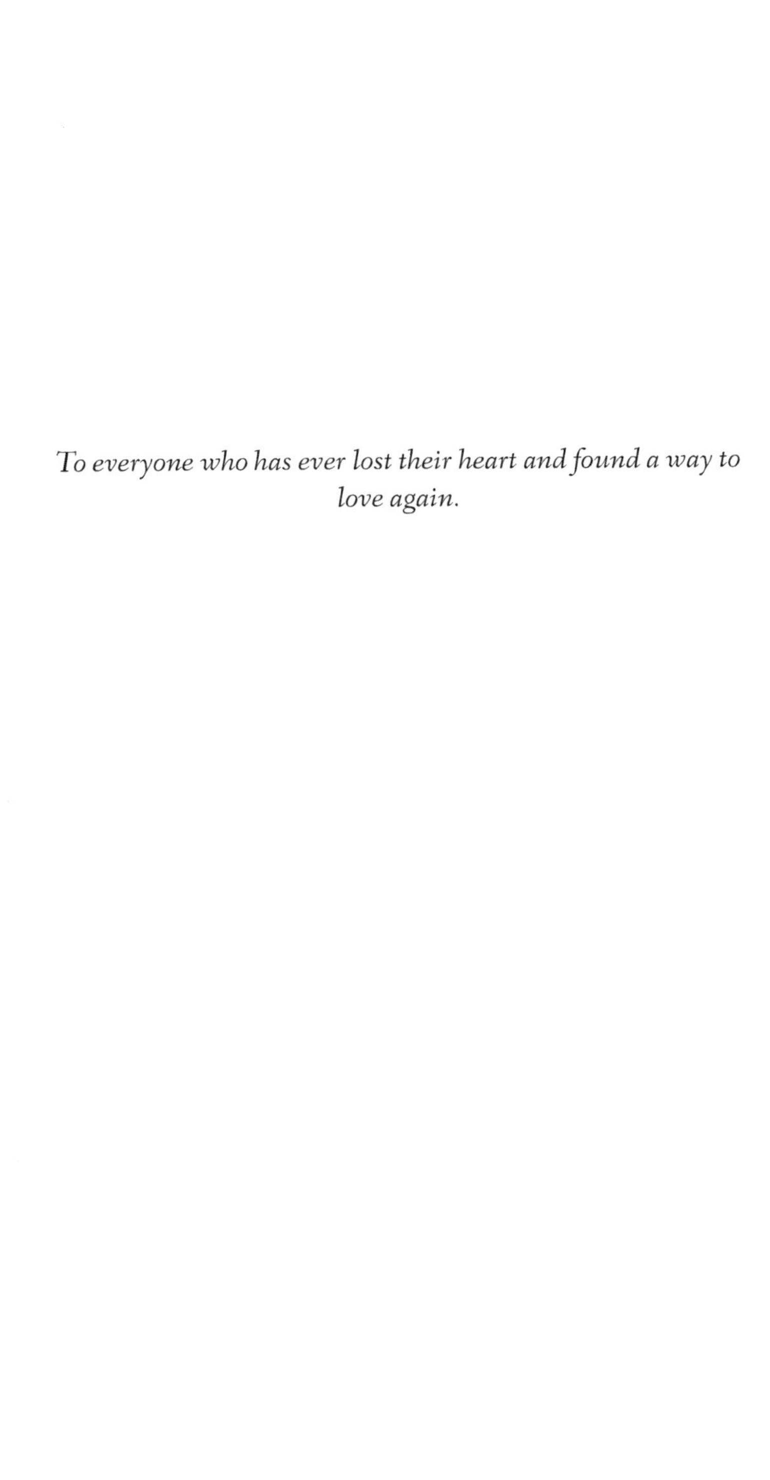

To everyone who has ever lost their heart and found a way to love again.

BEFORE YOU READ

This book contains content that may be triggering for some readers.

If you would like to learn more about the content warnings for this book, please visit Gwyn's website: https://www.gwynmcnamee.com/lumberjacksinlove

Chapter One

WELLS

Thick, black clouds billow above me, filling the heavens with the same tumultuous rage surging through my blood. Lightning rips open the sky, illuminating the heavy, dark woods around me for a brief moment, and the thunder rolls so close that it reverberates in my chest and shakes the soaked ground beneath my feet.

I slam the axe into the towering pine again, lodging the blade deep into the trunk, tearing open the bark and burrowing into the flesh, the same way I'm being ripped apart from the inside out.

Another flash of lightning rents the air, this one close enough for the electricity to crackle around me.

"You should go inside, Wells."

My fingers tighten on the axe handle, now slick from the rain. "I know, Di."

These summer storms on the mountain are the most beautiful—and the deadliest. The last place anyone should be is outside right now, holding a goddamn axe. If I wanted to live, if my life meant anything at all, I might listen to Diana and retreat to the safety of the cabin walls, but I've been an empty shell for two years.

I'd welcome the release right now—the sharp bite of pain, the electricity surging through my body, and then... sweet relief from the sheer agony of going on like this.

"You shouldn't be out here, Wells."

Muscles burning, hands blistered and stinging, body drenched by sweat and the cool rain—this is the only place I *can* be right now.

I swing the axe again, chopping wildly, blow after blow, until the massive pine finally releases the telltale creak, signaling it's close to falling.

So am I.

Close to jumping off the edge of the canyon to the raging waters of the river that flows at the bottom of it or standing out in the middle of the clearing, holding this metal axe to the sky. Whatever will get me there quickest, whatever will take away this anguish.

"This isn't you, Wells."

Diana's voice rings in my ears again, quickly drowned out by another rumble of thunder shaking the ground.

"It wasn't me..."

Before.

Everyone said it would get better. That eventually, I could go back to living, that this pain I carry, day in and day out, would eventually ebb. But all time has done is allowed the wound to fester, to hurt even more, to infect every fiber of my being. And now, I've reached the point of no return.

One more swoop of the axe and the tree releases a thick crack and starts tipping, only it doesn't go the way it should, the way I've notched it to. It starts leaning toward me ominously. The canopy of green hovers overhead, a beautiful piece of nature that's stood strong for over a hundred years but now threatens to crush anything in its path.

"Move, Wells!"

Her command comes strong enough for her to be standing immediately next to me, screaming in my ear.

I should jump out of the way, lunge to the side, and avoid the oncoming massive trunk, but instead, I stand on the forest floor and wait for the sweet liberation from all of this.

The wind picks up, swirling the scent of the wet grass, the damp moss, the cleansing rain—her favorite scents, the reason she loved being up here so much rather than in the city. The very things she commented on the last time we were up here together and watched a storm like this one roll in.

Her presence envelops me so completely, the gust so strong, it's like a physical push, knocking me to the side, and I dive out of the way just as the trunk of the massive tree falls right where I was standing.

I slam into the ground and stare at it—what could have been my vehicle to her, to them. Hot tears stream down my cheeks, mixing with the cool rain, and I release an agonized scream that fills the night.

"Why, God? FUCKING WHY?"

It's the same question I've asked a million times over the last two years.

What did I do to deserve this type of punishment, to have Him take them from me? What?

No matter how many times I ask it, I never get an answer. Only more pain.

I struggle to my feet and stumble to pick up my axe, then start hacking away at the fallen trunk, pouring all my anger, all my hatred of God and this world, all my frustration into the single act of violence.

Splinters of bark and wood fly up around me as the rain makes my hands slip on the axe handle, but I somehow maintain my grip—at least on that, but definitely not on reality. I haven't had that in so fucking long that I don't even remember what it feels like.

"It will get better, Wells. I promise."

Diana's assurance settles over me like a warm blanket, and for one brief moment, I can breathe without pain in my chest. But that warm, fuzzy feeling she always brought disintegrates just as quickly, doused by the honk of a horn.

Honk.

I freeze with the axe in mid-air, about to strike again. "What the fuck?"

Honk.

Honk.

The sound carries through the valley, echoing off the rock, a familiar sound I could do without hearing for the rest of my life. Still distant, yet near enough for me to hear it, which means it's far too close.

Who the fuck would be coming up here now, today of all days?

I climb over the felled tree, tightening my fist on the axe as I make my way toward the road. Every step ramps up my anger until my entire body vibrates the same way the thunder does around me. Trudging through the thick woods, my rage now redirects at whatever asshole decided they needed to invade my privacy.

Lightning shoots from the sky and strikes a tree up

ahead. It bursts into flames, the crack so loud I stagger away from it. Flames leap against the almost-black sky, but the pouring rain quickly dissipates the conflagration.

The smell of charred wood fills my nose as the honk grows louder.

They're coming up the damn mountain.

I make it to the edge of the road. The hard-packed ground loosely covered with gravel isn't easy to traverse, which means whoever is coming up here must have a definitive purpose or they wouldn't bother.

Hidden in the trees, I wait for the intruder to make the turn that will bring them into view. A black sedan turns the corner to my right and approaches slowly, the storm making the already-dangerous road even more so.

I can't make out the driver or license plate through the deluge, but it continues past me up the hill toward the cabin, intent on its destination. And they're going to turn right the fuck back around as soon as I get up there, if they know what's good for them.

This isn't the day for visitors, and anyone with any common sense would understand that and stay far away.

I trudge back through the woods, the most direct route to the cabin, even though walking the road would be far easier.

Easy isn't what I need right now.

My entire life was *easy*. Everything handed to me on a silver platter. All the hard work I did supported by an already billion-dollar business. A massive safety net under me at all times to catch me if I fell.

But it didn't do me any good when I needed it.

When they needed it...

So, I don't need easy anymore. What I need is the trees

around me, the cocoon of darkness they provide, lit only by lightning every few minutes and filled with the sounds of the forest creatures and the low rumbles of thunder.

Whoever the hell is in that car has a fucking death wish, maybe the same one I have today. They should have known better than to come up, but now that they're here, they're going to have to deal with me.

"Be nice, Wells."

Diana's familiar chastisement makes me snort and shake my head, ducking to avoid a branch in my way.

"I'm always nice, Di."

My typical response whenever I lose my temper floats from my lips so easily that it even draws a smile before I remember why I don't say it anymore.

Because she's gone.

They're gone.

The familiar gloom that has become my constant companion for the last two years settles back over me instantly, and the closer I advance toward the cabin, the more I allow my anger to consume me.

Whoever decided to interrupt me today is going to regret it.

LAUREL

Lightning streaks across the sliver of sky visible between the towering trees that canopy what is supposedly a road, quickly followed by a crack of thunder so close that it rattles the windows. Rain continues to pelt the metal loudly, the constant pinging so fast it almost becomes a roar enveloping the car.

I clutch the handle on the door and suck in a deep breath, trying to calm my racing heart. An impossible task when the forest surrounds us, closing in on what can only be called a rustic path—definitely not a "road" by any civilized means.

The farther we drive, the tighter I cling to the supple leather, as if my death grip on it might keep me safe from whatever lurks beyond the confines of the luxury vehicle.

Where the hell are we?

I lean forward slightly toward Allen, the driver tasked with bringing me up the mountain. "Are you sure this is the right way?"

He glances at me quickly in the rearview mirror, his kind hazel eyes offering me an apology even without the words. The old man gives a sharp nod and honks the horn again. "Yes, ma'am. I've been up here a few times over the last couple of years to bring documents and other personnel to see Mr. Lockwood. This is definitely the right way."

"Good God." I drop back on the plush leather seat and blow the hair out of my face with a heavy sigh.

What the hell is he doing living in the middle of nowhere, up a mountain, hours from Denver and corporate headquarters?

I thought billionaires like Lockwood reveled in all things ostentatious and lived in the lap of luxury, but this is about as far from that as is humanly possible.

Even the small town we passed coming to the mountain wouldn't be considered civilization to most people. After living in the city my entire life, this is as close to nature as I've ever been—and farther than I care to ever be.

Especially under these circumstances...

I peek at my companion in the backseat, who's still sound asleep. "This is so not what I signed up for."

The car hits a dip in the road, bumping me wildly in my seat despite the belt pulled across me. I tighten my grip on the handle just in time for a second jolt.

Allen glances at me in the mirror again. "Sorry about that, ma'am. The road is not a road at all." He chuckles and shakes his head. "I think Mr. Lockwood prefers it that way. Keeps too many people from coming up."

"He really lives up here all alone?"

Of course, people talk...but I always wondered how much was true and how much was simply rumors.

It would be impossible not to hear about what happened to Wells Lockwood, only son and heir to the Lockwood Brewing fortune, and I guess if I were in his shoes, I might want to hole myself up somewhere and avoid reality.

But *this*...is a bit extreme.

The man could *buy* any house he wanted anywhere on the planet. He could purchase his own damn island and live the lavish lifestyle he did in Denver, with servants waiting on him hand and foot, the world literally at his fingertips.

Yet...he's here...

The driver nods, swerving the car slightly to avoid another dip in the road now filled with rainwater. "Yep. And he isn't too keen on visitors, either. It's why he likes us to honk on the way up and announce we're coming." He peeks at me in the rearview mirror, his kind old eyes worried. "Is he expecting you?"

Hell no.

Mr. Lockwood is most certainly *not* expecting this visit today—or any day. And I would have preferred to make a simple phone call with this information, but Mr. Landry said Mr. Lockwood doesn't have a phone up here—on purpose—and this had to be done in person.

Which I can understand, given the situation.

Still, Landry would be much better suited to deliver this particular news.

"No, he isn't expecting me, but I was told this couldn't wait."

Allen offers a shrug. "Well, it's a good thing we got up here when we did. This storm's a doozy, and this road will be impassable if the rain keeps coming. Sometimes, it completely washes out."

I roll my eyes and huff again. "Lovely."

This is the type of place horror movies and nightmares are made. Remote. Dark and foreboding. Danger lurking in every shadow and behind every tree. The massive thunder-storm doesn't help things.

Poor Allen can barely see two feet in front of him, even with the wipers going full tilt.

"Go work for Lockwood," they said.

"It'll be a great opportunity," they said.

Yeah, right.

Drumming my fingers on the door, I stare at the dense forest through a wall of falling rain, trying to imagine the handsome man in the perfectly tailored suit in the photo on the wall at corporate living like this.

I turn back toward the driver. "Have you ever met him?"

The old man, who has been my companion the last several hours on our drive from Denver, shakes his head. "Not other than driving up and dropping someone or something off and seeing him open the door. Most of the time, I just leave it on the steps and knock so he knows to come get it. And if I'm dropping Mr. Landry or someone else to meet with Mr. Lockwood, I wait in the car until they're done, then drive back down the mountain. He prefers not to have to interact with anybody whenever possible."

So, this should be fun.

I drum my nails again, debating whether or not to ask the next question, but curiosity gets the better of me. If this man has been around as long as he claims, he'll likely know.

"What about his wife? Did you ever meet her?"

Allen stiffens slightly, then nods. "A few times, at headquarters. Years ago. Before..."

The emotion in his words prevents me from asking any follow-ups. A tragedy like that isn't something anyone wants to discuss, and guilt turns acid in my stomach for even bringing it up in the first place.

It isn't any of your business.

I need to do what I was sent here for and get the hell back to Denver, not explore the personal life of the enigmatic Wells Lockwood.

We turn a bend in the road, still enclosed between solid walls of thick brush and dense trees. Goosebumps break out across my skin. The hair on the back of my neck stands on end, and a shiver rolls through me that chills my blood as I stare into the pitch-black forest.

Something's watching us.

I can feel it as surely as I can my own heart thundering against my ribcage.

What the hell is out there?

Bears. Wolves. Mountain lions.

Angry billionaires.

I shift uneasily as we roll past the spot that gives me the heebie-jeebies and make our way farther up the mountain. "You're sure he'll be here?"

From the looks of things, we're not near anywhere a human could live. It would be almost impossible to even walk through the woods that surround us, let alone *survive* up here.

Allen chuckles. "Ma'am, as far as I know, Mr. Lockwood hasn't left this cabin in years other than perhaps to go into Lockwood Falls to get supplies. He'll be there."

"I hope so."

I want to get this over and done with as quickly as possible, so I can get back to Denver to the job I was actually *hired* to do instead of *this*.

We turn another corner, and the forest in front of us opens up slightly, revealing a small clearing getting pummeled by the rain without the benefit of the tree canopy over it.

The driver pulls forward, and a cabin comes into view on our right. Far smaller than I would've anticipated, the box building with a slanted A-line roof sits nestled in the break of the dense woods.

I stare at the tiny building—the only sign of human life I've seen for the last hour since we turned up the mountain "road." My stomach tightens. "This is it?"

Horror movies and nightmares.

The driver slows, puts the car into park, and nods. "Yep. This is it."

How can anybody live like this?

I'm about to ask the question, but motion flickers at the edge of my vision and I turn my head toward the woods on the left. Something small scurries through the underbrush, nearly impossible to see through the driving rain.

I shift across the seat slightly and narrow my eyes at it to try to get a better look. The bushes shift again, and a man steps out from between the trees—shirtless, tan pants soaked, long hair plastered around his face, down to his shoulders, a massive axe in his hand.

That same shiver rolls through me again as the fury in his gaze hits me even from thirty feet away through the downpour.

Before I can react, he storms toward the car, axe raised, ready to strike.

Chapter Two

WELLS

I step out from the woods, axe high, prepared to chase off whomever dared come up the mountain today with anything I have to in order to get them gone.

All the wrath and resentment for the world I've been fighting has built to a point I can't keep it contained. Not today.

"It will get better, Wells."

Diana says it like the words actually mean something, like it will somehow quell the rage boiling inside me.

"Be nice."

I won't be nice today. I don't have it in me anymore. Diana can judge me and be the voice in my head, reminding me of how badly I'm handling all of this, but it won't change anything. She and Maribel will still be gone. I'll still be here alone with my guilt and agony.

And I can't do that if I'm not *alone.*

Which means getting rid of these trespassers so I can go back to wallowing.

I approach the car, and my gaze lands on the front license plate.

LKWOOD1

Fuck.

It's one of ours.

The torrent of water falling from the onyx sky pelts the top of the vehicle and the windshield, obscuring the occupants, but if it's someone from the brewery, slamming this blade into the car would only end up costing me.

I slowly lower my weapon and take another step forward. My boots sink into the mud, and I strain to try to see into the driver's side window as the cool rain hits my bare skin.

Automatic wipers slash across the windshield, and a man I vaguely recognize as being up here before motions to the back seat, indicating this time there's someone in the car with him.

Fucking hell. If it's Landry again...

"Be nice, Wells."

I take another step toward the vehicle, and the back door opens, the rain violently pouring off the roof like the falls into the canyon on the property that gave the small town at the base of the mountain its name.

Black stilettos with red soles slide below the door, thin spiked heels settling into the mud. Auburn hair appears next over the top of the darkly tinted window, followed by Caribbean blue eyes peeking over the frame.

The woman stands fully, her pale, freckled skin and hair instantly soaked. Instead of stepping out farther, she keeps her body behind the door, as if that piece of metal will protect her from me.

Maybe she fucking needs the shield.

Sneering, I advance another step, so she'll hear me over

the rain hitting the roof. "Who the hell are you, and what the fuck are you doing here?"

The driver glances back at her, then at me, his gaze darting between us anxiously.

He should be nervous.

Bringing a stranger up the mountain...

He should fucking know better.

All my employees do. If you have to bring something, you leave it on the steps. If you bring someone, I better damn well be expecting them.

She clears her throat. Her fingers, with perfectly manicured nails, wrap around the top of the door. She squeezes it until her knuckles whiten, as if gathering her courage, then steps slightly to the side so I can see her fully.

The torrential downpour has already soaked her completely, her white blouse now see-through, clinging to her every curve. Her nipples pebble through a white lace bra, and a black pencil skirt hugs her hips and down her shapely thighs to end just above the knee.

This woman isn't dressed for coming up the mountain, and she certainly isn't from Lockwood Falls, either.

Who the fuck is she?

She levels an intense, determined, azure gaze on me, any trepidation she may have had climbing from the sedan pushed aside in favor of false bravado. "I need to speak with you, Mr. Lockwood."

I tighten my grip on the axe. "No, you don't." Another step brings me closer to her and farther out from the protection of the tree line into the full-on storm. I point to her open door with the axe head. "Get back in that fucking car and get down this mountain before the road washes out."

"Calm down, Wells. This isn't you."

Di's constant reminder of who I've become, of how

much I've changed since she left, only further ignites my fury.

This *wasn't* me. I was never the guy who lost my temper or who went on the offensive. But now I'm defending my property, my personal space, on the one day I absolutely *need* my solitude.

"Go. Now." I storm around the front of the vehicle toward the cabin, intent on leaving the invaders out in the rain.

The sound of her heels splashing in the small puddles behind me stops my progress, and I whirl back to face her, hand still clenched around the axe.

She stares up at me from under thick black lashes that cling together with the water streaming down her face. The blue shifts to an almost steel gray, and she fists her hands at her sides. "I *need* to talk to you, Mr. Lockwood."

The top of her wet head barely reaches the middle of my bare chest, and I purposely shift the axe into her line of vision to make my point—you don't come up on *my* mountain and make demands of me.

Her eyes widen, and she staggers back half a step. Her heel gives out on the uneven ground, but she manages to catch herself with a hand on the hood of the car. She rights herself and puffs out her chest, squaring her shoulders like she's preparing for a fight.

Not today.

I start to turn back toward the cabin. "Whatever you're here for can wait."

"No, it can't." She tries to stomp her foot, but the heel just sinks into the mud. A low growl slips from her pink lips, and she jerks it free and scowls at it, then me. "Believe me, I'd rather be *anywhere* but here right now. But this *cannot* wait, no matter how much you try to scare me away."

This little mouse has some bite in her.

Too bad it won't change my position on this. If she wants to talk with me, she can certainly *try* another day. But it sure as shit won't be now.

I whirl back to fully face her, take a step forward, and issue a low warning growl. "I'm telling you right now, you need to get the fuck off my mountain immediately."

She squares her shoulders again, drawing my gaze back down to her soaked shirt, and opens her mouth to reply, but a sharp cry sounds from the open back door of the car she just vacated.

My head turns toward the unexpected noise. "What the hell was that?"

The driver whips his head to check the back seat, and the mystery woman releases a heavy sigh, wiping water from her face and pushing her wet hair from her forehead.

I look between her and the car. "You want to tell me what the fuck is going on?"

Instead of answering, she marches to the opposite side of the car she came out of, yanks open the door, fumbles around inside of it, and steps out, holding a car seat with the top pulled down to protect whatever's inside from the pouring rain.

Sharp cries continue, and she lifts it in her hand and gives me a pointed look, her icy glare cutting through me. "You and I need to talk about *this*."

"What the fuck?"

This woman is nuts.

"Be nice!"

I retreat until I'm at the bottom of the two steps that lead up to the cabin. She approaches on unsteady legs, her heels encumbering her ability to find sure footing, and stops in front of me. Her jaw set with determination, she grabs the edge of the carrier cover and slips it up long enough for me to see a screaming baby inside.

The shrill noise fills my ears, and I clamp my eyes closed and stagger back a step against the hammering inside my head. "Why the fuck did you bring that here?"

"Because he's *yours*."

It takes a moment for her words to register.

Because. He's. Yours.

I shake my head to clear it, and a rumble of thunder rolls through the glen, vibrating in my chest and rattling the windows on the cabin behind me. The rain pounds down around us, continuing to soak this insane woman and me.

Lightning crackles and strikes a tree somewhere behind her in the forest, the electric energy sizzling through the air around us.

She jerks and whirls toward it, pulling the car seat toward her, trying to find the source of the sound. When she turns back again, true panic fills her eyes for the first time since she stepped out of that car. She holds up the baby again. "Mr. Lockwood, can we please go inside and talk out of this storm?"

"Go inside, Wells. Now."

The baby screams again, the sound cutting through my daze of confusion and Diana's voice. It is a dangerous storm —one of the worst this season so far. And while I may not care if I die in it, this woman and her baby don't have to.

I grab her arm and tug her toward the door, throwing it open and ushering her inside. She moves off to the side to allow me to enter behind her, mud covering the hand-hewn pine floors with every step she takes. I slam the door behind us. Her eyes immediately dart around the inside of the cabin, but I step around and in front of her, blocking her view.

This isn't an invitation to spy on the reclusive billionaire for some trash tabloid or personal curiosity.

"You have five fucking seconds to tell me what the fuck is going on."

She releases a heavy sigh, sets down the car carrier, and flips the top back, exposing the very angry baby in a pale-blue onesie.

Cheeks red.

Eyes squeezed closed.

Tiny fists clenched.

Mouth twisted in anger I can sympathize with.

Poor kid.

The spitfire redhead squats, digs around in the car seat, and pulls out a pacifier that she slips into his mouth, holding it there gently as she glances up at me. A brief moment of blissful silence allows her—and me—to take a deep breath.

She pushes her wet hair from her face and looks at her ruined heels. "Bob Landry sent me to talk to you about *this*." Her free hand points to the baby, who seems content with the pacifier—at least for now. "Because, apparently, he's *yours*."

There are those words again, but they still don't register.

Yours.

Because it isn't *possible.*

"Listen to her, Wells."

This is nonsense. Some sort of mistake. It *has* to be.

If I had ever met this woman, let alone *touched* her, I would remember it. She isn't the type you can forget. So, her words don't make any sense.

I shake my head. "I don't know what kind of fucking game you're playing, lady, but there's no fucking way this is my baby. I've never *seen* you before, let alone—"

She holds up a hand to stop me. "No, you've got this all wrong. This isn't my baby."

LAUREL

Confusion and anger flash in his bourbon eyes, and Lockwood clenches his hand tighter around the axe he still holds. His gaze darts from me to the baby. "Then whose is it?"

I could really do without his attitude, considering this is the last place I want to be, but antagonizing him will only make this tenuous situation harder to handle.

I've been trained to negotiate with difficult people and deescalate things when they become too tense. Mediation and arbitration clinics. Internships with judges. Now would be the time to put that real-world experience I got in school to use—though, I'd much rather be doing it in a boardroom or courtroom.

The baby finally calms, sucking hard on the pacifier, and I push to my feet and face Wells Lockwood, the billionaire a thousand times over who stands shirtless, wet, muscled chest heaving, long hair hanging soaked around his hard face, and clutching a deadly weapon like some deranged mountain man.

"Apparently...*yours*."

He gapes at me. "That's impossible." Anger tightens his jaw, and he shoves his free hand back through his hair as water pools under him on the wood plank floor. "I haven't been with anyone but my wife since we were sophomores in college."

I try to wipe some of the water from my face, but it does no good as it drips off my soaked shirt and skirt and down over my ruined Louboutins. "All I know is what I was told."

And that was a less-than-pleasant conversation, to say the least.

He takes an aggressive step toward me, his wide, chiseled, bare chest right in my face. "Yeah, and what the *hell* is that?"

Refusing to retreat, I stand my ground, widening my stance slightly, as if a bull is about to take a run at me. "You can tone down the attitude, Mr. Lockwood. You think I went to law school for this?"

"Law school?" His dark brows furrow. "Who the fuck are you?"

Shit.

With all the drama my arrival has caused, I haven't even formally introduced myself. "My name is Laurel Palmer, and I'm an attorney at Lockwood Brewing Company."

He immediately narrows his scrutinizing gaze on me. "I don't remember hiring you."

I prop a hand on my hip, straightening my shoulders, and his gaze drops to my chest.

Shit, this shirt and white lace bra are probably see-through now.

Crossing my arms over my chest, I tap my muddy toe. "I started at Lockwood Brewing a few days ago, and this"—I wave my hand—"is not how I expected my first week to go."

His haunted eyes darken. "Why wasn't I told about your hire?"

Crap.

There isn't any delicate way to say this.

"Mr. Landry said he would inform you of my hire soon but that this wasn't a good time to interrupt you."

His jaw clenches, and his entire body stiffens.

This man wants nothing to do with this baby or me and can't wait to get us out of his home, but Mr. Landry was insistent that I couldn't leave without working out this plan with Lockwood.

"I know this is all a surprise, Mr. Lockwood. But don't get angry at me. I'm just the messenger, or the temporary babysitter, as it may be."

"Whose baby is this?"

The ultimate question...

Though, this time, I think he's asking about the mother.

"A woman showed up at corporate first thing this morning. She told security at the front desk that she had to speak with you. When they told her you weren't available, she said it was urgent and this was your son."

He squeezes his eyes together and shakes his head. "No. Impossible."

"Mr. Landry was notified by security, and he immediately ushered her into a conference room where he could have some privacy to discuss the situation...and brought me in with them."

Lockwood rubs his hand on his stubbled cheek. "How the hell could Landry fall for this? It's just some woman trying to get money from the company, trying to milk the billionaire widower."

My heart clenches at his words. "That thought certainly crossed our minds. But..."

He narrows his gaze on me again. "But *what*?"

I shift uneasily under his accusatory glare. "But then she mentioned *Harry's* in Lockwood Falls and said she met you at the bar a year ago."

His eyes widen slightly, and I can almost see the wheels turning in his head. "A year ago...at *Harry's* in Lockwood Falls?"

"The woman didn't seem..." I try to think of the right word. "*Interested* in the baby. She said that she initially didn't know who you were, so she couldn't get in touch when she found out she was pregnant. But she claimed she recently saw an article in the paper that had your photo, and that's when she realized who the father of her child was."

"But it's *impossible*." He shakes his head, dropping his face into his palms. "I wasn't *with* anyone a year ago. I haven't been with anyone since my wife passed."

Shit.

This question will likely get another vicious response, but I have to ask it to accomplish the task I was sent here for. "Are you *sure*?"

His head snaps back up, and the fury swirling in his eyes sends a shiver through me. "Of course, I'm fucking sure. You think I wouldn't remember sleeping with someone?"

I recoil slightly, and he starts to pace, muttering unintelligibly to himself and rubbing at the back of his neck. This isn't the Wells Lockwood everyone saw for so long in the news, who I watched in the media through college and law school. That Wells Lockwood was strong, confident, sure, a rock of a man who took over the already-thriving family business and blew it into the stratosphere. This Wells Lockwood seems like he's on the edge of a total mental breakdown.

And given what today is...maybe he is.

He finally stops his pacing and glances at me. "A year ago..."

I nod. "That's what she said. Early June."

Some sort of recognition flashes in his eyes. "I *was* at Harry's a year ago. I went into town to pick up my order, to keep the cabin stocked because I'd need it, and I stayed and had a few drinks." He squeezes his eyes closed and winces, as if the memories coming back physically hurt him. "There was a girl at the end of the bar, a brunette with green eyes. She looked so goddamn much like Di—" He cuts himself off, his free hand tightening into a fist. Then he opens his eyes and meets mine. "That's all I remember until I woke up alone at the motel across the street the next morning."

Oh, hell...

"So...it's *possible* you did sleep with her."

"Fuck." He shoves his hand through his hair and stalks away from me, giving me his broad back. "I don't know. I had a lot to drink, and I was not in a good place with the one-year anniversary of their deaths approaching. So, it's possible, I guess." With a heavy sigh, he turns to fully face me. "What did she ask for? Money?"

That would certainly make this simpler.

I shake my head and glance down at the innocent topic of our conversation, who has returned to a peaceful slumber. "No. Like I said, she didn't seem at all attached to the baby, more like she was just going through the motions. She indicated she was leaving the country with her new boyfriend and that she couldn't take care of the baby anymore."

Lockwood's brow furrows deeply. "So, she just *left* him?"

I nod slowly. "She did."

"Without any sort of proof that he's even mine?"

It's a valid question. The whole scenario certainly screams of a scam to get her hands on the Lockwood fortune or some sort of set-up designed to taint the Lockwood name by creating a scandal for business reasons, which is precisely why I'm here.

"Landry and I are already on that. He had someone

from the security team go to your house to pull your DNA to compare to the baby's, and they took a sample from him before I left. Landry also has someone looking into the mother, searching for any potential motives here."

"Jesus"—he runs his hand over his face with a heavy sigh—"why'd you bring him here? Why didn't you take the baby to CPS?"

Because I didn't have a choice.

Because it's my first damn week on the job and my boss ordered me to.

But even if he hadn't, I never could have brought this little one to CPS—not after my experience in the system. Lockwood so casually acts like dropping off a baby to CPS is the obvious solution only because he has no idea what that could end up doing to this kid. He's had everything handed to him on a silver platter, and he probably believes it would be a safe place for the baby.

So damn wrong.

"Because Landry didn't want anyone else seeing the baby or knowing about the woman's claim. He didn't want to cause a scandal, especially—" I bite back the words until his eyes lock with mine. "Especially given what today is. He said I needed to bring the baby up to you immediately and that you needed to keep him concealed until all of this gets settled so you and the brewery don't get dragged through the mud."

Lockwood releases a humorless laugh filled with anguish. "You've got to be fucking kidding me."

"I wish I were, Mr. Lockwood, because like I said, none of this is in my job description."

I want to feel bad for him, given everything that's happening, but dealing with the fallout of a drunk billionaire knocking up some random at a bar wasn't what I signed on for at Lockwood Brewing. The fact that I have had to waste my entire day on this and ruined my favorite pair of pumps that—even though I bought them resale—I had to scrape and save every dime to even afford makes it ten times worse.

Thank God this is almost over.

Lockwood can deal with this on his own.

I grab the door handle and motion toward the outside world, where the tempest continues to rage. "I'll just grab the bags with the baby's things the mother left." The moment I open the door, wind and rain batter me. Ice-cold drops pelt me, and I shiver and turn back to Lockwood. "By the way, you might want to actually look at him."

As if he cares.

Chapter Three

WELLS

"You might want to actually look at him."

She offers me an annoyed glare, then steps out into the storm.

Her words carry immense disdain and heavy judgment I can't miss.

Can I blame her for that?

I haven't exactly been welcoming or friendly since she pulled up at my doorstep. Far from it. Diana's constant warning to be nice only emphasizes that fact.

And I acted like a lunatic.

I lift the axe still in my hand and cringe, thinking about how I raised it at the car earlier and probably scared the shit out of her and the driver.

A crazed man with an axe in the woods...

It wasn't so long ago that I was the cool, calm, and collected public face of Lockwood Brewing, when people came to me for answers, and I had them. Only a few short years have passed since my open-door policy for all employees that made them feel like we were one big, happy family working together to produce the best product on the planet.

Now, I run people off with weapons.

Things have changed so much so damn fast, and it seems they're changing again.

Vastly.

Something I'm wholly unprepared for.

This can't be happening.

Of all the things I might have anticipated for this anniversary, a woman showing up on the mountain claiming a baby is mine wasn't even *close* to on the list.

But he can't be mine.

Even if—and it is a *huge* if—I had sex with that woman from *Harry's* and don't remember it, I wouldn't have been stupid enough to do it without protection.

Would I?

Bits and pieces of memories try to push through the black fog all the booze that night created, but they come fragmented, impossible to put together into anything discernible.

I lean the axe against the wall near the door and squat in front of the car carrier. The baby shifts slightly, his eyes fluttering open slowly, and his unfocused gaze meets mine.

All the air rushes from my lungs at my own eyes staring back at me.

Holy shit.

I stumble back a step, my feet suddenly unsteady, legs shaking along with the rest of my cold, wet body.

What I was so sure was impossible only moments ago now seems absolutely certain. That baby shares the same bourbon eyes flecked with amber that Father and Grandfather before me both had.

This baby is a Lockwood.

And that woman is about to leave you here with him.

"Shit."

That can't happen.

She can't just show up with this baby, leave him at the cabin, and hightail it out of here like she didn't just drop a literal bomb on my already-destroyed life.

I find my feet and rush out the door toward the waiting car, where Laurel stands at the open trunk, a bag slung over her shoulder, reaching for a second one.

With the rain and wind whirling around us, she doesn't even notice my approach until I nudge her to the side and grab the small bag myself. Her head whips toward me, and I slam the trunk closed before it fills with water.

Rain pelts us relentlessly, not letting up for even one moment. The wind howls and batters us from the side, trying to push me closer to her. Lightning streaks across the sky again, and a boom of thunder draws a sharp cry from the baby just inside the open cabin door.

Laurel stares at me for a moment, the tempest surrounding us also swirling in the steely blue of her eyes. A question lies there, under all her attitude and determination, but another wail from the baby breaks whatever trance she has me under.

I hustle to the passenger side of the car and knock on the window, keenly aware of Laurel teetering on her heels behind me.

The driver rolls it down and leans toward me across the console. "Yes, sir?"

"You can go."

One of his bushy white eyebrows rises. "Sir?"

Laurel stumbles the few feet toward the cabin. "Let me just set down the bag inside, and I'll be all set."

Like hell you will...

I turn back to the driver, tightening my hands on the open window. "Go. *Now.*"

Laurel's hurried footsteps splash behind me in the puddles. "What the hell are you doing, Mr. Lockwood?"

The driver glances from me to Laurel, who comes to my side, her arms crossed over her chest again. "Excuse my confusion, Mr. Lockwood. You'd like me to leave Ms. Palmer here?"

It isn't rocket science. In fact, it was a pretty crystal-clear order. Yet, this guy obviously isn't getting the message.

I lean farther in the window, hoping the irritating redhead immediately behind me won't hear. "I said *go.* If you want to keep your job, you'll do it. *Immediately.*"

"What the hell are you doing?" Laurel tugs on my arm to pull me toward her, and I step back from the car.

The driver rolls up the window and pulls away to do a U-turn in the small clearing in front of the cabin. He gets the car facing back down the mountain, and he slowly advances toward the only escape from this place.

Laurel releases her grip on me and jumps out in front of him. He slams on the brakes, the large sedan slipping slightly on the uneven, muddy ground, wet metal squealing against wet metal.

The hood comes to rest mere inches from Laurel's thighs, and she releases a heavy breath, her chest heaving against the see-through fabric.

She points at him through the windshield, where the wipers work overtime to clear away the deluge. "You are *not* leaving without me."

I take a step toward her, my boots sinking slightly in the muck. "Yes, he *is.*"

Her eyes widen, red brows reaching her hairline. "Are you insane?"

"You're not leaving me here alone with that baby."

Her jaw drops open. "You can't make me stay here. I was told to drop off the baby to you and return to corporate. That's what I'm going to do."

"No, you're not." I take another step, the baby's bag slung over my shoulder bouncing against my hip. "You're going to stay here until all this is sorted out."

Those perfect bow lips twist into a scowl. "You can't stop me from leaving."

Taking the final step toward her, putting myself only inches from her small, wet frame, I issue a low growl. "Fucking try me, Ms. Palmer."

I grasp her upper arm, drag her out of the way of the car, and motion for the driver to take off. He offers one last apologetic look to the woman in my grip before he makes his way back down the mountain, going around the bend in the road and disappearing into the thick, dark forest.

Laurel struggles in my hold, trying to pull her arm from my fingers. "What the hell are you doing? This is kidnapping."

"No, it's a job. I'm your boss, and I'm telling you I need you to stay and help me."

An incredulous gasp slips from her lips. "You're keeping me here against my will in the middle of nowhere. That's the definition of kidnapping. I did go to law school, remember?"

Her fury might be entertaining enough to make me laugh if it weren't cold and pouring rain and there wasn't a screaming baby inside my cabin.

I offer her a smirk and tighten my grip on her bicep. "I am not keeping you from leaving. You're just not leaving in that car." My point made, I release her arm, and she lunges away from me, staggering back on the uneven, wet ground. "You're welcome to walk into town and try to find a ride there, Ms. Palmer. You can leave anytime you want."

A loud clap of thunder rattles the ground, and Laurel jerks at the noise and spins around, checking out the small clearing. "But we're like twenty or thirty miles from Lockwood Falls."

I examine her shoes, her torn nylons, the mud splattered across them, and her tight pencil skirt and the see-through blouse and lacy bra that do nothing to conceal her hard nipples in the cold. "It's going to be a cold, long walk in those." I motion toward the road her only means of escape just disappeared down. "I recommend you stay on the road. You don't want to get lost in these woods. A lot of predators out there."

As I turn back toward the cabin, her gasp of indignation floats through the air. "You-you can't *do* this."

Any other day, her plight and the distress in her voice might give me pause. It might make me reconsider what I'm doing to her. It could tug at something deep inside me that used to care, but I haven't had a working heart in two years.

There isn't anything left to tug at.

"I just *did*, Ms. Palmer." I glance over my shoulder at her, then point to the open cabin door. "Now, are you walking, or are you coming inside?"

LAUREL

Wells Lockwood is clinically insane.

It's the only explanation for how he can stand there and do *this.*

Sheer *insanity.*

The rain falls around us, thoroughly soaking me to the bone, but I refuse to give in to the psychopath. I stand my ground, digging my ruined heels deeper into the mud in the process.

He raises an eyebrow. "You're going to stay out here?" His broad, muscular shoulders rise and fall nonchalantly. "Suit yourself. This storm is supposed to last all night, and as soon as it's done, a lot of hungry critters are going to be snooping around out here in the pitch black. But...your choice."

A fucking lunatic.

Lockwood takes the two steps up into the cabin and disappears, closing the door behind him and leaving me standing in the middle of the muddy clearing, soaked, freezing, and utterly distraught.

I went to law school for this?

Years of busting my ass through everything life threw at me finally lands me my dream job, the one I need to have the things I always wanted, and instead, I end up stuck on a mountain with this asshole who seems intent on breaking me.

My hot tears mix with the cooling rain until I can't tell if I'm even crying anymore.

Never let them see you cry.

The sound advice my social worker gave me before yet another move rings loud in my head, bolstering my resolve not to bow to Wells Lockwood's demands, even if he technically *is* my boss.

I will *not* let this man get the better of me.

I didn't fight my way through foster homes and shitty schools to get a full-ride scholarship to college and law school just so some arrogant prick billionaire can treat me like I'm his personal bitch who has to jump at his every word and concede to his every command.

No way; no how.

There may be a fine line between what might be considered an appropriate task for an employer to assign, but Wells Lockwood crossed it so far that I don't think he could even see it if he looked back.

Coming up here, I was determined to make a good impression on the man who pays my healthy salary, to start our working relationship off on the right foot, but that ship sailed the moment he sent Allen back down this mountain without me.

Storming toward the cabin, my heels sink into the mud with each step. I jerk them free each time, wincing at the damage it's causing to my babies. "Motherfucker."

The *one* thing I've splurged on in my life, the shoes I always dreamed of owning, are now destroyed because of Wells Lockwood's dick.

I clamber up the two steps to the cabin, grab the door handle, and turn, but nothing happens.

He fucking locked it!

"You have to be kidding me." I pound on the door as hard as I can until the wood rattles and my fist hurts. "Open up, Mr. Lockwood."

That poor baby screams inside, likely terrified of the noise and the new face—that is, if Lockwood is even *looking* at him.

"Let me in, you psychopath."

Okay, maybe calling your boss a psychopath isn't a great idea for job security. But if the shoe fits...

I keep wailing on the door until a lock clicks, and he swings it open, a smug half-grin on his perfect lips.

"Ms. Palmer, how nice of you to come." He steps back and sweeps his arm like he's inviting me in for tea rather than trapping me in this godforsaken place for who knows how long. "Do come in out of the rain."

Any chance of my biting back the retorts that will probably get me canned disappears with his smug attitude.

"You asshole." I stalk in, water dripping from me into the existing puddles by the door where we stood earlier. "You cannot keep me here like this. I'll call Landry and HR...the police...*both!* Not only are you going to get arrested, but I'm going to sue Lockwood Brewing for every fucking dime you're worth for doing this to me."

He slams the door behind me and raises a dark brow. "Maybe you don't understand what's going on here, Ms. Palmer."

The baby wails, and I glance over at him in the car seat flailing, wanting to be comforted, but we're both dripping wet and cold, and I'm quite confident Lockwood won't pick him up.

"Not only are we an hour—by *car*—from the closest town, but that town is *Lockwood* Falls." He raises his brows again. "As in...I fucking own it. My great-great-grandfather set up his first brewery out here in the barn building on the far side of the clearing, and he eventually expanded and built a new brewery at the base of the mountain, employing people from all around the area. Lockwood Falls grew around it." He takes a step toward me, towering over me ominously, his wide, chiseled chest nearly brushing my face.

"I *own* that city. The police won't arrest me, and you can try to sue me, but as you know, I have an excellent legal department. I'm sure they can dig up something to tank your case and ensure you—and it—disappear permanently."

His threat sends a chill down my spine, but I *refuse* to bend. "This is *kidnapping*."

"I told you. You're free to walk back to town at any time. You must not have paid good attention in law school. This isn't kidnapping or even wrongful imprisonment."

"And how would you know that?"

A smug smirk crosses his lips. "I went to law school, too, Ms. Palmer. I just never practiced. I used what I learned to help Dad and the business. And right now, think of this as a work assignment for a tiny client. I don't have the first clue about how to take care of a baby." He glances over at the object of our discussion, still crying angrily. "I need your help."

I scoff at his choice of words. "My help? My *help*? Like you're asking for directions. You just forced me to stay up here with you against my will. Why the hell would I *help* you?"

His granite gaze softens slightly. "Don't do it for me." He motions toward the baby. "Do it for *him*."

Scowling, I cross my arms over my chest. That's fucking low. Make it about the baby so I'll feel bad and won't argue with him anymore.

Talk about manipulation...

"This is your problem, Mr. Lockwood, not mine."

"It became your problem when you took the position at the brewery. That means handling whatever legal situations might occur and anything else Landry might put you on. He's in control while I'm up here, for all intents and purposes. And he put you in charge of that baby."

"No"—I take a step forward and point a finger into his bare chest. This close, the heat radiating off his body seeps through my wet shirt and into my skin, a welcome reprieve from the chill—"he put me in charge of bringing the baby to *you*, giving *you* the baby, and returning to Denver. He never said I had to stay here, and I refuse."

He bats my hand from his skin and crosses his arms over his chest. "You know where the door is and how to follow the road out."

I sneer at him. "I need to call for help."

"That will be difficult, considering I don't have a phone."

"Of course, you don't." I scoff. "Radio?"

He shakes his head. "Nope."

"What if something were to happen to you out here? What if you were hurt, dying?"

His entire body stiffens, and his eyes go to a molten onyx—the type of dark I've never seen before in another human, even the ones who made my early life a living hell at times. Completely devoid of anything.

My question makes it clear—he doesn't care about living. If something did happen to him up here, he wouldn't worry about not being able to reach anyone.

That's exactly what he *wants*.

"That's none of your fucking business, is it, Ms. Palmer? That baby is, and you'll stay here and help me take care of him for as long as all this takes."

The command reverberates through me like the thunder that echoes overhead, and I shiver and take half a step back from his warm body.

That's it, then.

I'm trapped here for however long he says I need to be. I can't lose this job. I can't lose the money or the opportunity it will give me. This may be a shitty way to spend my first week, but once this is resolved, I can move on to reviewing contracts and handling other legal issues for the company—not Lockwood's personal troubles.

And with this man up here, my job down *there* will be far, far easier.

He stalks to the door and tugs it open, allowing the howling wind and driving rain in.

I shiver and retreat a step. "Where the hell are you going?"

It's a nightmare out there.

No human should be out in that unless absolutely necessary.

He glances over his shoulder at me, seemingly seeing right through me, and his gaze drops to the baby. "Wherever the fuck I want."

The door slams behind him, leaving me standing, dripping wet in the middle of his small cabin, a screaming baby in a car seat on the floor at my feet, and no prospects of rescue.

Chapter Four

WELLS

Night falling, coupled with the still-raging storm, allows pitch black to swallow me whole when I step back outside and slam the door behind me. But even the darkness can't stop the light from shining blindingly on what I just did to that poor girl.

Perhaps I went too far. Forcing her to stay crossed some invisible line.

Hell, a clearly visible, thick, black one where you don't kidnap *employees and force them to stay at your remote cabin in the fucking woods up a mountain.*

"It wasn't very nice, Wells."

Diana's censure throbs in my head like she's hammering it into my brain. The pain starts in my temples and radiates through my entire body, like she's physically telling me to stop being such a dick.

She isn't wrong, though. But I don't have a choice—I can't be put in charge of that baby. Not when I can't even take care of myself.

My head pounds, a jackhammer of guilt and shame slamming against my skull relentlessly, as I cross the clearing in front of the cabin and beeline toward the one place I might actually be able to find some solace.

Only having this entire property memorized allows me to make my way through the moonless night. Occasional flashes of lightning illuminate my path and the black sky above me until I move into the thicker forest.

Cocooned in the branches, surrounded by the sounds of the wildlife moving around, seeking continued cover from the rain, I try to push aside the feelings raging inside me.

It doesn't help.

Maybe nothing will or ever can.

Not if what that woman said is true.

Each step I move closer to my destination, just knowing I'll see them, the easier it becomes to breathe, until I finally step through the trees and out into the open area at the top of the canyon ridge where the small family cemetery sits.

My girls...

I take a sharp inhale, fighting back the sob threatening to escape my throat.

Of all the days for this to happen, for that damn woman to show up, why did it have to be today?

My feet might as well be lead weights, trudging across the muddy ground and over to the two newer headstones set amongst the old ones. Tears blur my vision so badly that I can't even make out their names, but I know they're there—exactly where they've been for two years.

Diana Lockwood.

Maribel Lockwood.

They shouldn't be here. They shouldn't be in the ground. They shouldn't be *gone.* And that woman shouldn't be here, either...or that baby.

How the hell did this happen?

I drop to my knees in front of the graves and bury my face in my hands, letting the rain fall around me, mixing with the tears flowing freely now.

It happened because I was weak, because I was drunk, because I wasn't in my right mind. As soon as Laurel mentioned *Harry's*, those broken bits and pieces soaked in a haze of booze trickled their way back.

And kneeling in front of Diana, the entire sordid night starts to coalesce into a clearer memory. One I had repressed and buried so deeply inside the darkest recesses of my brain because I didn't want to admit it. I didn't want to have to think about what I had done.

Resting my forehead on Di's headstone, I brush my fingers reverently over the lettering. The confession sits on my tongue, burning like acid. "I made the drive down the mountain to pick up beer and bourbon from Harry." I shake my head slightly, squeezing my eyes closed against where these memories will take me. "I'm sure you think I'm drinking too much, but I knew I wouldn't make it through the one-year anniversary of losing you without drowning myself..."

Swallowing thickly, I prepare myself to admit the thing I've never said out loud before, the ugly truth I've been fighting for two years.

"Part of me didn't want to make it through. I almost turned the damn truck around, almost gave up and leaped off this cliff to ensure I'd be with you and Maribel forever." My voice cracks. "But something kept me on the road into Lockwood Falls. Something kept me driving."

A boom of thunder rolls through the valley, low and ominous. The cold rain picks up, falling in sheets around me, but now that I've opened the floodgates, I can't close them until Diana knows everything—at least...everything I can remember.

"Harry insisted I stay for a drink." I can still taste the bourbon on my tongue. Feel the cheap tumbler in my hand as I raised it to my lips. "It was the first time I'd sat down with another human being for more than ten minutes in a year..." After I put them in the ground and locked myself away up here. I release a heavy sigh, one filled with the pain of what's coming. "And it felt good not to focus on my tragedy, not to have to wonder what he was thinking, not to see pity in his gaze everyone else seems to carry for me. He kept everything light, easy, talking about the weather and the Broncos' upcoming season and anything else that wasn't losing you and Maribel..."

It was what I needed in that moment.

A friend.

And I relaxed for the first time in what felt like forever.

For one brief second...I almost forgot my life had been shattered.

"Then I saw her..."

Sitting at the end of the bar, her green eyes sweeping over the place eagerly and settling on me.

She grinned, and my heart leaped into my throat.

Christ, she looked so much like Diana.

"I kept drinking. Far more than I should have. Harry insisted I stay at the motel and not try to drive home up the mountain in my condition. Only...I didn't go across the street to the motel alone."

Candace.

That was her name—Candace.

Vivid images of my lips on hers, my hands on her skin, my body moving with hers, race through my brain, and I pull my head back from the cold stone, drop it back, and release a primal scream into the storm.

It echoes through the canyon, sounding more like a wild, wounded animal than a human. A rumble of thunder follows it, rattling the ground violently, as if Diana is speaking from the grave and expressing her anger over what I did.

"What the hell did I do?" A sob slips from my lips. "I'm so sorry, Di."

How could I have betrayed her this way, betrayed what we had?

The baby's eyes flash in my head—that same amber I see every time I look in the mirror. It hits me like a runaway freight train, knocking me back on my ass on the wet, muddy ground.

I can't deny it.

Can't deny what's right in front of me.

No matter how much I might want to pretend it isn't happening.

He's mine.

The ultimate betrayal of my family, of Diana and Maribel, of the life we should have had together. A physical reminder of what I did in my moment of weakness...

"What am I going to do?"

I stumble to my feet and press a kiss to the top of Diana's headstone, the rough rock against my lips mirroring the way my actions tear at my heart, then lower myself to my knees and do the same to Maribel's.

Lightning electrifies the sky again, and the thunder rolls, almost in answer to my question. The rain picks up, a surge so heavy that I can barely see in front of me.

"Go inside, Wells."

Every day, her voice lives in my head, reminding me

that she's always here, forever a part of me, watching me struggle through this life without her. And now, she knows what I've done, yet she's sending me back to that place.

To *him*.

It's so Diana to care about someone else when she's the one who has been hurt.

I push to my feet and stagger back through the woods. Branches reach out like angry hands, pulling at my soaked pants and clawing at my exposed skin.

The light above the cabin door glows through the deluge, but I veer away from it to the barn to grab another axe, despite Diana's order to get inside.

There's only one way to work out this aggression, to try to decimate the guilt and anger and resentment. The tree I downed earlier will serve that purpose, will let me unleash it all somewhere no one else can get hurt.

"Go inside, Wells."

"I can't. I can't." I shake my head, barely seeing the ground in front of me through the storm and tears. They're in the cabin. The baby and that woman. "I *can't*."

I slog through the mud to the massive downed pine and immediately swing at it, driving the blade deep into the wood. Each time it bites into the trunk, I wish more that it was me taking the punishment instead of giving it.

I'm the one who deserves it, for betraying Diana, for creating that life.

My muscles burn with the exertion, but I keep going and going, battling the unseen enemy until, at last, I can't lift the axe anymore. It tumbles from my hands and falls against what's left of the tree trunk.

Air rushes from my lungs in hard breaths, and I stare at it for what seems like hours, letting my mind drift with the wind whirling around me.

My entire body vibrates, shaking so badly I can barely stay upright.

"Go inside, Wells."

I finally can't stand the cold or Diana's insistence anymore, and I stagger around the pine and make my way back toward the cabin. I stand with my hand on the doorknob for a moment, staring at it without feeling the metal against my palm at all, my entire body numb.

This is what you want, isn't it, Di? For me to come home?

"Go inside."

I turn the knob and shove open the door. The wind catches it, and it swings open, banging against the interior wall.

Laurel jolts toward the sound where she sits on the couch, wrapped in the afghan Diana knitted and used almost every night we were up here, the sleeping baby clutched tightly to her chest.

Fury flares through my veins, tightening my fists at my sides. "What the fuck are you doing? Take that off."

I storm toward her and rip the blanket from her shoulders.

Laurel jerks away from me, holding the baby to her protectively. Wide, confused blue eyes meet mine. "I-I'm sorry. I was cold. The fire went out, and..."

She trails off, and my gaze drifts to the dead coals in the fireplace.

Shit.

I've been so preoccupied all day, lost in my own head and agony, that I haven't even bothered to keep up with it. The chill in the air in here suddenly hits me as I stand in my soaked clothes, and my focus returns to the ones clinging to her shaking body.

She must be freezing.

"Fuck." I run my hands over my wet face and stalk to the fireplace. My fingers tighten on the afghan, reluctant to let it go, but I drape it over the back of the chair facing the fire so I can toss in a few logs and kindling and light it without looking back at her or the baby. "I'll get it lit again."

A heavy silence hangs between us, and she shifts on the couch, the slight movement enough to make her presence in the cabin that's always so empty loom large. "Are we really doing this, Mr. Lockwood? You're keeping me here?"

Wincing against the pain in my head, I rub my jaw. "I told you, you're free to go, but I need your help. I don't know how to care for a baby."

She's quiet for a moment, either resigned to the fact that she can't talk me out of this or figuring out a better argument. "Your dad, he was Wesley, right?"

I stiffen, staring at the flames as they finally catch on the bigger logs. "Yes. Why?"

"That's the baby's name."

Fucking hell.

The final nail in the coffin.

I must have told Candace Dad's name at some point that night. For some reason, I opened up to her. In that one moment of weakness, I let my guard come down.

My chest aches, and I try to search my memories for anything she told me about herself, but I can't focus on any one thing, just fragments of things she said. "You have no idea where the mother is?"

"No. She just said she didn't want to be involved anymore."

I grab the fire poker and nudge one of the logs. "Her name was Candace."

"Yes, Candace Shipley. Mr. Landry is looking into her, looking for any other family—"

Shaking my head, I glance over my shoulder at Laurel. "She doesn't have any."

Her brow furrows. "How do you know?"

"Because I remember her telling me that."

"So, you *do* remember her."

I nod and push to my feet. "I do. Some things. Enough... I'm pretty sure that's my baby."

LAUREL

Lockwood finally turns away from the fire, settling his gaze on me on the couch. It slowly drops to the baby cradled against my still-damp chest with only his baby blanket between us. Lockwood watches us carefully, like he doesn't know what he's supposed to be doing, probably because he truly doesn't.

If everything he said was true, then he has very little recollection of what actually happened that night. He wasn't lying with his initial reaction when I showed up. He wasn't being difficult or unwilling to admit what he did; he truly didn't think it was possible for him to have a child because he didn't know he had spent that night with Candace Shipley.

The combination of booze he must have drank at *Harry's* and the mental anguish he was under, he completely blocked it out. Given the loss he suffered, my just showing up like this had to have been more than a shock—it must have rocked his world off its already-unsteady axis.

He needs to find something to ground himself. He needs to find a connection with this baby, or I brought him up here for nothing.

Wesley shifts in my arms slightly, and I peek down at him, then back at Lockwood.

"Do you want to hold him?"

His eyes snap back up to mine, and he shakes his head, his lips twisting. "The last time I held a baby, she and my wife both died."

Shit.

My heart clenches so tightly that it hurts, and even though I want to be furious with him over what he's doing, forcing me to stay here, I can't help but feel for him, for what he's going through and what he lost.

I can't imagine loving anything the way he must have loved his wife and unborn child. Even just from the photos I saw of him with Diana in the media, it was clear in the way he looked at her that she was his world. Not only did he lose them, but now I show up here with this baby and drop the bomb—*"Surprise! It's yours!"*

It's no wonder he's so volatile and wants nothing to do with this little boy.

"I'm so sorry, Mr. Lockwood."

His amber eyes flash with a pain so deep it slices at my chest, making me wince. "Yeah, everybody's so *fucking* sorry."

He stalks away from me toward a kitchen set up along the south wall, jerks open the refrigerator, and tugs out a six-pack of Lockwood Ale. Staring out the window over the small sink, he grabs one, slams the cap against the counter to pop it off, then downs half the bottle in two large gulps.

His free hand tightens on the edge of the butcher block, his knuckles whitening as he tries to regain control.

I search for anything to focus on except the situation so I don't push him off the cliff he seems to be teetering on. "I'm glad to see you're drinking Lockwood beer. It gives me some job security."

If I even *want* to keep working for Lockwood Brewing after the man who runs it kidnapped me...

That remains to be seen.

Sitting here in cold, wet clothes, holding a sleeping baby that isn't mine, staring at an angry, broken man, it's hard to imagine going into the corporate offices every day and pretending none of this happened.

Lockwood freezes, then slowly peers over his shoulder. "If you do this, stay and help me figure all this out, I'll make sure you get a promotion and a raise when you get back to Denver. You won't have to wait to work your way up."

I narrow my eyes on him and adjust the baby, who starts to squirm. "I don't want anything handed to me, Mr. Lockwood. I've busted my ass my whole life to get where I am..." I give a pointed look around the cabin. "Or where I *should* be back at the office. All I want is what I've earned."

He turns around and leans back against the counter, watching me with Wesley. His eyes meet mine, an apology in them. "You've definitely earned more than whatever your starting salary is."

Releasing an incredulous laugh, I adjust Wesley to my other shoulder. "I won't argue with *that.*"

Lockwood takes a sip of his beer, his eyes trained on the baby. "You seem to know what you're doing? Do you have kids I'm keeping you from? A husband?"

Nice of you to think of that now—*literally* hours *since you forced me to stay up this godforsaken mountain.*

I shake my head. "No husband, no kids, but I grew up in foster homes that always had a lot of babies and small children running around them, so I got used to helping my different foster mothers with all the little ones."

His gaze softens slightly, some of the anger from earlier seemingly dissipating only to be replaced by a look of pity people always seem to give me when they find out how I grew up.

You should have kept your mouth shut.

None of that matters anymore. I'm not that lost girl seeking something solid to cling to. I've created the life I've always wanted for myself with no help from anyone else. And I won't let a man like Lockwood make me feel less than simply because I didn't have all the luxuries he did growing up as the Lockwood heir.

I square my shoulders, prepared to redirect the conversation should he push the issue, but another concern that's been lingering in my mind offers an alternative topic.

Christ this is awkward.

"Have you been...medically checked for...well, since you were with her?"

Wells cringes, massaging his temples. "Yes. I need an annual medical exam for my insurance. It was after..."

So damn awkward.

Wesley shifts again and starts wailing, his little fists clenched tightly on my shirt.

All of this must be disorienting for him—his mother disappearing, the long car ride, now being in a strange place with people he doesn't recognize for reasons he can't understand.

Poor kid.

I rock him gently and rub his back.

Lockwood shifts uncomfortably and clears his throat, concern furrowing his brow. "Is he okay?"

Loaded question.

Everyone always says kids are resilient, and at this young age, it's likely true. He'll adjust to his new surroundings, the new people caring for him, but this baby is far from okay.

A mother who doesn't want him.

A—probable—father who can barely look at him.

Unwanted.

A word and feeling I'm all too familiar with.

And I refuse to allow this baby to carry that weight—ever. If that means staying here until his uncertain future gets sorted out, I can suck up my anger and annoyance at the man who put me in the position.

I hold Wesley against my chest, his head to my shoulder. "He's probably hungry. I need you to make him a bottle."

Lockwood stiffens again and shakes his head, his long, wet, unruly hair floating around his face. He shoves a hand through it, glancing away. "I don't know how to do that."

Of course, he doesn't.

I push to my feet, now bare after I kicked off my ruined shoes and yanked off my destroyed nylons. "Either you make him a bottle, or you hold the baby. Those are your options."

He swallows thickly, then downs the rest of the beer in two gulps and sets the empty bottle on the counter before slowly allowing his uneasy gaze to meet mine. "What do I need to do?"

I incline my head toward the smaller of the two baby bags Wesley's mother left when she abandoned her child. "There are two containers of formula in this bag and a couple of bottles. Fill it with warm water, put in two scoops, shake it."

Lockwood glances at the stove. "It'll take a while to heat up the water. I don't have a microwave."

"As long as it isn't cold, he'll take it." He had no problem with the bottles I made him in the car with bottled water. "Room temperature will work."

He gives me a stiff nod, then walks farther into the kitchen and pulls open a tall door that appears to be a pantry. I take a few steps forward, eager to examine the rest of the cabin without prying.

Even when he disappeared earlier, I was too afraid of being busted snooping by a man who carries around an axe and a bad attitude.

Lockwood returns with a bottle of water, brushes past me to the couch, and digs through the baby bag to pull out the canister of formula and an empty bottle. "This?"

I nod. "Two scoops. Shake it well."

He brings it back to the kitchen and sets to work with his back to me. His broad shoulders bunch and flex as he scoops out the formula and shakes the bottle.

It shouldn't be hot, watching him do something so domestic begrudgingly, but no one could deny how attractive Wells Lockwood is. Far from the button-upped man in three-piece suits who used to appear in the media, this version is wild, reckless, dancing a fine line between control and chaos. The type of man women should avoid at all costs—yet I'm stuck here with him for God only knows how long.

Lovely.

He turns back to me, approaches cautiously, like he doesn't want to get too close to me or the baby, and hands me the bottle. His fingers brush against mine, and a tiny jolt ripples up my arm and through my entire body. He jerks his hand away, brushing it across his wet pants as if he felt it, too.

I tighten my grip on the bottle to keep from mentioning it. "Thank you."

"You're welcome." His gruff, stilted answer comes out lacking any warmth.

Maybe it's too much to hope that he'll come around to Wesley, that he'll be able to accept who he is and embrace him the way he would have the daughter he lost.

If he doesn't, where will that leave this baby?

He screams in my arms, seeking comfort and warmth that the man who is likely his father just can't give him. I adjust his position, settle back onto the couch, and slip the bottle between his lips. He sucks at it greedily, turning toward me and clenching his fingers around my shirt, clinging to me for what his mother once offered.

Lockwood stares down at us, his eyes shifting from amber to a golden hue before he buries his face in his hand and shakes his head. "I can't fucking do this."

The anguish lacing his words makes me wince.

Wells Lockwood is wholly unprepared for what drove up that road today, and he may never be ready for it.

He stalks back to the kitchen, grabs what's left of the six-pack from the fridge, and then snatches the afghan off the back of the chair. For a second, he stares at it in his hand, then brings it to his nose and inhales deeply.

Fuck.

No wonder he reacted that way. It was his wife's...

He tucks the blanket under his arm and stalks to one of two doors along the back wall of the small cabin. Pausing with his hand on the doorknob, he peers over his shoulder at me. "That couch pulls out if you'd rather sleep on an actual bed." Inclining his head to a small door to his right. "There are other blankets and sheets in the linen closet in the bathroom."

With that, he opens the door, steps through it, and slams it closed behind him.

The sharp noise makes Wesley jerk, and the nipple slips from his mouth. His sharp cry of surprise splits my ears, and I wince.

"It's okay, kiddo. None of this is your fault, and hopefully, your father will figure that out sooner rather than later."

If he doesn't, I worry for this child's future. Being the son of a Lockwood should mean endless possibilities and the best opportunities, but at what cost...

Growing up with a father who resents him does him no favors.

Wells Lockwood needs to get a grip on reality—fast.

Chapter Five

LAUREL

Sunlight barely trickles in the window on the far side of the cabin as I wake. I yawn and stretch out on the couch, which was surprisingly comfortable. Since I was too exhausted to pull it out and make it up like a bed last night, I had worried I'd be up all night, tossing and turning, on an uncomfortable piece of furniture. But of course, Wells Lockwood wouldn't buy anything cheap, and the soft leather and plush cushions helped me fall asleep before I ever realized it.

Having to let Wesley sleep in the car seat annoyed me to no end, and now waking in my still slightly damp, dirty clothes makes me cringe.

Jesus, I have nothing up here with me, and who knows how long I'm going to have to stay.

I scowl at the closed bedroom door, letting my anger at the man who has me trapped up here build until I can't stay quiet anymore. If Wells Lockwood thinks he's going to act like a grumpy asshole the entire time I'm stuck with him, he has another think coming.

Landry said he hired me out of dozens of qualified candidates because of my tenacity and what I said during our interview—that Lockwood Brewing Company was already a household name, but I wanted to be part of ensuring it always *would* be.

That loyalty to my new employer was the only reason I even *got* into that car and agreed to come up here in the first place, but it doesn't mean I have to accept the attitude of my *boss*.

I take a quick peek at Wesley to ensure he's still sound asleep beside me, then climb from the couch and march over to the bedroom door and pound on it.

"Lockwood, open up."

No answer.

Either the man is ignoring me, or he's still passed out.

I turn the handle slowly. It gives easily, but I still pause before entering. Somehow, walking into his bedroom feels like a violation of some sort of sanctuary. I *shouldn't* care since he basically kidnapped me and is holding me against my will, but after last night, the pain I saw in his eyes, a huge part of me understands his anger and his reaction to the situation.

A stranger shows up with a baby on the anniversary of your wife and baby's deaths, telling you you're the father—it isn't exactly the type of thing most people dream about, certainly not Wells Lockwood.

Understandably, if I'm truly being honest with myself. And intruding on his personal space makes unease bloom in my chest, but I can't stay in these clothes and Wesley will be awake and hungry soon.

I inch the door open farther and peek in.

The afghan Wells took from me last night lies across a massive king-sized bed with hand-hewn wood posts that occupies the center of the room, and handmade furniture—two dressers, nightstands, even a handmade lamp—fills out the rest of it. Early morning light streams in through the two windows, giving the space an almost ethereal glow, but other than the rumpled sheets, there isn't any sign of Wells.

I check the analog clock on the wall in the bedroom.

Not even 5:30 yet.

He must have been up and out of here early for me to have missed him, which means he won't be here to find me doing this.

I slip into the room and make my way to one of the identical dressers. A thin layer of dust rests across the top, and I trail a finger through it.

A tidy housekeeper Wells is not...

But removing that bit of dust exposes the true beauty of the solid piece of furniture.

Someone made this with skill and love. Chiseled the legs. Sanded the top. Lacquered the surfaces so the magnificent grain patterns would pop out of the wood.

Yet it's standing here collecting dust.

My heart aches for Wells, for what he might have had and lost. But if I let myself dwell on it, if I allow myself to feel bad for the man, I won't stay angry at what he forced me to do. And I *need* to stay angry, or he'll walk all over me with his abrasive attitude.

He needs to understand that I may be here, but I am *not* at his beck and call. I am here to help *Wesley*, not Wells. If it weren't for that sweet baby, I would be halfway down the mountain in broken heels with blisters bleeding on my feet.

Which leads to the current predicament—finding something else to wear, and, hopefully, something else to put on my feet.

I tug open the top drawer.

Empty.

The one below it.

Empty.

Bottom one.

Empty.

What the hell?

The truth of why comes to me slowly, and acid churns in my stomach at the reason *why* everything's empty.

This was Diana Lockwood's dresser. Wells cleaned out everything of hers. He couldn't handle the reminders of her being here.

That horrible feeling of invading his space creeps up again.

I close the drawer and move to the second dresser.

Top drawer—boxers and socks.

Next drawer—T-shirts.

Bingo.

I grab whatever's on top and try the next drawer down.

Sweatpants and dozens of pairs of jeans and work pants. They'll all be huge on me. My best bet is something with a drawstring, but it doesn't look like he has anything that will stay up on my waist.

I might be stuck in this skirt for a while.

Fucking hell. Just add that to the long list of reasons this is going to be epically painful.

My eyes are drawn back to the bed, the mess of sheets.

Did he even sleep?

He was a wreck last night...

Why do you even care?

I shouldn't.

He's my *boss*. And he's an overbearing, grumpy, rude man who has apparently lost all sense of how to act appropriately since secluding himself on this mountain.

But he's still a human being—one in pain who is suffering more than I could ever wrap my head around.

Who are you to judge when you've never walked in his shoes?

All I can do is pray today brings a better attitude from Wells Lockwood, and I'll be in a much better mood once I get out of these clothes.

I head for the bathroom off the living room, slip out of my ruined white blouse and still-damp bra, and tug on the oversized T-shirt. The soft gray Henley feels like butter against my skin, and a woody, masculine scent fills my nose.

Good God, is that what he smells like?

The closest I've ever been to the wilderness was going to REI to buy a new water bottle once, so the smells are unfamiliar to me. But this one stirs something deep inside me I don't want to even think about, and I bring the fabric to my nose to inhale again.

Hell.

I can't like anything about Wells Lockwood.

I *refuse*.

My body won't betray me by melting into a puddle of goo at his scent.

Not today. Not tomorrow. Not ever.

I use the bathroom and examine myself in the mirror hanging above the sink.

Christ, I look like a crack whore.

With my black mascara and eyeliner smudged under my eyes from the rain and my tears, my red hair matted and disheveled—both from standing out in the rain and from sleeping on the damn couch—I might as well have walked in off the streets after being ridden hard and put away wet.

Like a true professional, Laurel.

God, what if I showed up in court like this?

I release a heavy sigh, grab the toothpaste, and slather it on my finger since I sure as hell am not using his toothbrush. Scrubbing at my teeth, the fresh, minty taste helps a little to remove the feelings of being gross and scuzzy, but we're going to have to do something about the clothing situation if I'm staying here.

A girl can only take so much, and I have about reached my limit. Even someone with the patience of a saint couldn't handle more of what Wells threw at me yesterday.

Only Wesley and knowing he needs me will keep me sane. I step back out into the living room and check on him again, but he hasn't budged, his tiny lips parted, chest moving up and down rhythmically.

His mother—if you can call her that—said he was a good sleeper, and apparently, she was right.

Thank God because I could use a few minutes to think before he wakes up.

Maybe there's a way to approach Lockwood without it coming to verbal blows and threats.

I wander around the small cabin and examine the wall of books next to the fireplace—Clive Cussler, Dean Koontz, John Grisham. Somebody sure enjoys mainstream fiction, though somehow, I can't see Lockwood reading any of this. The dust covering them suggests they haven't been touched in as long as that dresser has, so they're probably his wife's.

Pictures fill the shelves along with the books—Wells with his father in front of the brewery, their arms wrapped around each other, smiling proudly. Wells and his late mother, him in a tux, her in a champagne gown, likely his wedding.

I grab it from the shelf and examine the man. Fewer lines on his clean-shaven face. Shorter, impeccably kept sandy brown hair. An easy smile from someone who is on top of the world. This isn't the forty-year-old, broken Wells Lockwood I met yesterday. This is a younger, happier version with his whole life ahead of him—one I wish I had met because I probably would have liked him.

Suddenly, the cabin becomes stuffy and suffocating, the tight walls closing in even more on me.

I return the photo to the shelf and move to the nearest window. The sun filtering in suggests the storm has fully passed, so I make my way to the front door and tug it open.

Immediately, bright morning sunlight hits me, and I inhale a deep breath, the scent of the recent rain, wet leaves, moss, and trees filling my lungs.

God, that smells good.

Though, my memory of yesterday taints it somewhat, and a shiver rolls through me, remembering how cold that rain felt and how icy my welcome was.

A pair of boots sit beside the door, far too big for me, but there's no way I'm putting my heels back on to walk around in the mud and muck left behind by last night's storm.

I slip my bare feet into them, leaving the door cracked open so I can listen for Wesley, and make my way down the two steps to the clearing in front of the cabin. Small puddles still stand throughout the area, the rest of it a sticky, muddy mess, but just beyond it, near the tree line, an array of wildflowers bloom, bright and cheerful after the rain.

Something rustles in the bushes, and I jerk away from it, narrowing my eyes at the shadows.

A lot of predators out there.

His warning from last night makes me cringe away, and I move in the opposite direction toward another patch of bright-white flowers.

I make my way over to it and squat. They stand out starkly against the lush green background, pristine and pure, the kind of brightness Wells Lockwood desperately needs in his life right now.

A bunch of these on his kitchen table might help liven up the cabin that feels more like a tomb.

I reach down and pluck several groupings of them. The tiny white flowers spray out on delicate, thin sprigs. Dainty. Beautiful. Almost peaceful. The kind of thing I'd expect to see in some fancy photoshoot posted on social media.

And they're just growing out here in the woods.

Maybe this place isn't *all* bad.

My manner of arrival may have skewed my initial impression, but I could definitely do without this mud. The rain has left everything so soggy that when I try to lift the heavy boots, they stay stuck in the ground. I pull on one to get it to dislodge, then the other.

Wesley releases a cry that carries out the open cabin door to me, and I hustle across the clearing as fast as I can in the oversized boots and up the steps to deal with Mr. Lockwood's son.

The kiddo slept like a champ, but he has to be hungry and in need of a change by now. I turn to close the door behind me, but a solid hand presses against the middle of it, pushing it back open toward me.

Lockwood stands in the doorjamb, his broad shoulders stretching from side to side, a dark, sweat-dampened T-shirt clinging to his muscular frame. His massive hand fanned across the door keeps it wide and allows the sunlight to pour in over me standing here in my skirt, the Henley he didn't give me, and the boots I also "borrowed" without asking.

Shit.

I expect a lecture about touching his things, but his eyes immediately dart to the flowers in my hand. The muscles in his neck strain, his jaw locking. He takes the final step up and sneers, any warmth in his eyes melting away to hard granite instantly. "What the hell were you thinking?"

WELLS

Laurel's soft blue eyes widen as she recoils from me slightly, stumbling back a step in my boots. "What do you mean?"

I step inside and grasp her wrist, casting a quick glance at Wesley, who cries in his car seat. As much as I hate leaving him in distress, he'll have to wait. This *can't.* I drag Laurel out of the cabin and down the stairs.

She tugs against my hold, trying to free herself. "Mr. Lockwood! What are you doing?"

"Be gentle, Wells. She doesn't know."

My grip on her arm might hurt, but she has no idea what she's done—how she's just put us all in jeopardy. Women like Laurel have no idea how dangerous this place is—or how the most beautiful things are usually the ones that come back to bite you in the end.

I pull her over to the edge of the forest, where she must have picked the flowers in her hand. To her, they're just pretty white blooms, but to anyone who knows anything about this mountain, they're an enemy we've learned to stay far away from.

Dragging her to a stop, I point to the patch she plucked

from. "That's *hemlock*, one of the most poisonous plants in the entire world."

Her mouth falls open, her red brows flying up. "What?"

"Drop it."

She looks to her hand and quickly throws them to the wet ground, staggering back a few steps from them, as if putting the space between herself and the offending plant might undo whatever damage has already been done. "Oh, my God..."

"Be nice, Wells."

This isn't the time to be nice. Not when I'm trying to keep another tragedy from happening on the mountain. I grab her bicep and lead her back toward the cabin. Wesley's cries flow out the open door and cut through the morning air.

"Hemlock?" She glances up at me, her eyes filled with tears. "That was *hemlock?"*

I warned her last night how dangerous these woods can be, how everything on the damn mountain will try to kill you in one way or the other. But the damn woman just didn't listen.

"Did you touch your face or the baby?"

Her head jerks toward me as we reach the steps. "What?"

Gritting my jaw, I ensure her eyes are locked with mine so she gets just how serious this question is. "Did you *touch* your face or the baby?"

"I-I..."

She stares at her hands, her mouth opening and closing like she can't form the words. Wesley keeps crying, completely unaware of the potential catastrophe he's just woken to.

"Be calm, Wells. Be steady."

I squeeze Laurel's arm tighter and shake her gently, drawing her closer to me, trying to get her to look me in the eye. "Laurel, I need you to answer me."

My attempt to keep the panic out of my voice fails miserably, but if she touched her mouth, touched him, or fed him, and either of them ingested any portion of the plant off her hands, we won't make it to Lockwood Falls in time.

The strong-willed redhead who stood her ground against me last night now looks up at me with tears flowing down her cheeks, all that sass and bravado instantly replaced by panic when she realizes why I'm asking. "Oh, my God." She shakes her head. "No. I just picked them and was walking back in. I was nowhere near Wesley."

"Jesus Christ, Laurel." A bit of the weight crushing my chest eases, but as I stare into her blue eyes, it would be so easy to get lost in, they morph into the vivid green ones I stared into for so many blissful years. "Did you touch your mouth, your eyes, your face at all?"

The same terror returns to her gaze, and she looks to me for the answer as if I will hold it. "I-I don't think so."

I turn her hands and arms over, scanning them quickly out here where we have better lighting. "Open wounds on your hands?"

She shakes her head again, panic beginning to make her shake. "I don't know."

Wesley's continued cries pierce my ears, and I usher her up the two steps, kick the door closed behind me, and rush her to the kitchen, where I throw on the water cranked as hot as it will go. "Get your hands under the water now."

What the hell was she thinking?

The first rule of thumb when outdoors is never to touch any plant or animal you can't identify. There are too many species that lure you in with vibrant colors and beauty only to poison you in an instant. If she or Wesley got any of the hemlock into their bloodstreams, they'd be sick within fifteen minutes and potentially dead within thirty.

"She didn't know. Be nice."

A massive vise tightens around my chest at that thought, making it impossible to draw in a breath.

They could have died...

Familiar dread I've lived with for two years settles over me, and I struggle to keep upright and focused on the woman in front of me when visions of another woman, another baby, another panic flood my head.

No.

"Concentrate."

I push away the panic threatening to control me. If I don't focus and get Laurel taken care of, she could develop a very uncomfortable rash from the contact. I squat to rummage under the sink until I find what I'm looking for—the massive bottle of dish soap.

Laurel's hands shake as violently as the rest of her as she moves them back and forth under the water, tears dripping into the sink to join the water swirling down the drain. "What do we do?"

I squeeze the soap over her hands, drenching them front and back. "Scrub them as hard as you can."

She starts lathering her hands together, and Wesley continues to fuss from his car seat. The poor kid is probably hungry, or he senses the tension in the air, but he will have to hold on a few more minutes.

I grab the small brush from the edge of the sink. "Use this."

"To do what?"

I step behind her, pressing my chest against her back,

and wrap my arms around her. Her body shakes so violently that she can barely keep standing. I grab her hands and start scouring as hard as I can with the brush against her nails, under them, all around them, in the crevices of each finger. The suds grow as the water pours down over them, filling the sink while I scour her skin raw.

She releases a sob, barely able to stand on her own without my body pressing her against the counter. "Am I going to..."

Die.

Am I going to die?

That's what she was about to ask me.

A question I never wanted to hear again. Words that shattered my entire soul. But this time, I can give her the real answer. I don't have to lie to her the way I did to Diana when she asked the very same thing.

"You'll be fine as long as you didn't ingest it."

Laurel sags back slightly against me. "Oh, thank God."

A little bit of the tension in her shoulders and panic in her voice slip away, but she continues to sob while I keep working on her hands.

"But you may end up with a rash and irritation on your hands from touching it. We need to get as much of it off as possible."

I pull her hands out from under the water and examine them for any sort of cuts or scrapes. "No cuts on your hand, so it shouldn't have entered your bloodstream."

Tears pour down her red cheeks, and she looks back toward Wesley in the car seat near the couch. "Oh, my God. What if I had come in and picked up Wesley? What if I—"

I slide my wet hand around her chin and force her to look at me. "You didn't. He's all right. You need to breathe. Calm down for me."

Her lips tremble, her eyes filled with so much uncertainty. "I-I don't know if I c-c-can."

"You can. Deep breaths."

She sucks in a ragged breath, then another, keeping her gaze locked with mine. The intensity with which she looks to me as her savior makes a rock lodge in my throat, and I swallow hard past it and return my attention to washing her hands.

I run mine over hers, adding more soap and letting the water get to almost-scalding hot. Her entire body violently shakes despite the heat of my own cocooning her.

If she doesn't calm down, she'll go into shock.

"You need to keep breathing, Laurel."

"I-I am."

"No, you're not." I shift my lips behind her ear, ensuring she'll hear every word I'm about to say. "Breathe. In and out."

Her back presses to my chest with her deep inhale, then she releases a long, slow breath.

"Good. Again."

She sucks in a big gulp of air and lets it out. Some of the shaking dissipates, and I keep my body pressed to hers, washing her hands under the hot water, adding soap, and ensuring she keeps breathing.

I don't need her passing out on me, but I also need to make sure she comprehends how dangerous things can be up here. She'll be staying for at least a few days, and she's already tried to poison herself and potentially Wesley on morning one.

"This is what I was trying to warn you about, Laurel." I try to keep my voice low and even, not laced with the panic this entire situation has set off inside me. "There are a lot of things that can kill you on this mountain, a lot of things that *will* hurt you, a lot of things that look beautiful but aren't."

She turns her head slowly to look at me, her cheek almost brushing my lips, her brow furrowed, but she doesn't say a word.

"Don't touch anything inside the cabin or outside without asking. Do you understand me?"

For the briefest moment, something flashes in her eyes that makes me think she's going to argue with me about it the same way she did yesterday, but instead, she gives me a sharp nod. I turn off the water and grab a towel, wrapping her hands in it.

"Dry those."

She moves mechanically, keeping her eyes on me as I rummage under the sink again and come up empty.

I point to where she stands, far steadier now. "Stay here."

Wesley continues to fuss in the car seat, and I hustle over to him and slide the pacifier into his mouth, hoping it will console him long enough for us to calm down the situation.

He accepts it and sucks, staring up at me with big, wet eyes.

Christ...she could have touched him, could have fed him. He could have put her fingers into his mouth.

I freeze at that thought, my heart seizing in my chest, a vise tightening until I wince.

"He's okay, Wells."

Diana's reassurance soothes me even as it reminds me I'm staring at the baby I made with a complete stranger.

I push to my feet and stumble into the bathroom, yank open the drawer, grab the cortisone, then return to the kitchen. Laurel stands wide-eyed, still at the sink, hands wrapped in the towel.

"Give me your hands."

Her eyes narrow on the tube, and she sets the towel on the counter and stares at her hands, now pink from all the hot water and scrubbing. "What's that?"

"Prescription-strength cortisone. It will help prevent any sort of reaction. How long were you holding them?"

She looks back up at me, her brow furrowed. "Not even a minute or two. I had literally just picked them and came right back in."

Then the chance of there being any lingering effects is pretty slim, but it's better to be safe than sorry in these types of situations.

I squeeze the lotion onto my fingers and slide them over her hand, rubbing it into every inch of her smooth, warm skin. The heat of her eyes on me as I do it makes my entire body tense, and I avoid looking up at her when that same crackle of energy I felt last night sparks between us.

It's just the charged air from the storm.

Nothing else.

I manage to complete my job, then step over to the sink and start scrubbing my own hands without meeting her questioning gaze. "You should be all right, but let me know if you start feeling strange—dizzy, nauseated, your skin tingling, anything like that."

"I will."

Her soft response makes me pause and glance back at her. She's been nothing but a spitfire since the moment she stepped out of that car yesterday, letting me have it and speaking her mind without hesitation, but suddenly, she's drawing in on herself.

"I'm serious, Laurel. You have to tell me right away.

We're an hour from Lockwood Falls. If you need medical attention up here ..." I bite back the rest of my words and look away, out the window at the woods filling the entire view. Drying my hands, I turn back to her. "We won't get to it fast enough."

She winces and stumbles backward, resting her ass against the counter next to me.

My gaze drifts over my T-shirt on her, hugging her breasts, her pert nipples straining against the soft fabric. Heat starts to unfurl through my body, and I toss the towel onto the counter near her and look away. "I see you went into my bedroom."

She doesn't respond, just keeps staring at her hands, but it's time we laid down some ground rules in addition to my warning about what lurks in the woods beyond the cabin.

"I want to make one thing clear, Ms. Palmer. While you're here, you will not go into my bedroom. You will not go into any other room except the kitchen, the bathroom, and the living room."

Her head tilts up, and she looks to the door at the far side of the cabin, opposite my bedroom. "What's the other door?"

Anger tightens my grip on the counter behind me. "It doesn't matter because you won't be in there. Do you understand?"

She gives a sharp nod, fear darkening her eyes slightly.

"Good. We're going to have to learn to live with each other, for a few days at least. I don't need you invading my privacy or causing any more trouble than you already have."

But something tells me this will be a losing battle with Laurel Palmer.

Chapter Six

WELLS

Laurel sits on the couch where I left her, trembling, wrapped in one of the blankets she pulled from the linen closet and slept with last night, staring at her hands as if she can't even see them anymore.

I think she's past the point of potentially going into shock, but she's been badly shaken by the whole experience. For someone not used to dealing with the various threats up here, who has likely spent her whole life in Denver, surrounded by traffic and the hustle and bustle of everyday living in a major city, it can be overwhelming on a good day.

And today definitely hasn't been a good day for Laurel.

I squat in front of her, getting myself eye-level with her terrified, red-rimmed blue ones. "We should probably get you out of that shirt in case any part of the plant ended up on it."

Her eyes open wide with renewed horror. "Oh, my God. I didn't even think of that."

She glances toward the baby. "What if I touch him? What if—"

I hold up a hand to stop her from spiraling into another full-blown panic attack and rest the other one on her knee. "You got your hands washed fast. It's all right. You'll be okay to touch him. And as long as you don't pass out from hyperventilating, you're going to be just fine. But you need to keep breathing for me."

Every few minutes, she seems to forget to do that and sits, holding her breath, frozen by fear.

I squeeze her leg, my calloused palm resting against her smooth skin. "Just breathe."

She sucks in a deep breath and blows it out, squeezing her eyes closed.

"Okay, sit tight. I'll be right back."

Her eyes fly open. "You're leaving?" She clutches at my shoulder, her nails digging in through my shirt. "Where are you going?"

That panic has returned with a vengeance.

"I'll be *right* back."

Her blue eyes beg me not to leave. I haven't had anyone look at me this way in so long that I've forgotten how hard it is to walk away when someone does.

"A few minutes. I promise."

She relaxes slightly and releases her death grip on me, and I rise and make my way to the door. Pausing with my hand on the knob, I peer back at her for a moment, then allow my gaze to drift over the baby.

He'll be waking up again any minute, and I need her calm and in control to help me with him because I sure as hell won't be cool and collected while he's here. My head has been a jumbled mess since the moment they arrived on my doorstep, and I don't know if it will ever get better.

"It will get better."

Those words I've never been able to believe fill my head, and I tug open the door and walk across the clearing toward the barn where I had been working prior to coming to the cabin to check on Laurel.

The wet ground squishes under my boots, the evidence of last night's rain hanging in the air, thick and heavy with moisture, but some of that electric charge has dissipated, so I can't blame it for the little spark I felt with that woman today.

"She's here to help you."

That one, I can believe, that she's here to help with Wesley and the entire fucked-up situation. But she isn't here willingly. Laurel will take the first opportunity presented to her to get back down the mountain and to the life I'm keeping her from. But her stay here doesn't have to be so horrible.

I can make it easier for her, even if it makes it harder for me.

And this shit isn't going to be easy.

I push open the sliding barn door and inhale the smell of old wood mixed with new. The chair I was working on the other day sits in my workshop to the left, and the large table in the center of the space immediately draws my eye. I walk past it, dragging my finger over the perfect top on my way toward the ladder that leads up to the loft.

Each rung I take up tightens my chest more.

She needs it. You have to do this.

Now I'm the one reminding myself to keep breathing when my lungs don't seem to want to work.

In. Out. Breathe.

I pull myself up onto the loft and slowly approach the pile of boxes tucked in the corner.

I'm sorry, Di.

"She needs them more now than I ever will."

It's exactly what she would have said. Always giving. Always worried about others. Always willing to give anything to anyone to make their life easier.

I walk over to the top box and flip off the lid. A familiar teal fills my vision before tears flood it, and I wince and squeeze my eyes closed, sliding the top back over it. But I stop myself when it's three-quarters closed, then reach in and pull out Diana's favorite sweater.

I bring the soft material to my nose and inhale deeply.

Fuck.

It still smells like her, even after all this time up here in the musty barn loft.

I knew it would—that's why I had to have it out of the house, why I had to lock it away up here and pretend it didn't exist for the last two years. It's why I had to do that with all her things, because if I had to look at them, smell them, touch them every day, I wouldn't be able to keep breathing.

Burying my face in it, I allow myself a few moments to breathe her in until a vivid image of how hysterical Laurel just was flashes through my head.

"Take care of her."

I shove the sweater back inside and grab the box, tucking it under my arm to climb down the ladder. The second my feet hit the old, cracked concrete floor, the tears flood my eyes again, and I have to swipe them away with my free hand.

Get a grip.

Laurel doesn't need to see you losing your shit. She's already in a fragile state after what happened today.

No need to upset her more.

I head back toward the cabin, and Wesley's cry hits my ears before I'm halfway across the clearing.

Shit. He's awake.

It couldn't last long, but a few more minutes to get Laurel calmed and settled would have made all of this a lot easier.

I hurry up the steps, grab the knob, and push in the door.

Laurel squats in front of the car seat, gently rocking it, her eyes filled with tears. "I-I'm afraid to pick him up. I don't want to hurt him."

My chest constricts at how much she cares, at how worried she is about hurting him when he isn't even hers. When she's being *forced* to stay here and take care of him by an asshole like me.

"I told you." I close the door behind me. "It's okay. But you should shower and change."

"Into what?" She shrugs and pushes to her feet, the tears back in her eyes. "I didn't bring anything with me. All I have are the two bags Wesley's mom gave us. I didn't even get a chance to grab my purse from the back of the car before you sent Allen down the mountain."

"Fuck." I scrub my hand over my stubble. "I'm sorry about that. Really." I hold up the boxes. "Everything you need should be in here. I'll put it in the bathroom."

I stalk past her before she can ask any questions and set the box next to the sink in the small single bathroom. When I turn around, she's standing just inside the jamb, watching me carefully, her brow furrowed.

"What's in there?"

The things that utterly destroy me.

I release a heavy sigh and pinch the bridge of my nose

against the headache forming behind my eyes. "All sorts of clothes. Some shoes at the bottom."

She pulls her bottom lip under her teeth. "Whose?"

My answer sits like a lead weight in my throat, and I lift my head and let my eyes meet hers. "My wife's."

She cringes slightly, then nods. "Thank you. I...know this can't be easy."

I hold up a hand. "Don't."

If she starts up a conversation right now about Diana and Maribel, I will completely lose the control I managed to regain back in the barn.

I stalk past her, my shoulder brushing against hers, sending a jolt of electricity through my body that mirrors what I felt during the storm last night and earlier when I touched her hands.

This woman has me all kinds of on edge, and it isn't just because of what she brought with her up here. Laurel is making me face things I've ignored for years at the worst possible time.

I can feel her eyes on me as I stride back toward the fussing baby, and I can feel the question, though she doesn't ask it.

Don't poke the angry bear.

Smart.

She is learning something about surviving on the mountain.

I glance back at where she stands just outside the bathroom, arms wrapped around herself protectively. "Don't worry. I'll take care of him until you're done."

Laurel swallows thickly. "Are you sure?"

"Do I have a choice?"

She presses her lips together, almost as if she's forcing

herself not to say anything else, then slips into the bathroom and shuts the door behind her.

I sag against the wall, dropping my head and releasing some of the tension from the back of my neck. Wesley continues to cry and flail, and I can't ignore it anymore, but I also can't make my shaking hands move to pick him up.

Instead, I push to my feet and make my way into the kitchen, mix up one of his bottles, and squat in front of Wesley.

"Is this what you need?" I slip the nipple between his lips, and he immediately latches and lifts his hands to rest on the side of the bottle. "Already holding your bottle yourself, huh, bud? Impressive."

Not that I know anything about babies, aside from what I read in that stupid book Diana gave me.

What to Expect When You're Expecting...

Yeah, fucking right.

There isn't anything in there to tell you what to do when your wife goes into labor six weeks early and you're hours from any major medical center. What to do when her placenta ruptures and there's so much blood all you can see is red. What to do when you have to bury her and your child instead of bringing them home to the life you planned together.

My legs give out from under me, and I fall to my ass on the hardwood floor, tears flowing down my cheeks as I stare at the little guy in front of me.

I reach forward and nudge the edge of the car seat, rocking it gently as he sucks down the bottle.

What Laurel said to him last night after I locked myself into my room was right.

None of this is his fault.

This is all mine.

I did this.

And I need to figure out a way to deal with it before it eats me alive.

LAUREL

A delicious scent wafts through the crack under the door and hits me in the bathroom. I inhale deeply, and my stomach rumbles.

Oh, my God, have I really not eaten?

Not since yesterday morning. Before that woman showed up at the office with Wesley. Before the long car ride up here. Before the enigmatic Wells Lockwood decided to keep me prisoner in his cabin...

Though, I didn't feel so much like I was a prisoner when he was taking care of me. When he rushed to ensure my and Wesley's safety. When he ran his calloused, rough hands over mine. When that same heat simmered between us. When he brought me these clothes, even though it must be agonizing for him to pull out his wife's things.

I glance down at the jeans and snug-fitting long-sleeved T-shirt. Something about wearing Diana's clothes makes a chill climb up my spine, but I don't have any choice. And Lockwood wouldn't have given them to me if he didn't want me to use them. That much I'm abundantly clear on. He isn't the type of man to offer anything without meaning.

You need to cut him some slack, Laurel. He's just had his entire world turned upside down.

My stomach rumbles again, and I finish brushing my hair with a brush I found in the back of one of the bathroom drawers and check myself in the mirror again.

It isn't much of an improvement from this morning, but at least the long, hot shower allowed me to cleanse the remaining mud and makeup from my body. Dark circles still rim my eyes, now red and puffy from tears, but given how the day has gone, I shouldn't be complaining.

Things could have ended so badly—for me and Wesley.

Bile climbs my throat at that thought I've been trying my best not to dwell on, and I swallow it back, open the door, and slip out into the main living space of the cabin.

Something clanks in the kitchen, and I scan the living room but can't find the car seat. I pad slowly with bare feet across the wooden floor and peek into the kitchen area.

Lockwood stands at the stove, stirring something. Wesley's still in his car seat near his feet, happily playing with one of the toys his mother put into the bags.

"Are you just going to stand there and watch?"

I jerk upright. "Sorry, I didn't mean to. I just didn't want to interrupt anything."

He glances over his shoulder and inclines his head to the small two-seat table under the window. "Take a seat. You must be hungry."

I rest my hand over my stomach, and it gurgles again in response. "You have no idea."

Stirring slowly, he snorts and offers a smirk. "I do have *some* idea. It's a long drive up here from Denver, and my guess is you didn't pack anything to eat on the way."

"Definitely didn't." I scowl at him. "Nor did I expect to be forced to stay."

His lips twist, but he doesn't respond. He just ladles whatever's in the pot into a bowl and shoves a spoon into it, then walks over and slides it in front of me.

I glance down at it. "What is this?"

"Stew. It's one of the only things I know how to make that doesn't taste like ass."

My barked laugh of response makes him take a half-step back. I press my hand over my mouth. "Oh, my God. I'm sorry. I don't know why that was so funny."

Something about a man like Wells Lockwood using that saying just doesn't fit—at all. Though, it seems like he isn't anything like what I was expecting. Not the man he was in photos. Not even the man he was yesterday when he stepped out of those woods with the axe, ready to do battle with anyone and everyone.

He seems softer somehow, or maybe I can finally see what's hiding beneath the layer of darkness that's clouded him since he lost his wife and daughter.

I inhale the steam floating up from the bowl, and my mouth waters. "It smells delicious." Poking at it with my spoon, I find carrots, potatoes, and chunks of meat. "What's in it, if I can ask?"

Lockwood crosses his arms over his chest. "That depends. If I tell you, are you going to refuse to eat it?"

Shaking my head, I dig in and hold a bite to my mouth. "No. I'm not a picky eater. When you grow up in foster homes and sometimes don't have a whole lot of food, you learn to take what you can get."

His gaze softens slightly, that same pity overtaking it I hated seeing before. "How long were you in the foster system?"

Shit. I need to stop mentioning that if I don't want him asking too many questions.

"Long enough to learn some life lessons that have stuck with me."

One of his dark brows rises. "Your parents?"

I try not to cringe as I take another bite. "This is really good."

He offers a half-smile but stands with his arms crossed, waiting for me to answer his question. I wouldn't have thought Wells Lockwood would want to delve into my troubled background, and a huge part of me screams that I shouldn't be telling any of this to my *boss*. But if there's any chance of my experience helping him in *this* one, then I have to share it.

I spoon stew into my mouth again, chewing slowly to buy myself a little time before I have to reply. Finally, I swallow and sit back slightly, stirring the bowl to keep from having to look at the man who suddenly unnerves me. "My mother wasn't exactly maternal. Kept leaving me with various friends while she went out and did...whatever." I release a heavy sigh. "And my father"—I glance up at him—"he knew about me but never wanted to be involved. Denied I was his."

Lockwood winces and turns away, heading back to the stove and keeping his back to me while he fills his own bowl and tosses a spoon into it. I think he'll flee again—back out to the barn or his bedroom to eat, where he doesn't have to face *everything* out here. But he grabs the car seat and carries Wesley over to set him on the floor next to us while we eat.

He takes the chair opposite me and digs in without verbally acknowledging my revelation or its connection to his current situation.

I tap my spoon on the edge of the bowl, then stir the delicious stew, more interested in forcing the conversation I probably shouldn't than in eating. "You said you're pretty sure he's yours..."

Lockwood stills with the spoon halfway to his mouth

and swallows thickly, then nods slowly before he takes a bite. He chews, watching the baby as if Wesley is somehow going to give him the answer. "It's the eyes."

I smirk, nudging the car seat with my foot and watching Wesley giggle and shake his toy. "I noticed it the minute you walked out of those woods."

"My dad has the same ones."

"Why didn't Landry want to call him?"

Wells drops his spoon into the bowl and leans back with a disgruntled groan. "Because my relationship with my father is very complicated."

"How so?"

He runs a hand back through his long hair, his bicep flexing and pulling against the T-shirt fabric. "I was groomed to take over the company, and that's all I ever wanted. He *made* me want it. He did a great job during his time running Lockwood Brewing, but he was forced to retire younger than he had planned due to his heart condition, so I had to step up."

"So, what was the problem?"

One of his shoulders rises and falls. "I wanted to push Lockwood Brewery into the new millennium while he was still set on tactics that worked in the '80s and '90s." His amber eyes meet mine. "It's a different world now. I wanted to focus more on craft brews."

"You mean the ones with the funny names?"

He smirks, and something deep in my core flip-flops at how handsome he really is. "Something like that. I had one called 'Locked and Loaded' that was almost double the alcohol content of our standard ale."

"Really?" I can't help but grin at the name. "That's actually clever."

He offers another half-shrug. "I thought so, but Dad hated it. He tried to go behind my back to get it nixed."

"Can he do that?"

An annoyed sigh slips from his lips. "He's formally retired. We don't have a board. We're one-hundred percent family-owned. So, while he still technically owns the company until he dies, nobody should be taking orders from him when I'm the CEO."

"Why *are* you the CEO?"

His eyes harden.

Shit, I shouldn't have asked that.

I shift forward in my chair toward him, offering an apologetic look. "I just mean, hasn't Landry been handling everything for the last two years? Isn't that kind of his role now? Why maintain the title?"

He leans forward, anger tightening his jaw. "Because no matter how fucked up in the head I might be, no matter how badly I may need to be *here,* this is still my family legacy. My great-great-grandfather built this company literally from the ground up, including this cabin that he lived in while he was doing it. I may have modernized things here"—he motions upward—"put in solar and a generator, dug a new well, added a water heater, a washer and dryer, things that make it easier to live up here. And I might have modernized some of our branding and product, but at its heart, this is a *family* company, and if Landry takes over as CEO, it won't be anymore."

The passion he holds for the Lockwood family legacy, for what they did, for how hard his predecessors struggled to put them in the position they hold today rings strong in every word. Staying up here, disconnected from the world, from the business, can't be easy for him.

"So, you plan to go back then?"

It's a simple question, at least it should be, but he runs his hands over his face like I just asked him to donate a damn kidney and pushes his bowl away.

"I don't fucking know." He glances down at the baby, who coos and shakes his rattle. A few moments pass with him staring at the boy who must be his son, undoubtedly wondering what kind of future he will have and how to secure it properly when he feels like his own life is up in the air—and up this mountain. "I have a lot of shit to do around here."

Lockwood pushes away from the table and motions toward the stove. "Help yourself to more if you're hungry and put the rest in the fridge."

He stalks toward the front door and tugs on his boots, bending down to lace them with more aggression than necessary for the task.

"When will you be back?"

The pain in his eyes when he looks back at me almost knocks me off my chair. "The fuck if I know."

Chapter Seven

LAUREL

Day three of captivity. Maybe I should keep a diary or something. Documenting my days with Wells Lockwood like prisoners do the time in their cells. The small cabin feels like a prison today, despite the progress I *thought* we made yesterday.

One step forward, six steps back.

That's the way it seems to work with Lockwood. All the demons that attack him lash out whenever we're getting somewhere, leaving me here again, stuck in his home, with nothing to do but wait for Landry or someone else from corporate to appear magically with the answer Lockwood seeks so he's finally *forced* to make some decisions,

At least I have an adorable cellmate.

"You're such a handsome little guy, aren't you, Wesley?"

He gets that from his father.

As soon as Candace told us he was Lockwood's, I could see the family resemblance, and when he opened his eyes, it sealed the deal. Landry must have seen the same thing because his whole demeanor changed toward the woman who showed up with this baby—from a confrontation with a perceived enemy to trying to do damage control with someone who could severely tarnish the company and the Lockwood name.

But I can't see him as anything other than an innocent, sweet, adorable little baby wrapped up in the center of drama he has no control over.

I tickle his tummy. He giggles and smiles up at me, staring with the same big bourbon eyes his father has. No one could look at this baby and not see Wells in him, and that's likely exactly why he refuses to look at him.

Seeing the very real consequences of one's actions can be a major blow, especially when he's already spiraling from his other traumas. But that leaves the two of us bored and antsy in a way I'm not sure I've ever felt before.

I push up from the floor where I've been playing with Wesley on the mat his mother rolled up in one of the bags to pace around the living room with him on my hip. My short path leads me back over to the bookcase.

"Maybe we should just read something—anything—to get our minds off having nothing else to do." I scan over the same titles I did yesterday, but nothing leaps out at me as something that might keep me occupied. Then I pause at one of the pictures and point. "This man right here is your grandfather. You're named after him."

The baby coos and opens and closes his fingers, reaching out toward the picture. I pull the dusty frame from the shelf and let him hold it on one side. He stares at it quizzically before I take it and put it back so he doesn't somehow knock it down and break the glass.

I blow out a puff of air off to get the bangs out of my face, continuing to pace around the small room, seeing all the same things over and over. Sitting still has never been my forte, and after yesterday's almost-poisoning-myself-and-the-baby incident, wandering around outside doesn't exactly seem safe, either.

And it isn't as if Wells has offered me any options or suggestions on how to fill my time while I'm here. The man was out the door again this morning before I even woke.

Perhaps I could cook something?

I *do* know my way around the kitchen after helping my various foster mothers over the years, but curiosity has nagged at me all day. And it finally gets the better of me when I stop at the closed door on the other side of the room.

Sunlight peaks out from underneath it, but it's dead quiet in there—no whir or thump of machines, so it doesn't house any equipment Lockwood uses to run this place.

I try the handle, but it's locked.

Dammit.

What are the chances there's a key easily accessible somewhere that I can find it?

Wells probably keeps it on him even though there isn't anyone else up here who could try to access the room—under normal circumstances. This lock might stop someone with a mild curiosity, but luckily, I learned a thing or two in those foster homes.

I settle Wesley back in his car seat and head to the bathroom to dig around in the drawers until I find what I need—a bobby pin.

"Pretend you're not seeing me do this. Okay?"

He smiles and grunts, completely oblivious to the crime I'm about to commit. Though breaking into a locked room seems mild in comparison to what Lockwood has done to me.

I grab the car seat and settle him next to the door before

I drop to my knees and quickly work on picking the lock.

Just like riding a bike.

It pops easily within a few seconds, and I offer him a satisfied grin.

"We did it, Wesley."

He giggles and reaches for me, and I scoop him up, push open the door, and carry him into the room.

My steps immediately falter.

Oh, God...the nursery.

A stunning handmade crib stands directly across from me under the sole window in the room. Beautiful turned spindles painted bright white. A matching rocking chair sits unused in the corner, a hand-knitted gray and white afghan draped over the back. Another handmade dresser, similar to the ones in the master bedroom, except zoo animals are etched on the front of the drawers, occupies the far wall with a built-in changing table on top of it.

No wonder Wells kept this room locked.

It represents all his dreams and the greatest nightmare he's now stuck living, all rolled into one small space.

I take another step in, then another, running my fingertips along the beautiful crib rail.

"They never got to use this, Wesley. They never had the chance..."

Tears well in my eyes for what he's suffered, and it makes it so much easier to dismiss his anger and attitude over the last few days. With everything he has been through, no one could handle my showing up with Wesley well.

I move over to a small bookcase already a quarter filled with brand-new baby books that were never even cracked open. A thin layer of dust hangs on everything, and a tear falls from my eye and streaks down my cheek.

The wood floor creaks behind me, and I spin around with my heart in my throat.

Lockwood stands just outside the room, hands clenched into fists at his sides, his jaw locked so tight, it looks like his teeth might shatter. "I told you to stay out of here. How the hell did you get in?"

"I ..." I glance at the baby, still oblivious to everything going on around him, now focused on the new arrival, who shoots daggers in his gaze. "I'm sorry. I didn't mean—"

"You didn't mean what?" he roars, taking another step forward but not daring to cross the threshold into the room. "To invade my fucking privacy? To violate the one sacred space I have?"

I've never seen a volcano, but I imagine this is what it looks like right before it's about to erupt.

And I'm directly in its path.

WELLS

I open and close my fists at my sides, trying to control the rage boiling inside me, but it doesn't help any of it dissipate. Not when Laurel stands there, holding Wesley in the room meant for Maribel.

Everything I thought I'd have. Everything I ever wanted. Everything *we* dreamed of. All of it was snatched away from Diana and me in a matter of minutes.

And Laurel has the audacity to defy my wishes and come into the one place that's still pristine. Where I can still imagine they're alive and happy and okay in here as long as I keep the damn door closed.

My whole body vibrates with my rage, though it isn't

really all directed at her. "What the hell makes you think you have the right to be in here?"

Laurel opens and closes her mouth a few times. A wet trail of tears stains both her cheeks. "I'm sorry." She glances at Wesley, then back at me. Her soft-blue gaze holds an apology, but the fire is still there, the one that wants to defy and push. "Curiosity got the better of me. I didn't know..."

Didn't know.

She knew I told her to stay out.

She knew I warned her not to snoop at the cabin or go outside exploring on her own.

She knew I was trying to protect her from *this,* from turning me into the person I hate being. One who lashes out to hurt someone else to try to ease my own pain.

"Be nice. She's here to help you."

Of course, Diana would make her displeasure at my attitude known. She was never afraid to call me out on my bullshit or to demand I make an apology when I stepped over a line I never should have crossed.

She was the very best of me, the thing that kept me in check, that stopped me from working too hard or getting too deep into my own head. But since she's been gone, I haven't had anywhere else to go. Nothing else to do but wallow in my own personal nightmare.

I take another step but stop at the jamb, refusing to enter the room I haven't set foot in since they died. Even after boxing up Diana's things, I couldn't bring myself to go into the nursery. I preferred to imagine it with life in it as we had planned rather than as the dead, empty space it became.

"Of course, you didn't fucking know what was behind this door because you didn't *think.*"

There's no way she went to work for Lockwood

Brewing without doing her research. She couldn't live in Denver and not see the massive news articles about Diana's death. If she had actually thought about it, she would have known what was behind that door and why I kept it locked, and she would have respected my wishes instead of rebelling.

"You don't have free rein over my place while you're here, Laurel. This isn't a fucking vacation."

"You think I don't know that?" A sob slips from her throat, her pretty pink, bow lips trembling. "This is the last place I want to be, Mr. Lockwood. I should be at the office right now, learning my role, working on contracts, doing what I've always wanted to do my entire life and busted my ass to be *able* to do for a company like *yours*. But instead, I'm your goddamn babysitter."

Wesley chooses now to yank on a hunk of her hair, and Laurel winces and reaches over to pry his little fingers from it.

"No, kiddo." She presses her lips to his hand affectionately. "Ouch."

He giggles and opens and closes his fist, reaching out toward a colorful abstract painting of an elephant on the wall—just one of many that adorn the space and give it a sense of playfulness and movement.

Diana insisted on them since we wanted to be surprised about the sex of the baby. She said all the gray and white décor needed to be livened up with something gender neutral until he or she was born.

Had they lived, I have no doubt she would have filled the nursery with pink everything, and staring at Wesley in the space now, I can almost see another life. One where we had a boy and Diana didn't die.

I force my eyes closed against the onslaught of memories and dreams I don't dare allow to overtake my mind. If I fall down that rabbit hole, I'll never get out.

"Mr. Lockwood?" She waits for me to reopen my eyes and look at her again. "I understand why you have this room locked, why you wouldn't want me in here, but—"

"But what?" Another migraine pounds at my head, increasing in intensity the angrier I become. Diana's expressing her disdain for the way I'm tearing into this poor girl. "Don't tell me you understand when you can't possibly."

Laurel shakes her head, her red hair flying around her. "No one can understand. You're right. That was a poor choice of words." She takes a step toward me, defiantly, her shoulders back. "But you have everything you need to take care of a baby in here, yet you act like this one doesn't even exist."

She holds him up toward me, and his whiskey colored eyes meet mine as he giggles and flails his arms and legs, reaching out to me.

I stumble back a step, wincing, hand at my throbbing temple. "Because..." I shake my head. "Because I just *can't*."

"You're not going to be able to ignore that he exists forever, Mr. Lockwood. You and I both know what that DNA test is going to say. He's your son, your responsibility now, not mine. You may be able to force me to stay here with promises of money and promotion, but eventually, I'm going to leave. I'm going to go back to work, and you are going to be stuck here alone with him." She advances, stopping right in front of me, cradling him to her chest. "And you're going to have to figure it the *fuck* out."

She storms out of the room past me, slamming her shoulder into mine with purpose, but there isn't anywhere to go, nowhere to hide from me in the cabin.

I follow her across the living room, intent on continuing our conversation, but she darts into the bathroom and slams the door, throwing the lock before I can stop her.

Fucking hell.

Laurel Palmer is the definition of a spitfire. No wonder Landry hired her. She'd be an asset to anyone in any legal situation, and if everything she has said about her childhood and what she's had to endure is true, then she isn't ever going to break, which is good because something tells me the longer she's here, the closer she's going to get to it.

I shove off the doorjamb and stalk back toward the door.

The only reason I even came back to the cabin was to check to see if she needed help with anything for lunch. Here I thought I was doing something nice to show her I appreciate her assistance—however reluctant it might be. But she broke in to the damn nursery.

I stare back at the open door, the one that has stayed locked since the day I buried them.

A vision of Diana standing there, her brunette hair tumbling down around her shoulders, holding our little girl who looked so much like her flashes through my head so vividly, it's like I can reach out and touch them.

"We're okay, Wells. And you will be soon."

My lungs seize in my chest, and I can't seem to pull in any air. Darkness creeps into the edges of my vision. I squeeze my eyes closed and shake my head to try to clear it and stumble down the steps out into the bright sunshine.

Even the heat and beautiful day aren't going to be able to eradicate the darkness seeing them in the nursery has brought down upon me again.

There was a reason I kept that door locked because I knew that nursery would take me down into the depths of the abyss, one I'm not sure I can get out of.

Chapter Eight

WELLS

The harsh bourbon burns my throat, but I chug it anyway—two quick glugs that leave my belly on fire. I wince and set the bottle down on the concrete floor beside where I sit, leaning against one of the massive old posts of the barn that houses some of the livestock and doubles as my workshop.

I stare at the long table, the one that sat untouched for two years in the center of the space, the one I haven't been able to bring myself to work on since they died.

It was supposed to be for us, for the family. Somewhere we could eat together—the three of us. Where Diana and Maribel would color and do art projects and all the other things little girls love to do with their mothers.

"It's beautiful, Wells."

Even only two-thirds finished, it truly is a work of art. Perhaps the best piece I've ever made. The perfect slabs of wood for each portion. Stunning grain patterns shaped and molded by my hands into exactly what we wanted.

"This isn't how it's supposed to be, Diana." I take another sip and wince. "You should be here right now. Maribel should be here right now."

My statement hangs in the chilly night air, and I drop my head into my palms and release a frustrated sigh filled with all the emotions I can't seem to get a grip on.

"Things are exactly how they're supposed to be."

"How can you say that?"

My anguished question echoes through the high ceilings and off all the old metal implements and equipment I barely use anymore. I've let things go to shit here, only doing the bare minimum to keep the place and myself alive and running.

I shove up from the ground, not even bothering to brush off the sawdust that covers my legs and back. It doesn't matter anyway. I stumble toward the table and run my hand across the perfectly smooth surface that Diana watched me spend hours sanding.

"How can you say it's supposed to be like this? How?"

She doesn't answer my question this time, and the heavy silence weighs on me so hard I might finally crumble under it after all this time.

Instead, my eyes drift over to one of my axes leaning against the wall with the rest of my woodworking tools. My fingers itch to grab it, to use it to get out my aggression and frustration the only way I know how.

"Don't do it, Wells."

I push off the table, grab the axe, and turn back to face it.

"You'll regret it later."

Ignoring her warning, I lift the axe and swing it down with all the power I have straight into the center of the perfect oak table. It slams into the surface, the force reverberating up the handle, my hands and my arms, through my entire body. The blade cuts in deeply, and I jerk and wiggle it free, then raise it and slash it down again.

Over and over, I hack at what was supposed to be our family table, at what should have been a place where we sat together, where we enjoyed being here on the mountain, where we started our lives together, where we fed our daughter and watched her grow into the person she was meant to be.

This should have been a happy gathering place, but instead, it's become a symbol for everything I've lost, and I can't stand to look at it anymore.

Again and again. I slam and bang the axe into the surface, making my way around the table, striking the legs, the sides, chopping off a big chunk of the corner, destroying all my hard work because none of it means anything anymore.

Not without them.

Finally, I can't even lift the axe anymore, my arms aching and floppy like Jell-O.

I stagger over to the almost-empty bottle that I swear was full when I came out here earlier, grab it from the floor, and tip it back, downing what's left. Welcoming the searing pain down my throat.

"That's enough, Wells."

Shaking my head, I chuck the bottle against the concrete. It shatters into a million pieces, the same way I've felt inside for years.

I stumble over the broken shards and out into the chilly night. A billion stars blanket the heavens above, but my eyes won't seem to focus on any of them, a blurry, dark expanse dotted with fuzzy lights.

That single light shines above the cabin door, and I

slowly advance across the small clearing back toward it, each step more unsteady than the last. I grip the handle and shove open the door.

The light on inside causes me to jerk back slightly.

Why is it so bright in here?

Laurel turns from where she stands next to the fireplace, holding the baby, rocking him gently in her arms. Her eyes narrow on me, then widen slightly when she takes me in. That stark blue gaze travels from my muddy boots, up over my dirty, sawdust-covered pants, across the stained T-shirt, and to what can only be my completely disheveled hair.

She mutters something to herself, then goes and sets the baby in the car seat as I stagger in and collapse on the couch.

The soft leather cushions sag slightly under my weight, but finally getting horizontal feels so damn good. I release a sigh and let my eyes drift closed, which only seems to make the world spin around me more.

Fuck.

I let one foot fall to the floor, trying to ground myself so I don't spiral down into whatever tornado is whipping around in the cabin right now.

The click of the door closing hits my ears, followed by hurried footsteps against the creaky floorboard in the living room. I turn my head slightly toward the sound.

"She's here to help you."

Something warm brushes against my arm, and a soft hand tucks hair off my face.

"Mr. Lockwood..."

Fuck.

The formality brings with it annoyance, and I lift my hand and wave it off. "Wells...I think you should call me Wells."

She is living with me and caring for the baby that's likely mine. It makes the *Mr. Lockwood* moniker almost a mocking name. I haven't been that man in so damn long; I don't even know if he's still in here.

"Wells..."

My name from Laurel's lips makes warmth spread through my chest, and her light touch along my arm makes goosebumps spread across my skin.

"Are you all right?"

I bark out a sardonic laugh, and she shushes me and presses a hand over my mouth.

Warm breath flutters across my cheek. "Quiet. The baby's asleep."

"The baby?"

Right. There's a baby now...

I let my eyes flicker open and find bright-blue ones staring back at me with concern. She feathers her fingers over my face, tracing my cheeks and down over the scruff on my chin.

Concern and regret fill her gaze, so different from the confrontational attitude she had with me in the nursery before I blew up at her and went on my bender. "I'm sorry about earlier, Wells. I didn't mean to—"

I shush her this time and reach out to capture her face in my palm, slowly brushing my thumb across her plump lips. "No, I'm sorry."

More than I could ever put into words. For so many things, I can never count them. So damn much in my life has been fucked up because of me, because of what *I* did, because of *my* choices and actions. All of it could have been prevented. I could have changed the outcome, altered it so this future, this present wasn't happening.

But I fucked it all up, and I'm doing it again with the woman who is only here to help me.

"I'm such an asshole."

The corners of her mouth twitch into an almost-smile. "I won't argue with you on that, but I also won't repeat it, since you're technically my boss and I really do need this job."

That's why she's here—the job.

It's hard to remember that when she's invading my space, pushing against my walls, driving me to face the things I've put off and ignored for so long.

And Christ, is she beautiful.

Her red hair spills around her face, a halo on an angel who I'd be lost without right now. If she had gotten in that car, left me here with Wesley, I don't know what I would have done, how I would have coped with any of it.

I drag my thumb over her pinkened cheek. "I don't know how to act around people anymore, and it's been a long time since I've had a beautiful woman in this house."

She stiffens slightly but doesn't pull out of my touch, just examines me with a new curiosity in her assessing gaze.

I don't want her to see any of this, to see me at my worst, to witness what a fucking mess I am.

Closing my eyes, I shake my head. "None of this is the way it's supposed to be. *She* should be here. *They* should be here."

She gently caresses the side of my cheek. "I know, Wells, and I'm so sorry. None of this can be easy for you, and you don't have to apologize to me."

"Yes, I do. None of this is your fault." I lift my head slightly, bringing me even closer to her, and my eyes zero in on her lips. So soft, so pink, so tempting. "It isn't your fault I did something stupid. It isn't your fault you picked the wrong fucking job. It isn't your fault you're so damn beautiful."

She sucks in a sharp breath and slowly leans closer to me, searching my face for something I don't think she can find. Something I'm not even capable of anymore.

Wesley's cry fills the room, and she jerks back as I collapse fully onto the pillow, letting that darkness creep even further in.

LAUREL

A deep, agonizing groan comes from the couch behind me, and I wince before glancing over my shoulder to where Wells has been passed out since late last night.

He releases another groan and rolls onto his other side, facing me in the kitchen, his eyes still clamped closed, like he's afraid to open them.

I would be, too, if I were in his shoes.

I anticipated this morning wouldn't be pretty. Wells was annihilated when he stumbled in here last night. Clearly not thinking with his right mind when he said what he did, when he looked at me that way, touched me like that.

No way it was real.

Even if it felt like it. Even though my body heated. Even if I *wanted* it to be real.

I intentionally bang the heavy cast-iron pan a little too hard on the stove, and his eyes fly open.

He winces and presses his fingers into his temples. "Fuck."

"I thought you might have a rough morning."

He cringes and pushes himself up to sitting, then drops his elbows to his knees and scrubs his face. When he lowers his hands and looks up at me, the heavy red bags under his eyes tell the tale of how bad it really was for him last night.

"I made coffee. Bacon and eggs will be ready in a minute."

Wells cringes and presses his hand over his stomach, looking like he might throw up. "I don't know if I can eat."

"You *need* to, whether you *want* to or not. Whatever you got into last night is just sitting in your stomach. You need some grease and caffeine to soak it up."

"Are you an expert on hangovers?"

I chuckle as I flip the bacon in the frying pan. "You could say that. My roommate in undergrad was a very heavy partier. Any frat that threw a shindig, she had to be at it. She was the girl dancing on tables."

He scoffs. "I bet she did really well in school."

Like Wells Lockwood didn't drink in college...

I cast a glance over my shoulder at him. "Actually, she's an assistant United States attorney in New York."

"Really?"

"Really." I nod. "I went to law school at the University of Denver Sturm, but she headed out east—Harvard."

His dark brows fly up. "Really?"

I nod again. "Yep. So maybe you shouldn't be so judgmental, considering your current condition."

Wells scowls at me and pushes himself up. He wobbles slightly and grips the edge of the couch to keep himself upright. For a minute, it looks like he won't make it without losing his stomach or falling back onto the cushions, but he stumbles to the kitchen and leans against the counter next to me, looking into the pan.

"Was I..."

I glance at him. "You were pretty fucking ripped."

"It certainly feels that way." His brow furrows, and he rubs at the back of his neck, averting his gaze from mine, suddenly interested in his bare feet. "I didn't say or do anything..."

Does he remember the way he touched my face? The way he leaned in like he wanted to kiss me? Does he remember saying I was beautiful?

I shake my head. "No, you didn't. It was the alcohol."

Of course, he's not going to remember.

The man was soaked in what smelled like bourbon, and anything that was said or done last night was only a side-effect of his being completely sloshed.

That's all it was.

It's what got him in this situation with Wesley in the first place. When the man drinks, he latches on to women to help ease the pain of losing his wife.

I don't know if I can really blame him for that, but it certainly doesn't mean I have to let him do it to me.

No matter how handsome he might be.

I'm here for one reason—to take care of that baby until Landry arrives with some sort of plan. Until then, things will remain professional between me and Wells Lockwood.

"Bacon's ready. Grab me that plate."

He snags the plate from the counter and hands it to me. Our fingers brush, and the little spark that jumps between us makes me jerk my hand and the plate away.

Wells doesn't react, though. He just continues to stare at me as I plate the bacon, leaving the fat in the pan. He hasn't had anyone cook for him in a long time—or had a woman in his kitchen.

Don't get used to it, Lockwood.

I crack three of the eggs I found in the fridge into the pan and freeze. "Why do these look weird?"

He glances into the pan and chuckles, his face lighting up in a way I haven't seen since arriving. "Because they're duck eggs."

"Duck eggs?"

"Yep." He inclines his head generally toward the front of the cabin. "Out behind the barn, there's a small pond, and I raise ducks. Their eggs are delicious, and there's nothing like a properly cooked duck breast."

"I don't think I've ever had duck."

One of his eyebrows wings up. "Really?"

I stare down into the pan, waiting for the perfect moment to pull them from the bubbling fat. "It wasn't really served at any of the places I lived growing up."

Hell, I was lucky to get boxed mac and cheese most nights.

"What about since then? You've never been to a nice restaurant that served duck?"

I listen to the eggs pop and sizzle. "Not really. I went to school on scholarships, so I didn't have a lot of extra cash lying around for fancy dinners."

Wells crosses his arms over his chest. "And no boyfriend ever took you out and paid for it?"

Snorting incredulously, I shake my head. "Who had time for boyfriends?"

He offers a shrug. "Diana and I dated for half of undergrad and all through my law school."

"Yeah, but you two were already together by the time you hit one-L year. I wasn't about to start up a relationship with somebody when my entire focus was academics."

Not when I had to work so hard to even get there.

I had tunnel vision, and there wasn't any room in that tunnel for a boyfriend. The light at the end was a stable life, filled with all the things I never had—a home, a family, the ability to buy whatever I needed or even *wanted* without having to think about whether or not I could afford to eat if I did.

Wells studies me for a moment. "I can appreciate that. You're focused, driven."

I glance at him. "I am, which is why being stuck up here playing nanny isn't exactly where I thought I'd find myself my first week on the job."

He releases a heavy sigh and shoves his hand through his sandy light-brown hair, the long strands hitting his shoulders. "I know. Believe me. Hopefully, we can get some sort of resolution to all this soon."

Resolution to all this.

The way he says it makes it seem like a business transaction, not his damn life. Not Wesley's.

I grab the spatula and slide the eggs out of the pan and onto the plate, then shove it into his chest a little more aggressively than I had intended. "Eat."

He stares down at the food, his skin taking on an almost green hue.

"I don't care, Wells. Don't argue. Eat it."

Suddenly there are two children here who need to be mothered.

But Wells hasn't had anyone to take care of him for a long time. By his own choice. I have no doubt he has dozens of employees at the mansion he lived in with Diana in Denver who would wait on him hand and foot had he chosen to remain there instead of hiding out up here in one of the remotest parts of the mountains.

He groans and takes the plate over to the table, but rather than sit across from him, I lean back against the counter, wanting to put some distance between us. My skin tightens with both his proximity and my annoyance at the way he's addressing his entire situation.

Tapping my bare foot on the wooden floor, I watch him examine the food in front of him. "What are you going to do?"

He cuts into the eggs, the yolk running out across the plate. "What do you mean?"

"About Wesley?" I incline my head toward the car seat where he's been sleeping since I gave him his last bottle.

Thank Christ they mostly sleep at this age because, without more to entertain him and do with him around here, this could get very tedious very quickly.

"Let's assume the test comes back and he's yours, which I think both you and I know is true."

He stills with his fork halfway to his mouth, swallows thickly, then shoves the eggs in and chews slowly, staring at his plate. "I don't know. I can't really think about that right now."

"You're going to have to think about it soon. They were going to try to rush the tests at one of the local labs anonymously. I think he said three days, maybe four, and then Landry will be coming up here with the results."

"And you'll be leaving."

"The first chance I get."

His gaze drifts over to Wesley, and his eyes soften slightly. *Something* is there, buried beneath this wall he's built around himself.

Wells Lockwood isn't a bad man. He's a broken one.

And all of this, the timing of it, is just too much for him to handle rationally.

I can't really blame him for that, and the way he looks at the baby is starting to change. Maybe because he's beginning to realize this isn't going away. That he's going to have to face the consequences of his actions, including the very real little boy in there who's going to need him.

Chapter Nine

WELLS

"*You know what you need to do.*"

Di's voice echoes through my head in time with the throbbing in my temples as I stare at Wesley. I take a bite of my eggs and chew slowly, trying to buy myself some more time to think. Because even though she's right—and so is Laurel—I'm not ready to say the words, not just yet.

They sit like acid on my tongue, and all the things I've been holding inside for so long try to pull it back down into my gut. I've lived with my pain-fueled anger driving me forward for so long that it's almost impossible to let it go.

I cling to it the same way I cling to the dream life I thought I'd have by now. But no amount of money or prayer or sacrifice can ever bring Diana and Maribel back.

I've always known that, but having Laurel and Wesley here makes it abundantly clear that I can try to run from my life, from the real world, but eventually, it will find me and force me to face it head-on.

Laurel bangs around in the kitchen, washing the pans and putting things away, casting me curious glances every few moments. The heat in her eyes has altered slightly from the sheer hatred she had when she arrived to an almost resignation and something else I can't quite place.

Unease creeps over me, and foggy memories of drinking in the barn come floating back as I clean my plate and push it away, my stomach already feeling better.

"Thank you for breakfast, and for…" I trail off and rub my hand at my nape, unable to look at her full-on when I can't gather the entire memory of what happened. "Whatever you did last night…" I finally meet her gaze. "I imagine I wasn't very easy to deal with in that state."

I'm not an angry drunk—at least, I never was *before*—but when I fall down that black hole, I can be volatile. It's one of the reasons I locked myself away up here so no one would get caught in the crossfire when I'm lost in myself.

She leans back against the counter and crosses her arms over her chest in one of Diana's favorite low-cut V-neck T-shirts. Her breasts peek out slightly, and I avert my eyes, dropping my focus back to the empty plate and then over to Wesley.

"Do it, Wells. You know it's the right thing."

It is the right thing. Something I should have done the moment Laurel showed up here with Wesley in tow. And I'm a fucking asshole for not doing it.

"You should put him in the nursery."

Laurel's heated gaze rakes on me, and I glance at her.

Her red brows draw low. "Are you sure?"

I nod slowly, push up from the table, and grab my plate to bring it over to where she stands next to the sink. She doesn't move out of my way, and I stop in front of her and reach around her to set it into the soapy water.

With our bodies mere inches from each other, the heat radiates from her and into me. That same crackle of energy sparking between us even though we don't touch.

"He shouldn't be sleeping in that car seat. We don't know how long this is going to take. He should be comfortable. I built that crib for a baby; that's where he should go."

Her eyes soften as she stares up at me. "Thank you."

Why the hell is she thanking me?

I've done nothing but be a total ass to her over something that's completely beyond her control and that she had nothing to do with. If anything, I should be thanking her *endlessly* for the patience and restraint she's shown through all of this.

"Thank you for breakfast."

A half-smile curls her lips. "You feeling better?"

I nod slowly, even though my temples still feel like a hammer's being slammed against them. "Yep."

"I did the best with what I could find in the kitchen."

Shit, I haven't even given her a tour of the property or told her where anything is.

"Besides the ducks, I also have a cow and three goats, and there's a garden on the side of the house."

Her eyes widen with interest. "There is?"

"My wife's. We spent most of our summers up here, and she loved to cook."

Laurel winces slightly.

"I've done what I can with it, but it's nothing like it was when she was the one taking care of it. I do *not* have a green thumb, but there should be more carrots and potatoes, ready to harvest, herbs, things like that. And if you go down into the cellar, I have several deep freezers with some things in them."

"Oh!" Her face lights up. "Well, why don't I go find something that I can make for dinner and let it defrost?"

"You don't have to do that."

"Do what?"

"Cook. I'm perfectly capable of taking care of myself and feeding you."

Her cheeks flare pink, and she shifts uncomfortably. "I don't mind. Really, sounds like you have other things to take care of on the property, which is, I imagine, where you've been the last couple of days."

That and intentionally avoiding you and the baby.

"Yes, and now that I don't feel like I'm about to puke my guts out, I should probably go take care of those things."

She glances at her watch. "He'll probably be waking up soon."

"I'll leave you to get him settled."

While I might have finally accepted that it's time to put him in the nursery, it doesn't mean I have the strength to be here when that happens or to see him in there.

Not right now.

Laurel and I stare at each other for a moment, like she's waiting for me to say something, but I turn and stalk to the bedroom, closing the door behind me.

I drop back against it, resting my head on the solid wood, letting my eyes drift closed. Releasing a heavy sigh, I rub my hands over my face. "What the fuck are you doing, Wells?"

So much has changed in only a handful of days.

I thought what happened two years ago was the most upheaval I would ever have to survive, but now this—a baby in the nursery, a baby in the crib I built for Maribel, *my* baby, only it isn't Diana's. And the woman here taking care of him *and me* isn't anything I could have ever anticipated.

"It's all right, Wells. She's here to help you."

"No, I forced her to stay here and help me. Those are two different things."

"She's here to help you."

I push off from the door, unable to have this conversation in my head again. Not when something bashes against my skull relentlessly and there's so much to do around the property.

Every muscle aches as I change out of my dirty clothes, likely from whatever I ended up doing last night. I have a good guess, but I don't want to think about the damage I may have caused.

I sneak out while Laurel still has her back to me, washing my plate, and I release a heavy breath of relief that I don't have to face her again.

A strange tension hangs between us today that wasn't there yesterday. When she arrived, animosity and hatred laced her words and glares. But now, some tiny bit of that has slipped away. What's left is even more disconcerting.

Laurel Palmer didn't have an easy life; that much is abundantly clear based on the very little she's said about her childhood. And her comment about her parents felt like an ice pick being driven straight into my heart.

No matter the issues Dad and I have had, I never doubted he and Mom cared. That I was cherished. That I was the paramount thing in their lives. At least, I felt that way until Dad made the business more important than our relationship.

That baby doesn't deserve to ever feel that way, and Laurel was right to call me out on it, to ask me what I'm going to do. I just don't have an answer. But I know where I might be able to find one.

The fresh air fills my lungs, and I slowly cross the clearing toward the barn to grab the feed for the animals.

I tug open the partially ajar door and freeze. "Holy shit."

All the breath rushes from my lungs, and my heart stops for a second, quickly replaced by a sense of dread and a painful ache. I rub my fist against the spot and take a step inside the place that has always been mine. Where I come to think, to work with my hands, to create beautiful things from the beauty of nature all around me.

There isn't anything beautiful in here anymore. That sense of peace has been destroyed, shattered by whatever deep pit of despair I fell into last night.

Shards of glass litter the concrete floor. Tools lie strewn across every surface. The destroyed table stands where it always has, only it looks nothing like it did the last time I remember seeing it.

Hours of work.

Nights spent out here, carving, sanding, and lacquering, while Diana looked on.

"It was beautiful, Wells."

It was.

And now, it's utterly decimated.

"What the fuck did I do?"

LAUREL

Wesley stretches and shifts slightly where he lies in the crib but slips back into the relaxed, soft breaths of sleep. Content to slumber on the fresh sheets I found in one of the dresser drawers in the new bed that's never been used.

After spending a few minutes dusting the rest of the room, it doesn't feel like a tomb anymore. There's finally life in here—the way it was meant to be. It may not be what Wells anticipated, but it's the reality now.

I just hope Wesley can't sense all the turmoil and upheaval his tiny presence has caused. Running my hand across his fuzzy little head, the same question that's been haunting me for days rushes back.

How could Candace just walk away from him?

A vise tightens around my chest, and my eyes burn with coming tears.

The same way your mother walked away from you...

At least he's too young to have memories of her, and that's so much better than these flashes that keep coming back to me. The curls in her auburn hair. That floral perfume. Her soft voice singing along with the radio.

Only it was never to me.

I never got lullabies or rocked to sleep, never had comforting arms to run to when I needed it, aside from a few good foster moms over the years. My mother was never one in any sense of the word, and I don't want Wesley to suffer the same fate.

"Things are a little messed up right now, kiddo, but I think your dad will eventually get his shit together. He doesn't really have a choice."

Candace had made it clear she wasn't coming back, that she was expecting Wells to take care of Wesley. And even though this whole situation might have stunned him and left him a bit off-balance, I can see the change.

Every day, he looks at Wesley a little differently. Eventually, whatever's holding him back will finally crumble, and this baby will get a father who would burn down the world for him. Because everything I've discovered about

Wells since I've been up here says he's the type of man who would do just that for anyone he loves.

"Sleep tight, kiddo."

I lean down and press a kiss on his cheek, then slip out of the nursery and close the door behind me with a soft "click." He should be down for a few hours, which gives me time to explore the garden and the cellar Wells mentioned while he's out doing whatever it is he has to do around the property.

And gives me some much-needed space from the man who continues to give me whiplash with his moods.

I open the door and slip out into the beautiful summer afternoon, wearing the shoes I found at the bottom of the box. Up here, the sun seems brighter, warmer, everything more alive, and I inhale the freshest air I've ever smelled in my entire life.

I'll never admit it to Wells, but that is one major benefit to mountain living over city life. The stunning plants and trees aren't bad to look at, either, but now I see them in a whole other light after the hemlock incident.

As interested as I am in exploring, I know better now.

Stick to the cabin unless you're with Wells.

I scan the small clearing for him, especially over near the barn on the far side, mostly concealed behind the trees, but there isn't any sign of my reluctant host. So, I make my way around the side of the cabin until I stumble on several raised garden beds.

Wells said it was nothing compared to what Diana had done, and I can see exactly what he's talking about. Half the beds remain empty, others already starting to fill with weeds.

He isn't doing a very good job taking care of it.

Can you blame him?

He's out here alone, surviving, doing everything he has to in order to keep living day-in, day-out. I certainly couldn't do it.

How will he with a baby?

The thought of him being up here alone with Wesley makes my gut tighten.

It isn't your problem, Laurel.

That's what I keep telling myself. Wells has all the money in the world and a support system in place in Denver. He'll figure it out without my butting into his life.

More than I already have.

I walk between the beds, scanning to see what I might be able to use to throw together something for dinner. Things may be tense and awkward between us, but the man clearly needs some help. The least I can do is cook a nice dinner.

When I hit the end of the row of garden beds, the cellar door is just visible on the backside of the cabin. I head for the large wooden doors and tug them open.

"Jesus, these are heavy..."

They creak as I lift them to expose a pitch-black hole going downward with cracked cement steps. And I don't even have a flashlight or my phone to illuminate whatever's down there.

Horror movies and nightmares.

"Just go."

I slowly descend, one hand balanced against the uneven dirt wall so I don't stumble down the steps. The light filtering in from above and behind me illuminates a string hanging from the ceiling.

Please be a light...

The cool air down here sends a shiver through me and

makes goosebumps pebble on my skin, doing nothing to put me at ease being in the dark, dank space.

I reach up and pull the string, and a single bulb overhead flares to life, casting an eerie glow across the small cellar. Two large chest freezers sit against the far wall of the tight space with an extension cord running down from the ceiling where he tapped into his solar power.

Thank God he has at least some modern conveniences.

I don't know if I would've survived here without a flushing toilet and electricity. Wells may make fun of me if I ever admitted it to his face, but I am a city girl—through and through. This mountain living will never be my thing—like having to walk through a creepy cellar to a freezer to find dinner.

Nope.

Another shiver rolls through me, and I hustle to the freezer and tug open the top.

My scream pierces the air, and I bolt away from the freezer, rush up the steps, and slam smack into a hard, warm body.

Strong arms wrap around me, and Wells pulls me to him, holding me tightly. "Laurel, what's wrong?"

"I-I..."

He pulls back and shakes me gently. "Laurel, tell me what's wrong. I heard you scream as I was about to head inside."

"D-down there..."

His dark brows drop low over his eyes, his grip on my arms tightening. "What? Is there something in the cellar?"

"I...the freezer....I opened it, and something was staring back at me."

His brow furrows for a moment, then he tips his head back and barks out a laugh so loud that it echoes around us.

His entire body shakes as he completely loses it, almost doubling over with laughter.

"What's so funny?"

He returns his gaze to mine, the first true smile I've seen from the man since we met gracing his lips and brightening his entire face, making him even more handsome—which I didn't know was even possible. "You mean the rabbit?"

"He was looking at me, and it moved."

"It didn't move." Wells shakes his head, still having trouble controlling his chuckle. "You probably bumped the freezer with your knee when you were opening it."

"No, I swear, I—"

He grips my chin and holds my face steady, gazing deeply into my eyes. "Calm down, Laurel. I guarantee you that rabbit is plenty dead. I caught it in one of my traps a few days before you came up here."

"But..."

He keeps grinning at me, barely containing his laughter.

"It's not funny! My heart's in my goddamn throat!"

He chuckles. "It *is* funny."

I shove at his hard chest, but it doesn't move him a single inch. "Knock it off, you asshole."

He smirks at me. "Yeah, maybe I am being an asshole for laughing, but I have news for you, Laurel."

"What's that?"

He leans down slightly, his face just inches from mine. "It *is* funny. A city girl like you up here, you'd never survive."

I square my shoulders and step back out of his hold. "How do you know?"

It doesn't matter that I just thought the exact same thing before the *definitely* not-dead rabbit almost leaped out at me. Hearing it from Wells feels like an insult that I have no intention of standing here and taking.

He barks on another laugh and points to the open cellar doors. "A dead, frozen rabbit just scared the shit out of you. You showed up in thousand-dollar stilettos and picked a poisonous plant on your first day. That's three strikes."

I scowl and cross my arms over my chest, his smug grin only making me angrier. "First, I was dressed for *work*. You know, at corporate fucking headquarters, not up on a godforsaken mountain. Second"—I point back at the cellar—"that rabbit *definitely* moved. And third, how the hell was I supposed to know those beautiful white flowers were goddamn hemlock?"

He takes a step toward me, some of the humor evaporating from his stance. "All you need to know is that this place is dangerous. Pretty much everything on this property could kill you in an instant, could tear you limb from limb, and destroy you."

Wells shifts closer, his massive chest and frame towering over me until we stand only inches apart, staring each other down—neither willing to admit defeat.

Heat floods my body, starting at my core and spreading out through my limbs under his fiery gaze. "Are *you* dangerous?"

He narrows his eyes on me. "Very."

I shake my head. "I don't think you are."

"Then you haven't been paying much attention."

"I think you're lonely and confused, and your whole world has been thrown off its axis too many times for you to regain balance. But you aren't dangerous."

His jaw tightens, along with his fists at his sides. "You have no idea what you're talking about, Laurel."

I take a step toward him until my chest brushes his, my

nipples pebbling instantly against the fabric of the shirt. "I do, Wells."

He stiffens at my use of his first name.

Staring up at him, the confusion in his eyes makes me equal parts annoyed and relieved. This tension between us, the electric sizzle that seems only to intensify when we touch, hasn't dissipated. It's only grown the longer I'm here.

Wells feels it, too, but he's too stubborn or too damaged to acknowledge it.

I raise a brow at him, resting my hands against his rock-hard abdomen. "You don't remember last night, do you?"

He stiffens, his muscles under my hands solidifying even more. "What happened last night?"

Too much. Not enough.

I thought this attraction to Wells Lockwood would go away. That sanity would prevail and the fact that he's my boss and beyond emotionally unavailable would convince my body that this is a terrible idea.

Yet the almost kiss last night keeps replaying in my brain on an endless loop, and I can't stop wondering if it would have been as good as I dreamed it was after he fell asleep.

I push up on my tiptoes and hover my mouth over his. "You did this..."

He sucks in a sharp breath, so close that I can feel the air shifting.

"But then, you stopped."

I murmur the words just short of his lips, and we stand frozen for what feels like hours, staring at each other, willing the other to back away, to end the madness the same way Wells did last night.

Wells finally breaks, but this time, he crushes his lips to

mine so hard it knocks me back a step and only his strong arm wrapping around me keeps me upright.

He kisses me with an intensity I've never experienced before. A primal need, as if stealing my breath and my will can somehow keep him alive, and a growl rumbles deep in his chest. The vibration rolls through my ribcage to my heart and down between my legs to make my clit throb.

I moan into his mouth, clinging to his shirt, trying to get him even closer, but he jerks away from me, leaving me panting and breathless.

His eyes wild, he releases his hold on me and takes a step back. "Don't ever underestimate how dangerous I can be, Laurel. It could be a deadly mistake."

Chapter Ten

LAUREL

Even the roaring fire in the fireplace and the warm tea in the mug in my hands can't alleviate the chill that settled over me this evening. I snuggle deeper under the blankets on the couch, my knees pulled up to my chest, staring into the flames.

Wells' warning to me this afternoon rings loudly in my ears, and the feeling of his lips against mine makes them tingle again. All that anger and heat and passion being poured into that kiss.

A shudder rolls through me, and I take another sip of the warm liquid and then stare down into it. All it does is remind me of why he is the way he is. Because given the way the tea was tucked into the back of the cabinet, it was likely Diana's and has been sitting there untouched for years.

Just like Wells.

He's been locked away up here, a broken man with

nothing to do but dwell on his loss, and bringing that baby up here only crushed the already-shattered pieces into dust.

One strong wind is all it would take to destroy him completely, to blow away all the parts of him that are good and strong. The ones I *know* are still there, that I see glimpses of when he has moments of clarity.

I tighten my hands on the mug and take another sip. The click of the bathroom door opening makes me freeze. He snuck in there to shower while I was cooking dinner and has managed to keep himself locked away since then. He'll likely just duck into the bedroom without even coming out to see me, and I can't say I blame him.

I'm not sure either of us is ready to face what happened or the way my body reacted to his strong hands on me, his warm mouth moving against mine.

It was exactly what I said I would avoid. I can't be attracted to my boss, especially when that boss is Wells Lockwood and completely unavailable.

I squeeze my eyes closed and wait, listening for the sound of his bare feet on the wooden floor heading to the bedroom. One of the boards creaks, and I open my eyes and find him standing just inside the living room, long hair damp and falling to his shoulders, eyes narrowed and full of that same confusion as earlier today.

Firelight dances across one side of his face—half illuminating him while leaving another half in the dark. The perfect physical representation of the man I'm staring back at.

I swallowed thickly. "Do you want dinner? I made rabbit pot pie."

For a split second, his eyes soften before they go back to hard granite. "Not hungry."

It shouldn't hurt so much to hear him say that, to have

him reject the meal I made for him, but my chest aches, and to avoid saying something else I might regret, I take another sip of my tea.

He scans the room, and I incline my head to the closed door of the nursery.

"He's already down. Took his bottle about half an hour ago."

"Oh."

The slight tinge of disappointment in his voice gives me hope that maybe the tide is turning, that maybe, just maybe, Wells will be able to accept this child the way he would have the one he had with Diana.

He turns his back to head toward the bedroom, and I drop my feet to the cool wooden floor.

"Are we really not going to talk about it?"

His shoulders stiffen, and he freezes. His hands fist at his side, and his neck muscles tense.

Wells glances over his shoulder at me. "There isn't anything to talk about."

"Like hell, there isn't."

He releases a heavy sigh and turns his head away from me again. "Please, Laurel." He shakes his head. "I can't." He sucks in a heavy breath. "I can't right now."

His words are so final. It's like a bullet through my heart, but I shouldn't care. It shouldn't bother me. There's no reason I should care if Wells Lockwood kissed me in a moment of heated anger and passion. It was a fluke. It will never happen again. He and I both know he's lonely. He's been up here with very little human contact for two years. People can't live that way. Not for long, not without going completely nuts. And he seems to already be on the brink of that. Then I show up here with all of this.

Maybe pushing him to talk about what happened earlier is too much tonight.

"At least...don't run away. Come sit."

He stands stock still for a moment, turned away from me, contemplating his choices. Then slowly, he turns toward me, his face an impassive mask, though his eyes give away something else completely different.

All the turmoil raging there makes my stomach clench.

"I made tea. It's in the pot on the stove."

Wells winces.

Shit, I was right. It was hers.

He inhales deeply. "Chamomile. I can smell it."

I nod slowly. "Yes, I needed something comforting tonight."

His brow furrows slightly. "Are you all right?"

Fucking hell. Of course, he'd ask that like everything's fine.

I release a sardonic laugh and shake my head, tucking my legs up again. "You think anything about this situation is all right?"

He runs a hand through his hair. "No. And I can't offer any more apologies than I already have."

I shake my head. "I don't even care about this, you keeping me here anymore. I'm worried about that baby."

His entire body stiffens again. "What do you mean?"

I stare into my tea rather than look at him when I say this because it'll hurt him. "I'm worried about what's going to happen when that DNA test comes back and you can't pretend you don't know the truth. I'm worried about leaving you here with that baby alone. And I'm even more worried that you're just going to pawn him off on someone else—a nanny, a babysitter, even adopt him out to someone rather than have to look at him."

He winces and takes a step forward to rest his hands on the back of the chair opposite the couch. His fingers tighten on it, and he drops his head, staring down at the cushion. "You don't think I'm scared of that, too?" His voice almost breaks, like he's fighting back some unstoppable emotion. "All I ever wanted was what Diana and I had. We waited so damn long." He sucks in a breath. "Through two years of college, three years of law school. And even then, we put off having a family because I was so damn busy with Lockwood Brewing.

"I was so intent on building up the business, on showing my father that I could take over his role, and she supported me a hundred percent through all of it. Putting off having kids, the family we always said we wanted, that by the time we started trying..." He trails off slightly. "We were both over thirty-five, and that made it all the more difficult. It took us three years to finally get pregnant."

I want to go to him, to wrap my arms around him and offer him some comfort, but he wouldn't want that now. Maybe not ever.

Wells finally lifts his head to look at me, and the pain in his tear-soaked eyes physically knocks me backward farther onto the couch. "We thought we were finally going to have everything we ever wanted."

"I'm so sorry, Wells. I can't imagine how hard this must be for you."

"You have no idea." His bottom lip quivers. "You can't fathom what it takes for me to wake up every day without her, without them. And to keep going when all I want is to join them."

WELLS

It's the first time I've ever said those words out loud, the only time I've admitted to anyone how close I've come, how close I've *been*, to doing something I can't take back over the last two years. Especially the day she showed up...

Why the hell would you tell her that?

The look of sheer horror on Laurel's face right now makes me want to take the words back, makes me want to shove them down with all the other emotions I've been clinging to so tightly for so damn long. I've never been one to share my burdens, to lay them on anyone and expect them to pick up any of it. But now I've just laid it out for her in no uncertain terms—what a fucking mess I am and how utterly useless I'll be to Wesley.

She sets her mug on the end table and swipes at a tear that trickles from the corner of her eye. "I can understand why you'd feel that way, but I'm really glad you didn't do something stupid."

I wince and squeeze my eyes closed, unable to look at her. Too embarrassed by what I've confessed to her, by what she knows about who I am and what I've done. She knows about Candace, and now she knows the thing I've held closest to my chest.

"Because if you had, that baby asleep in that beautiful crib you made wouldn't be here. That baby is a miracle, Wells, whether you see it that way right now or not. But I have faith you will see it that way, *eventually*."

My lungs seize in my chest. There's something about this woman that allows her to drive right to the heart of the matter and force me to see things in a different way. She's a breath of fresh air I so desperately needed after suffocating alone for so long.

I swallow back a sob that clogs my throat with the uncertainty of whether what she says can ever really happen. "What if I never can?"

"You can."

The words are said with so much surety that I open my eyes and slowly lift my head to meet her gaze again. She looks at me with so much kindness and understanding that it shatters everything in me again.

"You shouldn't have so much faith in me, Laurel. You don't even know me."

She sighs and runs a hand through her hair, offering me a humorless smile. "You're right, maybe I don't, but I know enough. You think I would've just taken a job with Lockwood Brewing without doing my research on who was running it?"

"Obviously, you didn't do a very good job if you didn't know I went to law school."

The corner of her mouth twitches into a smile. "I may have skimmed a few parts, but I know how hard you work. I know how much you loved your wife. I could see it in all the photographs I found of the two of you at events together. And I'll tell you something that I learned all the years growing up without any parents who loved me..."

I cringe at the pain in her words, at how close to home they hit. Guilt claws at me from the inside out, tearing at the heart I thought was buried in the ground with my girls.

"People who can love the way you did Diana don't just lose that ability. Eventually, you're going to be able to look at Wesley and see something other than pain. You're going to be able to look at him the way you did Diana and the way you would have your daughter."

A tear slips from my eye and falls to the floor beneath me. "I'm not so sure about that. His mother...Christ..." I push off the chair and scrub my hands over my face. "I was drunk. I only have bits and pieces of the memory, but it was fumbling and quick and meant nothing. It wasn't the way a baby should be made."

Laurel lets out a mirthless laugh. "I hate to break it to you, but that's the way a lot of babies are made. But it doesn't matter how he got here. What matters is that he *is* here now. And I think we both know that as soon as that DNA test comes back, you're going to have to make some very hard decisions, which is why I'm worried for both of you."

I walk over to the fireplace and grip the mantle, staring into the flames, rather than looking at her. "You shouldn't be worried for me."

"But I am because I can see all of this tearing you apart."

"So that's what you want? To fix me?"

It explains why she kissed me back, why she clung to me like she needed me so badly this afternoon, why the way she's looked at me has changed so much in the last few days.

This isn't an attraction; she needs a project and I'm it while she's here.

"No. Look at me, Wells."

I force myself to turn my head to meet her eyes.

"The only person who can fix you is yourself, and you have to want to do it. I could have let my childhood, what happened to me and how I grew up, affect me. I could have let the beatings and everything else that happened to me in some of those homes destroy my faith in people."

I whirl back to face her fully. "What do you mean what else happened in those homes?"

She shifts uncomfortably on the couch and tugs the blanket tighter around her. "They were good homes, ones with foster parents who tried really hard, who really cared about the kids, who did everything they could for us, who protected us and treated us like their own children. But for as many good ones as there were, there were also bad. And when a foster family wasn't available, there were group homes. Those were always the worst." She shivers and looks down at her feet. "They were run like a business without giving a damn what was best for any of us. Thankfully, I was in more good ones than bad. But the ones that were bad..."

Laurel finally looks up, and without her saying another word, I know exactly what she went through.

"Jesus, Laurel."

She holds up a hand to stop me from saying anything else. "I'm not telling you this because I want your apologies for the way I grew up, or your pity. I just want you to understand that you can make a choice not to let your past affect your future with that baby, and I think you need to. You're all he has. I'm telling you, Wells, that woman isn't coming back, which means you're going to have to take that DNA test to a court and get full custody of this child. You're going to be the person who molds him for the rest of his life, who protects him, who cares for him, who ensures the type of things that happened to me never, ever happen to him. That's *your* responsibility, and you can't ignore it forever, just like you can't stay up here locked away in this cabin, ignoring the rest of the world."

"I don't need the rest of the world, Laurel. The world is a dark, scary, empty place. You, of all people, should know that. This is the only place I'll ever want to be."

Because this is where *they* are.

Where I belong.

Chapter Eleven

WELLS

No matter how long I stare at the ceiling, what I see there doesn't change and sleep never comes.

How can it after that conversation with Laurel tonight?

I cover my eyes with my hands and groan, rolling onto my side toward the hauntingly empty bed.

What the fuck was I thinking telling her all that?

"You weren't thinking. Just feeling. And that's not a bad thing, Wells."

Diana's reassurance does nothing. It certainly feels like a bad thing, and what she said to me has been running on repeat in my head since I came to bed. It's what's kept me awake, staring aimlessly at the ceiling.

Because she's right.

Every *single* word she said was right, like getting struck with the painful truth disguised as a young, smartass attorney. And I've been too damn stubborn and stuck in my own grief to see it and to act how I should. To act like a fucking decent human being.

I've taken it out on Laurel, and myself, and worst of all, that baby. The guilt eats away at me until, finally, I can't stay in bed anymore.

I climb out and tug on a pair of jeans before I slip into the living room. Laurel lies on the couch, her back to me, sleeping softly. Her lips slightly parted, her auburn hair falling over her face.

She looks so sweet, so innocent, but she's far from it. The bravado she carries like armor was a necessity in her life, something she clung to in order to be able to deal with all the horrific things thrown at her. And she came out on top, despite all the reasons for her to fail.

I swear to God, if I ever find out the names of any of the people who hurt her...

Rage builds through every fiber of my being the same as it did when she said those words to me earlier tonight, and I clench my fists to keep from reaching out and brushing the hair back from her face.

Everything she went through, yet look where she's come. She has a great job at one of the most profitable businesses in the country...

Working for an asshole like me...

I push away from her and make my way toward the closed nursery door. For the first time in two years, I turn the knob and ease it open slowly, not even sure what I'm doing or why.

Wesley lies on his back, sound asleep, arms splayed out on either side above his head. Soft little puffs of air slip from his tiny lips. His chest rises and falls rhythmically.

Sleeping soundly. Completely unaware of the turmoil surrounding him.

What I wouldn't give for that.

Something draws me in deeper, my hands shaking. He shifts slightly, turning his head from one side to the other, and I freeze.

"Didn't mean to wake you, buddy. I don't know what the hell I'm doing in here. If I were being honest with myself, I don't have a fucking clue what I've been doing with my life for the last two years, and now, you are in it."

I take the final two steps to the crib and rest my hand against the wood I cut and sanded and painted as I stare down at him.

So sweet, so innocent.

He doesn't deserve any of my bullshit.

"You don't deserve it, either, Wells."

What would Diana say if she could see you now, if she could see how you've been acting?

"I would tell you to grow the fuck up."

I snort and shake my head as her voice rings in my ears.

"That's your son."

It is.

I feel it deep in my soul. A connection that I can't explain, that I can't deny, even if I wanted to. Which I don't. That may be the biggest thing to come from the agonizing conversation with Laurel earlier.

This baby is here for a reason. I may not understand what it is right now, but there *is* a reason.

His tiny little face crinkles up, and he releases a sharp cry, squirming in the crib. My chest tightens immediately, and I reach down and scoop him up, lifting him and settling him against my chest.

"It's okay, I got you."

Resting my hand against his back and rubbing gently, I make my way over to the rocking chair in the corner, the one

Di and I never got to use. I lower myself into it, and the image of Diana sitting here, her belly huge, watching as I set up everything in the room, flashes through my head.

It feels like only yesterday and an eternity ago at the same time. This may not have been our main residence, just a getaway for the weekends and times she convinced me to take a real vacation, but this was where we felt most at home. This nursery would have been a second home for Maribel.

I squeeze my eyes closed against the sting of tears and slowly start to rock, rubbing Wesley's back. He fusses and fidgets for a few moments, then settles against me, his fingers tightening around my hair.

The sweet smell of fresh, clean baby surrounds me, and I inhale deeply, letting it relax me and calm some of the turmoil raging inside me.

Is this what it would've been like if they'd survived?

Would I have been in here every night with her so Diana could sleep, or would I have been a selfish father, one who made his wife do all the work?

I'd love to say the former, but I honestly don't know anymore, not with the way I've behaved the last few days. But now that I'm holding Wesley in my arms, in the quiet stillness of the middle of the night, everything feels so different.

"I'm so sorry, kiddo, about everything. Your mom, how I've acted since you've been here."

So many things I now regret.

"Laurel was right. And I have no idea what to do with you or how I feel about her. I've been a total asshole, and none of it's your fault. You don't deserve any of it. You deserve the world, a perfect dad and a loving mom, and the big house, and the dog, and brothers and sisters. I just don't know if I'm the person who can give that to you. I've been broken for so long, I don't even remember what it feels like to be whole anymore, and I'm not sure if that's even possible." I sigh and press my lips against his head. That baby smell invades every inhale, and for a moment, I just breathe him in, relishing the peace and quiet and feel of him safe in my arms. "I'll do whatever's best for you, though. I promise, whatever it takes."

He shifts slightly, and I continue rocking him for a few moments, trying to figure out what I'm supposed to do with any of this—with him or my feelings for Laurel.

"I hate that Laurel is right. I hate that I couldn't see it myself. And I hate the way she makes me feel because she does, buddy. She makes me *feel* again, and it fucking hurts."

She charged up here on a mission to bring Wesley to me and ended up burrowing under my skin, reaching into the heart of me where I didn't think anything was left, and finding that one tiny, tattered piece that still hangs on.

Her unwillingness to back down, to force me to take a long, hard look at my life and how I've been living it, has only made me appreciate her more, but it doesn't matter because I don't have anything to offer her.

There isn't anything left to give.

LAUREL

Something stirs me awake, and I turn and scan the living room, even though I can barely see it in the dark. It's still late or early rather, far too early for even Wells to be up.

A low rumble of thunder rolls above the house, likely the sound I heard.

I close my eyes again, but the now-familiar sound of footsteps creaking on the floorboards makes me freeze. It isn't coming from the bedroom or the bathroom but from behind me, toward the nursery.

What's going on?

The haze of sleep fully evaporates, and I push myself up slowly and peek over the back of the couch to see him twist the handle and push open the door slowly.

Oh, my God.

I slap my hand over my mouth to keep myself from saying or doing anything that'll stop whatever's about to happen. Wells hasn't set foot in the nursery since he told me to put Wesley in there, and I didn't think he would anytime soon.

He squares his shoulders, like he's gathering strength to move forward, and my heart stops as I hold my breath and wait. Every fiber of my being screams for me to approach, to wrap my arms around him from behind, to bury my face against his back and offer him any support I can give for this pivotal moment.

But I keep myself still because he has to do this on his own.

This may seem trivial to anyone who doesn't know Wells Lockwood, but over the last few days, I've come to understand the man who tries to keep so much of himself protected and restrained.

This is a massive step for him, one I don't want to interrupt. One that absolutely *needs* to happen before he'll be able to move forward with Wesley and his new reality.

Wells finally steps into the room slowly, one foot, then the other until I can't see him anymore.

Stay out of it, Laurel.

I should leave him alone to do whatever it is he needs to

in peace. I should give him space, but I can't help myself. Not after witnessing everything I have over the last few days. Not after what he told me standing by the fire tonight.

Something deep inside me yearns to confirm he's okay in there, that Wesley is okay. That they'll get through this so when I leave, they won't be as lost as Wells has seemed.

I swing my legs off the couch and stand carefully, keeping the blanket wrapped around me as I tiptoe toward the open door. The fire has died down but still radiates heat and light from behind me, like it's urging me to go in when I can't.

He needs to do this.

And I won't interfere.

When it's just the two of us, I have no problem telling him exactly what I think about the situation, about what he should be doing, but this isn't the time or place to butt in with my unwanted opinions.

I stand with my back against the wall and listen. Wesley releases a sharp little cry, and I turn to go in and take care of him, just like I have every single time he's needed anything since the moment his mother arrived at corporate headquarters.

But I don't make it one step in before Wells bends over and lifts him from the crib.

Oh, my God.

I slip back to my hiding spot quickly and hold my breath, happy tears forming in my eyes.

Progress!

He's never held the baby before, and a huge part of me worried it might never happen, that he might never be able to push past that wall preventing him from touching his son.

This huge moment has my heart thundering against my ribcage, and I dare to peek around the doorjamb and watch him settle into the rocking chair in the corner of the room. Wells cradles Wesley against his chest, rubbing his large hand up and down his son's tiny back.

Thank you, God!

I've never been one to pray. I've never even set foot in any church. But this, this *is* a miracle if I've ever seen one.

The angry man who wouldn't even *look* at that baby when we arrived rocking him and comforting him...

Tears finally spill from my eyes, and I return to the wall and listen.

It's none of your business. Go back to the couch and pretend you didn't see or hear any of this.

But I can't, not when I care so much about that baby and the man holding him, not when I want so badly for Wells to accept his new role and what he needs to do for Wesley.

Wells' deep voice reaches me through the still night air, and I hold my breath again, listening to him unburden his heart to the baby who doesn't understand a single word of it.

Tears spill down like a waterfall now, impossible to restrain, and I keep my hand over my mouth to fight back the sobs that would tell him I'm eavesdropping on what is meant to be a very private conversation with his son.

He says all the things he needs to, and if he truly believes them, then it means there is hope.

"I hate that Laurel is right. I hate that I couldn't see it myself. And I hate the way she makes me feel because she does, buddy. She makes me feel again, and it fucking hurts."

I whip my head toward the door.

What?

It takes a moment for the words to really register.

He feels the same thing I do. That this is bigger than what both of us can possibly fathom or what we may want to accept. Wells might be lost, but he isn't alone. He wasn't supposed to be.

I thought I was sent here to bring Wesley to him, but maybe I was meant to be here the whole time.

I've never been one to believe in fate, but the way he held me, the way his lips moved over mine, the way he looks at me has me questioning that.

You can never have him.

Not really.

He will always belong to Diana.

That reality slams into me like a Mac truck, and if I weren't leaning back against the wall, my legs might crumple beneath me.

It's true, though.

After two years, he still grieves for them the same as he did the day they died.

And why shouldn't he?

He lost the only things he loved in this world. I've never loved anything that much, never let myself grow close enough or care enough about anyone to ever allow myself that kind of pain if anything were ever to happen to them. So, I can't understand it, but I can see that he's not in any place to explore his feelings for me, either. Not when this baby's just been brought to him, not when he's not over his loss.

Something rustling in the nursery and a floorboard creak break through the uncertainty in my head, and I peek around the corner again to see what's happening and freeze.

Wells stands just inside the door, staring back at me, a mixture of anger, confusion, and something I can't quite place filling his amber gaze. He knows I've heard everything, knows I've been standing here, listening to something I was never meant to hear.

He doesn't say a word, but he doesn't have to. The way his eyes rake over me, the way his hands fist at his sides. The tension in his shoulders, neck, and jaw. The man is near his breaking point on so many levels.

And he's afraid I'm going to push him beyond that point.

What he just said to Wesley wasn't for my ears. It was never meant for anyone else's, yet I heard it. And now that I have, I can't unhear it. I can't pretend I don't know what Wells just said about me, about this buzz we've been feeling. The way I'm drawn to him, even when he's pissing me off and acting like a true prick.

I open my mouth to say something, but he holds up a calloused palm to stop me and takes two steps forward until the heat of his body radiates into mine.

"Don't."

A single word.

A command.

Then he brushes past me, his shoulder bumping mine the same way I did his when he caught me in here without permission, sending a zap of electricity coursing through me.

He stalks across the living room to the door, throws it open, and steps out into the still-dark early morning.

Too bad for Wells, I've never been good at following commands.

Chapter Twelve

LAUREL

Thunder booms ominously as I reach the wide-open door that Wells didn't bother to close. The rumble from the sky should act as a warning to stay away, to let him go and not chase after him into an oncoming storm, but I can't stop myself.

Something about Wells Lockwood calls to me, his pain like a siren song that draws me toward the jagged, rocky pieces of his heart and drags me down into the deep waters when I know I can't swim and he can't help me.

I step out the door barefoot just as the sky opens up and the rain starts to fall.

Where the hell did he go?

Cool drops hit my exposed skin and quickly dampen my shirt, but I can't just turn around and go back inside. I care too damn much to let Wells go drown himself in bourbon again.

Scanning the clearing, I catch the faintest glimpse of movement on the far side near the barn. I don't even bother looking for shoes. If I give him enough time, he'll disappear into the woods, and I won't see him again until he is forced to come back up for air or food.

And this is the time to talk to him, to force the issue, when he's more open than I've heard him in the past three days, when he's finally maybe starting to realize the truth and sees what he has to do.

The rain starts falling harder, and the mud squishes under my toes.

It's probably stupid to go after him now. As he loves to remind me, there are things that can kill out here—a lot of them, especially when I'm barefoot, in a tank top and shorts, and a storm is raging around me.

But I can't bring myself to care.

I run through the blinding rain as lightning streaks across the sky. The massive barn tucked behind the grove of trees looms ahead, ominous and foreboding. Another warning I don't bother heeding.

The large door stands open despite the oncoming storm.

So this is where he's been hiding out.

Well, he can't hide from me anymore.

I won't let him.

I *can't* let him, not if I want any sort of resolution to all of this—for Wesley and for me.

Because I will eventually go back down that mountain. In a few days, all *this*, whatever *this* is, will all be over. And I can't let that happen without at least discussing it with the man who I'll be returning to work for.

I make my way toward the barn, but as I approach, Wells appears in the open doorway and glares at me. The fire in his eyes burns with anger rather than the heat I've seen him looking at me with.

"What the fuck do you think you're doing following me

out here?" His gaze dips over my soaked shirt, exposed legs to my bare feet. "You don't even have shoes on."

"You think I care? You know I heard what you said in there."

His jaw tightens along with his shoulders. "You shouldn't have been eavesdropping."

I take another step forward, cautious like I'm approaching a wounded animal because that's what Wells is right now. He's been living feral up here, not having to answer to anyone for his actions or for what he says.

"You're right. I shouldn't have been. But now that I've heard it..."

He takes a step toward me into the rain. "Now that you've heard it, what?"

"Now that I've heard it, I can't pretend that I didn't."

"Yes, you can. People pretend all the time." He throws up his hands. "They pretend to be happy. They pretend to care. They pretend that their lives are exactly what they want. They pretend all the damn time. You do, too."

"What the hell is that supposed to mean?"

"You"—he waves a hand over me—"coming up here in thousand-dollar shoes you can't afford."

I recoil slightly at his comment. "Fuck you, Wells."

He shakes his head, his now-soaked hair plastered to the side of his face. "No, if you're going to eavesdrop on me and act like you know all the answers, then you're going to listen to me, too." He points a finger at me. "This job, you took it because you wanted the stuff you never had. You thought money could buy you things—a stable home, food, expensive clothes and shoes, anything else you could ever want. But you wanted *things*."

Tears start to burn in my eyes, but I shake my head. "No."

"Are you really going to stand there and lie to me?"

I take another step toward him. "Just because I told you something about my childhood doesn't mean you know me, Wells."

Yes, I wanted things, but that wasn't all *I wanted.*

A family. People who would truly love me. Someone to rely on who always had my back. *That's* what I wanted. The job, the *things*, they were just a means to that end. I could put myself in a position to meet someone who could give me all of the things I *couldn't* buy for myself. The things that only come from the heart I never let anyone into.

Wells takes another step toward me until our chests almost brush. "And just because you eavesdropped on me talking to my son doesn't mean you know a damn thing about me, either."

My son.

He probably doesn't even realize he said it, but my breath catches at his words. Another gigantic step for him, one I thought I'd never witness. It melts away some of the anger toward him for his accusation, and I swallow thickly and take the tiniest half-step forward, pressing my soaked chest to his.

"I do know you, Wells. I *see* you. I see all the pain you've buried yourself in. I see you fighting everything and everyone who tries to help you. You've scared them all away, locked yourself up here with your grief. But you can't stay hidden up here forever. You can't keep yourself and your feelings bottled up inside. You can't just suffer for the rest of your life."

A growl rumbles in his chest. "I can do whatever the fuck I want."

"Then do it." I square my shoulders. "Do what you

want, Wells, not what you think Diana wants, not what you think other people expect. Do what *you* want."

He's on me so fast I don't even have time to breathe. His lips crash to mine as the rain picks up around us, coming down in solid sheets. Strong arms pull me to him, and he groans into my mouth, a deep, needy sound. One that goes straight between my legs and makes me clench my already-damp thighs together.

Wells devours me like a starved man, like a man seeking something that's never been given to him, or that he hasn't tasted in so long that he doesn't even remember it.

He ravages me, his tongue sweeping against mine, his hands clinging to my hips and digging in so hard that it'll likely leave marks. He kisses me ruthlessly, not holding back for even a second, pouring years of frustration and loneliness coupled with all the tension we've felt into the action.

And when he finally tears himself away, both of us breathing hard and stares into my eyes, I see it there. The acknowledgement that he feels something for me other than anger. That he just doesn't know what to do with it or how to control it. I see how badly he wants to fight it.

"Do it again, Wells."

He issues another low growl, then spins me and backs me against the weathered wood of the barn, smashing his mouth to mine. His hands fumble at my waistband.

Fuck.

Despite the cool rain, my whole body heats instantly. Each drop sizzling as it strikes my skin.

I cling to his soaked shirt, gliding my tongue along his, releasing a tiny little moan to let him know I'm with him one-hundred percent, even if he can't be.

Whatever holds him back, whatever he's constantly fighting, whether it be his own guilt or his unwillingness to let anyone else in, melts away the longer he kisses me. Replacing it, a feral, mad, frantic desire that pours out of him the way the rain does from the violent sky above us.

I flip open the button and slide down his pants zipper, as he shoves down my shorts enough to slip his hand between my thighs.

"Fuck..." He mutters the word against my lips as his finger glides easily through the wetness already pooling there.

No one can deny Wells Lockwood is a handsome man, but this isn't about that. It isn't just a sexual attraction drawing me to him and making me clutch at his neck like he's the only thing keeping me grounded to the Earth. Wells feels harder, loves stronger than any man I've ever met in my life. The passion bottled up inside of him needs to go somewhere, and I want it directed all at me.

I grind my core into his hand, and he groans against my lips, taking me again in a bruising kiss. My body shakes in anticipation, coiling so tightly I might snap in two.

He shoves his pants down to his thighs, and I slide a hand between his legs.

Hell.

I wrap my fingers around his hard cock and give it one long, slow stroke. He groans and bucks his hips, driving himself into my palm slick with the rain.

This is stupid.

I know it.

He knows it.

But we both need it.

Need to release this tension that's been building between us. Need to acknowledge, for once in our lives, something that we want, even if we shouldn't.

His finger slips up into me, and I gasp and immediately

clasp around him. He issues a low groan of approval as I continue to stroke him.

The rain pours down around us, utterly soaking us to the bone, but neither of us seems to care. With so many bigger things to worry about, getting a little wet while finally getting what we both crave so badly is the least of our concerns.

He probes into me, adjusting his hand position so his thumb can find the apex of my thighs. The rough pad rolls against the tiny nub, and my body jerks in response, clenching around his finger again.

"Fuck, Wells."

One of those growls he's so fond of tossing at me shakes his chest, and he mutters something I can't hear over the driving wind and rain. His hand disappears from between my thighs, and he grips my hips and lifts me to wrap my legs around his waist.

I align him to my slick core, and he shoves home in one hard, determined thrust that steals my ability to breathe.

WELLS

My cock glides into her wet heat easily, her body welcoming me as if it was meant to be there. A sense of relief rushes through me, like I'm coming home for the first time after being at war and finally finding some semblance of peace.

Even though this is all kinds of wrong...

On so many levels.

Wrong for her.

Wrong for me.

Wrong for this life and this place.

Thunder rolls, shaking the ground beneath us and rattling the old glass in the windows of the barn just to our left, but even the wrath of God wouldn't be able to stop this now.

I pull back my hips and drive into her again, pushing her against the worn wood with far more force than even I expected. She gasps and loops her arms around my shoulders, clutching the back of my neck and digging her nails into the flesh there.

"God, Wells."

My name falling from her lips acts as gasoline thrown on the already-raging inferno searing between us. Everything this woman has said and done since the moment she stepped foot on my property has pushed me to this.

She showed up full of piss and vinegar, determination, and a smart mouth she couldn't keep shut even when it would've been best for her. Even when it would've been safer for her to just stay away, to leave me alone to deal with everything that's going on in my own time and way, she had to push, she had to prod, she had to force me to this moment.

A single act that will change everything, that will destroy me further and put both of us in a place neither of us should be.

I wrap my hand around her neck, tilting her chin up until her eyes meet mine as I slowly roll my hips and thrust up into her again. Her mouth falls open slightly.

"Is this what you wanted, Laurel?" My words come out as almost a snarl, more animal than human because that's what I feel like in this moment. A train off the tracks barreling toward destruction. "For me to lose control?"

She gasps and shakes her head slightly, struggling to

speak as I pummel her. "No. I just wanted you to *feel* again. Feel *anything*."

"Fucking hell..."

My confession in the nursery only a few minutes ago gets thrown back at me, and I can't deny that it's exactly what she's done.

She's made me *feel*.

Rage.

Lust.

Frustration.

Hatred.

Need.

All of it rolled into a giant bomb sitting in my chest, slowly ticking down until it finally exploded. And now that it has, there's no undoing it. There's no way to push it all back inside, to pretend none of it ever happened. There's no wishing I made different decisions where she's concerned. It's far too late for that.

We're so far gone, lost in each other, that nothing, not even the storm around us can make us stop.

I redouble my efforts, slamming into her and grinding my pelvis against hers with each thrust. Her pussy clenches around me, catching the head of my cock in that perfect spot that makes my balls tingle almost immediately.

Fuck, fuck. What the hell are you doing, Wells?

She's twenty-six years old. She's my *employee*. I'm her *boss*. I have absolutely no business being inside this woman. But I can't stop myself either, not with her warm, lush body pressed to mine, her sweet, hot cunt wrapped around my cock.

Her lips against mine feel so damn good, every kiss filled with the same frenzied hunger I share, desperate to consume and be consumed by her just as badly.

I press my lips against the throbbing pulse on her neck, sucking there hard enough to make her jerk on my cock. Sharp nails score the back of my neck, and she drags my mouth back to hers, frantically kissing me and moving her hips to meet mine, seeking madly something she can only get from me.

What is it?

She came up here because it's her job, and she has every intention of going back the moment the next car shows up.

So, what is it she really needs and wants from me?

Dropping my head back, face to the rain, the question lingers in the back of my head as I rail into her, driving away my demons, trying to keep them at bay long enough to reach climax.

She grips my face and tugs it down to meet her gaze. "Don't. Don't get lost in that."

Christ, she can read me too well.

Laurel knew exactly what I was doing, where I was going, and her words and her mouth pull me back from that edge and make me dance along another one.

"You stay right here with me, Lockwood."

I press my forehead to hers while I plunge into her, trying to get deeper, to reach that part of her that no one else ever has. "Fucking hell, Laurel."

"It's all right, Wells."

Her pussy clenches around me tightly, and I grit my teeth at the desire to unload inside her, but coming before her would be the ultimate dick move, even worse than everything else I've done to her since she got here. I clench my jaw and keep going, rolling my hips and doing the little twist at the end that makes her mouth fall open on a strangled gasp.

"Oh, God."

Laurel's entire body twitches, and she seems to float in mid-air for a second before she's coming. I keep thrusting through her beautiful release, gripping her hip and holding her steady, her pussy rippling and clenching along my cock.

Any modicum of restraint I may have held onto shatters when she leans forward and bites into my neck, and I finally fall over the edge with her, stilling and emptying myself deep inside her.

The storm continues to rage around us, thunder and lightning shattering the sky and shaking the ground, and I bury my face against her soaked skin and press my lips to her neck. That familiar crisp scent of the rain blends with one that's all Laurel, one that smells like salvation and damnation mixed into a volatile concoction that could destroy us both.

What the hell did I just do?

I release my grip on her thighs, letting her feet slide down to the wet ground, and stagger back a step, wincing as my cock slips free from her. Her eyes fly open to meet mine, heavily lidded, still filled with lust, now morphing to confusion.

"Wells, I..."

She swallows the rest of her words.

An apology?

It doesn't matter. There isn't anything she can say right now to fix what I've done.

I stumble another step back, grab my pants, and jerk them up as I run a hand through my soaked hair. Lightning flashes overhead, and the low rumble of thunder vibrates through me.

"Fuck, I'm sorry, Laurel." I bury my face in my hands. "I shouldn't..."

Have kissed you...

Have touched you...

Have let myself fall into your arms and sink into your body...

She reaches down and pulls up her shorts with shaking hands, and I stare at her for a moment. Utterly soaked, her hair darkened and matted from her head down to her shoulders. The white tank top she wears clings to her breasts and torso, accentuating every perfect curve. The tiny running shorts barely covering her long, thick thighs. Her bare feet now covered in mud.

"Jesus Christ..." I squeeze my eyes closed and stumble back a few steps. "What the fuck did I just do?"

She takes a step forward and wobbles with her hand up. "Wells, no, don't."

Fuck.

I turn from her and stagger away from the barn, toward the woods.

What did I do?

You fucked your employee, the one you forced to be here in the first place.

I need to get control of myself.

I need to get out of here.

Away from her.

Away from all these feelings she brings up.

From all the things that she makes me want to do that I know can never be real, that can never happen.

"Wells, please."

Her footsteps slapping on the wet ground behind me follow me toward the edge of the forest, and I whirl back toward her.

"Don't follow me, Laurel. You aren't going to like what you see."

That damn plump bottom lip quivers slightly, but she

squares her shoulders as if she's ready to battle again. She hasn't backed down once since she's been here, so I guess I should expect the same now, the same fight that helped her survive her childhood, that helped her get the job with Lockwood Brewing in the first place.

"We can't do"—I motion between us—"this. I can't." I shake my head, a migraine blooming and slamming against my skull. "I never should have touched you. I never should have..."

"Fuck you, Wells." Anger seeps into her warm blue eyes, turning them to ice instantly. "I'm a big girl; I can make my own decisions. I don't need you making them for me, especially when you're so fucked up in the head right now."

She isn't wrong, but her words still flare an anger deep inside me.

"I *am* fucked up in the head, Laurel. I'm a goddamn mess. So, what the fuck do you think you were doing chasing after me?" I grip my soaked shirt, twisting the fabric in my fists. "You *knew* what would happen. You knew."

"I did, and I still came after you because I wanted it, Wells, because I wanted you. Because even though you're fucking broken, you're kind and loving and beautiful."

My entire body stiffens, and I shake my head as I wobble a few steps into the woods. The trees loom behind me, their canopy falling over me the farther away from her I retreat, already starting to envelop me into the dark quiet I've always sought when things spiral so badly.

Laurel watches me, and another flash of lightning illuminates her perfectly. Standing at the edge of the clearing, drenched, cheeks pink, lips kiss swollen, her hands hanging helplessly at her side.

She looks so young. So innocent, even though I know

she's experienced far too much in her short life. But she thinks she sees something in me, something that isn't there. Maybe it was once, a long time ago, but not anymore.

"No, I'm not."

With that, I turn and stalk off into the woods, leaving her alone in the clearing as God's wrath rains down on us again.

Chapter Thirteen

LAUREL

I ease the nursery door closed, and despite moving into the living room where I'm closer to the fire, another chill rolls through me. Even rubbing my arms doesn't relieve them of the goosebumps I haven't seemed to be able to get rid of all morning.

No amount of hot tea or thick sweatshirts helps, either.

I grab the blanket from the couch, wrap it around me, and go stand near the fire, letting the flames seep a little bit of warmth into me.

Wells must have come home at some point because when I woke, it was roaring away, and it would've gone out by now if he had never come home last night. But I was passed out, utterly exhausted by the emotional upheaval, and didn't hear him come in.

Or maybe I didn't want to wake up.

I was lost in another dream, only this one was different than the ones that normally haunt me. Instead of sneers and angry, violent touches, the ones I dreamed about last night, or I guess early this morning, were heated, needy, breathless, the kind of pure, unadulterated passion I never thought I'd experience with anyone.

But I got it.

Far more than I bargained for.

My body remembers every second of it, and right now, only those memories keep me warm.

I rest my head against the mantle and release a heavy sigh, remembering the panic in his gaze as he stepped back from me, leaving me cold and empty against the barn wall.

He called it a mistake.

Maybe Wells was right. Maybe I shouldn't have let it go that far, shouldn't have given in to my attraction to him or let him give in to his for me. Maybe he wasn't ready and pushing him only made the crack that runs through the center of him open even wider, leading him even closer to further splintering.

All the reasons it was so wrong have run through my mind since I woke this morning, and at the top of the list is the fact that he is technically my boss. But it doesn't feel that way when I'm here with him.

We've developed an almost friendship over the last few days. Something I didn't think was possible with a man who literally forced me to stay on this mountain against my will. But deep down, it's more than that. I know it, and I just don't want to admit it to myself.

I'm falling for the broken man because I can see what's there if all the pieces were reassembled.

If that's even possible.

I shiver again and tighten the blanket around me. The storms must have brought through one hell of a cold front, and another long, hot shower sounds incredible, even though I took one just after Wells left me standing alone in the clearing.

The door clicks open behind me, and I freeze.

Don't turn around, Laurel. Don't give him the satisfaction of thinking you're eager to see him, not after how he acted last night.

I lift my head from the mantle but keep staring into the fire as heavy footsteps cross the living room.

Despite my best efforts not to, I shiver again, and a little groan escapes my lips at the ache the movement brings to my body.

"Are you cold?" His low gravelly voice sends a new round of goosebumps skittering across my skin.

"Yeah, I can't seem to get warm this morning. Must be the cold front."

More footsteps fill the room until he's standing next to me, his amber eyes narrowed at me in concern. "You don't look so good."

I snort and roll my eyes. "Gee, thanks. Just what I want to hear from the guy I—"

"No, I mean, are you feeling all right? You're very pale."

I'm *always* pale. Between my pasty-white skin and the red hair, it gave endless fodder to the bullies in school and my foster homes. But those trials only made me stronger, gave me a thicker skin to deal with the bigger challenges—like Wells Lockwood.

Another shiver makes me wince, the fight knocked out of me instantly. "I don't know."

He closes the distance between us with two steps and presses his hand against my forehead. "Jesus, Laurel, you're burning up."

I jerk out of his hold, not wanting to feel his calloused

fingers on me right now. Not again. Not after last night. "No, I'm fine."

"You're not fine. You're sick."

Almost as if to prove the point, a cough slips from my throat that I can't bite back, and I tuck my head into my elbow to keep from spewing germs all over the living room.

Shit.

"I'm fine. It's probably just a cold or something. I'm not used to all this wet wilderness air or being out in the rain multiple days."

He takes a step back and holds out his hand. "Come on."

"What?"

Where the hell are we going?

Wells waits a moment, his hand hanging out between us without mine in it. His scowl deepens, and he stalks over to me, drops his shoulder, and scoops me into his arms easily.

"Hey!" With my arms trapped inside the blanket, I don't have any way to fight him. "What are you doing?"

He glances down at me, a determined set to his stubbled jaw. "You need to rest."

I push my elbow into his gut. "I'm fine."

He growls low, the sound reminding me exactly how and what that sound did to me last night. "Do you always have to argue?"

I almost get out my answer, but a wave of dizziness sends the room spinning, and I have to clench my eyes closed. It could be I am sicker than I realized. "Where are we going?"

Ignoring my question, he stalks toward the bedroom, clutching me tightly against his strong chest.

"Wells, what are you doing?"

He glances down at me again, his bourbon eyes swirling with concern. "You're not sleeping on the couch."

"But this is your bedroom."

"I know." He sets me on the edge of the bed, the mattress sagging slightly under my weight, then tugs back the covers behind me. "Get under."

"Excuse me?"

His brows rise to his hairline. "I said, get under the covers."

I heard exactly what he said, but given his insistence that I don't enter his room for any purpose, sliding between the sheets wasn't high on the list of things I thought he'd be demanding of me—especially after last night.

And I'm not sure I *want* to be in his bed—the one he shared with Diana. I start to argue with him, but another cough wracks my body, and I cover my mouth until the hacking subsides.

Wells squats in front of me, resting his hands on my knees. "I'm going to make you some tea. When was the last time Wesley ate?"

"Um, I don't know, half an hour ago? He'll be down for a little while."

"You rest. I'll handle him."

"But—"

"No buts." Something dark crosses his gaze, and he presses his lips together in a firm line, his jaw tightening. "This is my fault."

"What is?"

"That you're sick." He shakes his head. "I never should have kept you out here. You sat around in wet clothes, and then last night..." He squeezes his eyes closed and winces, then pushes to his feet and turns away, running a hand through his hair. "All of this is my fault."

I can see the path he's barreling down now, and it's a dangerous one for him when he already takes on so much responsibility and guilt. If he goes down it, I may never be able to coax him out of that hole again. No one will be able to.

"Wells, look at me."

He stiffens but doesn't turn back; he just stares out the door into the living room, as if something in there might hold the answers to whatever questions he's asking himself.

"Wells, please, look at me."

A second passes before he turns slowly and his eyes finally meet mine, filled with regret. The last thing you want to see in the eyes of the man you're starting to fall for.

"I'll be okay." I force a smile I don't feel. "It's probably some little bug. I just hope you and Wesley don't get sick, too."

Renewed concern tightens his fists at his sides. "I'll keep an eye on him, make sure he's all right."

Sheer exhaustion settles over me so quickly that I can barely keep my eyes open. He turns to leave, but I reach out and grab his hand before he can move away.

"Wells?"

He looks back at me with so much turmoil in his gaze that I know exactly what he's thinking—the very thing I was worried he would.

"It's not your fault."

I mean that about a thousand things—not just my being sick.

What happened to his wife, to his baby, wasn't his fault.

His rift with his father wasn't his fault.

Even Candace and Wesley weren't his fault, not really.

Things happen in life that are beyond our control. One action creates a ripple effect no one can ever anticipate, but

Wells is the type of man who will always blame himself, who will always bear that burden and carry it on his shoulders until it finally makes him collapse.

That's the reason my heart is breaking right now because he's a good man. A good man who tries to do the right thing and somehow ends up in the places he least wants to be, including with me last night.

He pulls his hand from mine and stalks away without another word, and I settle down into his bed, the covers pulled up over me.

The woodsy rain scent I've come to associate with him invades every breath, and I snuggle down against his pillow and release a little sigh. I hadn't realized how tired I've been, how exhausting all of this is—taking care of Wesley, taking care of Wells, taking care of my own demons that seem to want to destroy the first good thing I've found in a long time by making me push when I should step back.

But they all seem to evaporate as darkness creeps in on the edges of my vision.

I close my eyes and start to drift, that comforting scent enveloping me in a cocoon of calm and peace even though the man who holds it is a never-ending enigma who might be my undoing.

WELLS

Wesley's piercing cry practically shatters my eardrum as I bounce him on my hip and pace the living room, only increasing the pressure in my head beating against my skull "Shh. It's okay, buddy. I know you miss Laurel."

The truth I don't want to admit to myself sits on the tip

of my tongue, and I glance toward the closed bedroom door and back to him.

"I do, too."

How is it possible to miss someone who's one room away?

Maybe because I've pushed her so far away that it feels like she might as well be back in Denver. And now she's sick because I was a selfish prick where she was concerned. Over and over again, I did what I wanted, what I thought was best for *me*, and I ignored how it was going to impact the woman who has been nothing but generous and giving and caring when she has every reason not to be.

"It's okay, Wells. Everything will be all right."

I wish I could believe what Diana tells me, but even after giving Wesley his bottle, I haven't been able to get him to settle down.

He's fidgety, cranky, inconsolable.

This is the part of parenthood I'm not ready for—where I don't have a fucking clue what to do and don't want to disturb Laurel when she's sick.

Christ, what if it's something bad? What if her fever doesn't break? What if...

Acid crawls up my throat with a thousand potential scenarios that all end badly, and I swallow it back.

No. If I start to think like that...

Just no.

I can't let myself go there again, not when Wesley and Laurel need me to hold my shit together long enough to take care of both of them.

What would Diana do if she were here?

All the things I'm not capable of...

I already got Laurel tea and Tylenol, but that's all I have

here—the very basics since I haven't exactly been worried about my health over the last two years.

This is one of those times when I really wish I had a phone up here, or even a radio, so I could get a doctor up the mountain, or hell, even send Laurel back to the city.

Fuck.

Wesley continues to wail, and I lift him up and hold him to face me, his little eyes squeezed closed, his mouth open in a twisted, pained expression that tugs at something deep in my chest.

"Come on, buddy. You've got to tell me what's wrong."

He doesn't have a fever, but he certainly isn't acting like himself. At least from what I've seen, he's been relatively calm since they arrived. Eating well, sleeping well, content to play with the few toys his mother sent along in his bags and then the ones in the nursery once Laurel moved him in there.

But you haven't exactly been around the cabin much, have you?

Fuck.

All the time I spent avoiding this little man and Laurel here at the cabin is coming back to bite me in the ass because I have no idea how to ease his distress.

"He'll be okay."

Diana's soothing words act like a balm to my soul, but they do nothing to help the frantic baby in my arms or the headache growing with each minute he wails.

I cradle him to my chest and press my palm against the back of his head, hoping the pressure helps. He nuzzles against me, still screaming, but he seems to settle slightly.

Didn't Diana say something about skin-to-skin contact being calming to babies?

I try to think back to the many conversations we had

during her pregnancy, the things I didn't really pay much attention to because that was her world—being Supermom. So anxious, yet so ready to bring Maribel into our lives and do all the mommy things with her.

"It's okay, kiddo." I bounce him again and pace the living room. "We'll figure something out."

At this point, I'm as desperate to ease his pain as I am my own. I bring him back to the nursery, change his diaper to make sure that isn't the problem, and he continues to wail, so I pull off my shirt and rest him against my chest.

Almost instantly, his screaming falters, and after a few seconds of fidgeting, he settles in and slips his hand flat against my chest, over my heart. A vice tightens around my lungs, and I struggle to suck in air as I stare down at him.

Jesus, I'm a father now.

The reality that this tiny little bean is going to be looking to me for comfort, for care, for fucking everything for the rest of his life, hits me so hard I stagger back and lower myself into the rocking chair before my legs completely give out from under me.

Shit.

I drop my head back and close my eyes, rocking gently. "I don't know how to do this, Wesley. Not without Diana, not without..."

A heavy breath rushes from my chest.

You're not going to think Laurel because she isn't yours to have, and she isn't staying.

She's going back as soon as someone from corporate comes up here with those DNA tests. And after what you've done to her here, she won't be returning.

Why would she?

I've given her every reason to despise me and this place, including apparently making her physically ill.

I push up out of the chair, keeping Wesley snuggled against me. He's so small that one hand on his back is enough to secure him to me as I ease open the door to the bedroom.

Laurel lies on her side, facing the door, her red hair spread out on my pillow, normally pink lips pale and parted, with steady breaths slipping from them.

She looks exhausted but also somehow stunningly beautiful.

I'm sorry, Diana.

Another betrayal. I always swore I'd never have another woman in this bed, that I'd never be with another woman after I lost her. Now I have a child with a woman I don't even know and have another, one who *works* for me, in the bed Diana and I shared.

What the fuck are you doing, Wells?

I tighten my hand on the doorknob, and Laurel stirs slightly, her eyes flickering open, almost like she can sense me staring at her.

"Wells?" She blinks a few times and finally focuses on me. The corner of her lips twitches slightly when she finally sees me and Wesley, then her gaze narrows. "Is he okay?"

The slight panic in her voice makes me take the few steps into the bedroom to offer her a reassuring smile. "Fussy, but he doesn't have a fever. I got him to settle down."

She smiles and closes her eyes again, snuggling back down. "He just wanted his daddy."

Daddy.

Laurel says the word so casually, like it's the simplest thing in the world, to refer to me as his father.

Maybe it is. Maybe everything that brought us to this point doesn't have to define Wesley's life. Maybe he doesn't have to be haunted by his conception, by his mother abandoning him, or the fact that his father, at least initially, didn't know how to handle his appearance in his life.

He doesn't have to *be* any of those things. None of them will matter as he grows up as long as he knows he's loved and there's someone taking care of him. At least, that's what I have to keep telling myself if I want any hope of being able to make it through this.

Laurel's steady breathing returns, and she slips back into sleep.

I slowly lower myself to the edge of the bed and reach out to brush the hair off her forehead. She rolls to her side and presses her face against my hand, nuzzling into it, and something warm lights in the center of my chest at having Wesley in one hand and her in the other.

For a moment, things feel...*right.*

But this is so wrong, all of it.

I jerk my hand away from her, push up from the bed, and quickly hustle from the room, pulling the door closed behind me quietly.

Fuck.

I lean back against it and close my eyes, listening to the silence of the cabin.

It should have been full of Diana and Maribel's laughter and joy. Our favorite place in the world, an escape from the busy life filled with meetings and media events in Denver. But it's become a tomb, an empty, silent place where I came and stayed to die.

And now, new life has been injected into it by the feisty redheaded attorney and this little man who needs me so much.

I just hope I can give him everything he needs because

if I fail him, if I fail at this, it's not something I get a second chance at.

"This is your second chance, Wells."

There might be some way for me to believe that was true if I wasn't messing up every single thing put in front of me. From the second that car horn honked and dragged me from the depths of my misery, I've done precisely the wrong thing every chance I got.

When it was just me, that kind of idiocy never affected anyone else, but now Wesley and Laurel have appeared in my life, and if I fail either of them, that crushing darkness continually threatening me may finally win.

Chapter Fourteen

WELLS

The half-broken neon sign for Harry's hasn't changed since the last time I was here. H-A-R flashes and glows red against the smoke-stained front window.

I glance down at Wesley asleep in the car seat in my right hand, then back up at the building. My gaze naturally drifts behind me and across the street to the Lockwood Falls Motel.

None of my memories from that night are fully clear, but I remember enough, enough to make coming back here awkward as hell, especially carrying this baby.

Still, I don't have a choice. I have to find Doc.

I tug open the door and step into the dimly lit space. Harry stands behind the bar, filling a pint for an older gentleman I don't recognize near the end of the long slab of lacquered wood.

Harry glances toward the door and does a double take. His gaze drops to the car seat and narrows as I approach.

"Well, look what the cat dragged in." He smacks his hand against the bar and offers me a half-grin. "It's been a long time since I've seen you in here."

I nod slowly. "It has."

I've picked up the last few shipments out of the back rather than have to set foot in here again. Even then, I did it as quickly as possible, almost like my subconscious didn't want to be anywhere near this place, though I couldn't remember anything about that night until recently.

"Who's your little friend?"

I set the car seat up on the bar rather than the dirty floor, and Harry examines a snoozing Wesley.

"A friend of mine brought him up to the cabin and has been staying for a few days."

Not a lie, not the full truth, either, but I'm not about to tell Harry, the biggest gossip in Lockwood Falls, what's going on in my fucked-up personal life, especially when he's the only person who might be able to actually make the connection between Candace and me.

He glances up at me, the corner of his mouth quirked. "Handsome kid."

I nod and gently rock the seat to try to keep Wesley asleep while we're here. "He is."

"Very handsome."

When I don't offer anything else, Harry leans his elbows on the bar and raises a bushy white brow at me. "What can I do for you, Mr. Lockwood?"

I run a hand through my hair and sigh. "I've been trying to track down Doc. I went by the clinic, but it was locked up. And I tried his house, but he wasn't there, either. I know he sometimes takes his lunches here, so I thought I might catch him."

"Oh, no." Harry shakes his head. "Doc took a fishing

trip this week. He won't be back until Saturday, I think. Maybe Sunday for church."

I drag a hand over my cheek, the whiskers there coarse against my palm. "Shit."

Harry's brow furrows. "What do you need him for?"

"My friend is sick. It might just be a cold or the flu or something. Fever broke this morning, but I'm worried. I was hoping I could talk him into taking a ride up the mountain with me with the promise that I'd bring him right back and buy him a case of beer on top of his usual fees."

"Well, you're out of luck there." Harry offers me a kind smile. "My wife used to be a nurse, though. She worked with Doc for a while. You want me to give her a call and see if she would go up with you?"

I sigh and slide onto the stool, dropping my face into my hands. The exhaustion of the last several days finally hits me, every fiber of my being sagging and screaming for the sleep I haven't been getting.

Would I really be capable of driving up the mountain and then back down today?

Probably not. And if Harry's wife saw Laurel, it would start the gossip mill churning, which is exactly what we don't want.

"You won't be able to hide forever, Wells."

"Maybe just call her so I can talk to her, see what she thinks?"

He nods and raps his knuckles on the bar top. "Sure thing. Can I get you anything while you wait?"

"Something with caffeine, please."

He smirks and walks over to grab a coffee pot. "Cream or sugar?"

I shake my head. "Black."

And hopefully strong as shit.

Between the stress the new arrivals brought and my already-shitty sleep patterns, I'm barely keeping it together.

Harry pours the dark brew into a chipped coffee mug and slides it over to me. "Let me call Phyllis." He pulls out his cell phone and dials, leaning a hip against the bar while I take a sip of the scalding-hot, bitter liquid. "Hey, hon. Good, good. I have Wells Lockwood here. No, I'm not joking. He has a friend who's sick, wants to talk to you. Okay, here he is."

He hands the phone across to me, and I pull it to my ear. Wesley starts to fidget slightly, and I return to rocking the car seat, constantly keeping one hand on it to ensure it can't tip off the bar.

"Mr. Lockwood?"

"Hi, Phyllis. I appreciate your help."

"Of course, dear. What's going on?"

My life is in literal shambles, and I have no fucking clue what to do about it.

The words sit on the tip of my tongue, ready to fall out as a rapid confession to the kind old woman who used to give flowers to Diana at the summer markets whenever we came to town.

But this isn't about me and how badly I've messed up everything; it's about ensuring Laurel is all right.

"I have a friend who developed a fever yesterday morning. She has a slight cough and is pale and exhausted, but she really has no other symptoms. The fever seemed to have broken this morning, but I'm still worried. I came into town to try to get Doc and some medication, but I heard he's gone."

"Oh my, yes." The genuine concern in her voice makes me stiffen as much as it does warm my chest with the reminder that the people of Lockwood Falls truly do care about each other. "You said the fever broke?"

"Yes, at least, I think so. I checked early this morning and temp was normal."

Phyllis releases a little relieved sigh. "Well, that's certainly a good sign. Is your friend eating and drinking?"

"Tea, a little bit of soup."

"That's good. Keeping hydrated is important. But no other symptoms?"

"Nope. At least, none I was told."

As stubborn as Laurel is, it's certainly possible there are other things going on that she never shared with me. It would be just like her to hide it rather than admit what she might see as defeat to whatever illness has taken her down.

"Well, as long as the fever broke and your friend seems to be doing better, I wouldn't worry too much. It's likely the flu. Grab some Gatorade or other electrolytes and over-the-counter cold and flu medicine while you're in town. Make sure your friend stays hydrated and gets lots of rest to give it time to pass. But if there's a turn for the worst, get your friend down the mountain and come straight to our place."

The tension I've been carrying around since I walked in and found Laurel sick releases slightly, and I let out a long sigh of relief. "Thanks, Phyllis. I appreciate it."

"Anytime, Mr. Lockwood." She pauses for a second, silence lingering awkwardly through the line while Harry watches me. "I know how hard it is for you up there, being cut off from everyone, how dangerous it can be if something were to happen..."

She doesn't say anything else, but vivid memories of the day that destroyed me race back.

Diana's screams...

So much blood...

Maribel so tiny, not yet ready for the world...

Sitting there with both of them, knowing there was nothing I could do...

Dragging myself off the ground to load them into the truck and come down the mountain for help that was far too late...

The same torment that keeps me awake at night and tortures me during the waking hours crushes my chest. There isn't anything I can do to keep the memories at bay, and I try to breathe through them, shaking my head and squeezing my eyes closed.

"She'll be all right, Wells."

With Diana's reassurance ringing in my ears, I finally manage to gather air into my lungs. "I'll make sure I get her down here if she needs help."

"Good. Drive safe, Mr. Lockwood."

I end the call and slide the phone across the bar toward Harry, who's kept close enough to overhear my end of the conversation.

One of his brows rises. "So, your friend will be okay?"

"Sounds like it."

Thank fuck.

I was prepared to throw her into the truck with me and bring her down the mountain this morning, but then I slid my hand across her forehead and found the fever had broken. She was sleeping so soundly, so comfortably snuggled in my bed, that I couldn't bring myself to wake her and force her to endure the bumpy, long, uncomfortable drive down the slick road to see Doc when I could just bring him to her.

But now that Phyllis' words have helped allay my fears, I need to get back up to Laurel as soon as possible.

Harry tops off my coffee. "Can I get you anything to eat?"

I shake my head, taking another sip. "No. I'm all right. I need to make a stop at the grocery store and drugstore before I head back up the mountain, and I want to get going as quickly as possible."

He nods his understanding, casting a quick glance toward the man at the end of the bar to ensure he doesn't need attention before returning his focus to me. "You come back if you need anything."

"I will." I chug half the coffee, letting the hot, harsh liquid fill my stomach. "Thank you."

Wesley releases a tiny cry from the car seat, and his eyes finally flutter open.

"Look who joined us." Harry approaches and turns the car seat to face him, smiling kindly. "Well, look at that." His eyes dart between me and the baby. "He sure has striking eyes, doesn't he?"

Shit.

"Yep, he does."

And given that Harry has spent his entire life in Lockwood Falls, he knows damn well everyone in my family has them, which means that this secret isn't one anymore.

Fuck, where the hell is Landry with the DNA results and a fucking plan? Because I have no idea how to handle any of this.

I scoop up the car seat and down the rest of the coffee as I stand. "What do I owe you for the coffee?"

Harry waves a dismissive hand. "On the house." He inclines his head toward Wesley. "It looks like you could use it."

"Thanks."

I slip out of Harry's and avoid looking at the motel as I

hustle back toward my truck. Two quick stops at the grocery and drugstores, then I'm heading back up the mountain to let Laurel know I may have just exposed the very thing we've been trying to hide this entire time.

LAUREL

I come back to the world slowly, my brain reluctant to reengage with my surroundings. I'd much rather stay buried under the covers, surrounded by the masculine scent, dreaming about things I can't have in real life, things that were never meant to be mine.

Dreams are so much easier to navigate than real life, especially when that real life involves the enigmatic Wells Lockwood and a maelstrom of conflicting feelings.

Stretching, I blink awake and stare at the bright sunlight streaming in the eastern-facing bedroom window.

What time is it?

I roll over and check the clock.

Almost dinnertime.

Hell, I slept the whole damn day.

I twist my back, releasing some of the tension there from lying in bed for so long. Almost two full days without leaving except to use the bathroom. Wells even insisted I eat in here rather than waste my energy walking the few feet to the kitchen.

It was a bit...overbearing and overprotective, but he might have been right about what my body needed because I finally feel better, stronger.

Thank God because I can't stay cooped up in here any longer.

I roll to the side of the bed and slip my feet to the floor, then slowly stand, expecting my legs to be far wobblier than they are. The room doesn't spin, and that chill that's encapsulated me since yesterday morning has fled.

It couldn't have come soon enough. I've left Wells alone with Wesley for too long already. He may have made some strides toward accepting his new role as a father, but that doesn't mean he was prepared to handle it all on his own yet. Nobody is ready to be thrown into the deep end without some swimming lessons first.

A piece of paper on the nightstand catches my eye, and I grab it, staring at the unfamiliar, meticulous handwriting.

Went to town to get medicine for you and talk to the doctor. Took Wesley. Be back soon.

He went to town?

How?

I open the bedroom door and step out into the quiet living room that has become my home over the last several days. It once felt like a tomb or a prison, but I've come to appreciate the cozy warmth of the small space.

It's easy to see why Wells and Diana loved it so much. Not only does it hold an immense amount of family history, but it's so different from the city and everything living there requires.

A low rumbling sound comes from outside the cabin.

What the hell is that?

I rush to the front door and yank it open just as a massive truck pulls from between the trees and stops in front of the cabin with Wells behind the wheel. His eyes dart over to meet mine, and his gaze narrows on me as he takes me in standing at the cabin door.

He throws the huge vehicle into park, shuts it off, and hops out of the driver's seat. His boots crunch on the gravel as he walks around the hood and approaches me cautiously, worried brow furrowed deeply. "What are you doing out of bed?"

I cross my arms over my chest and lean against the door-jamb. "What are you doing with that truck?"

His eyebrows wing up. "What do you mean?"

"What I mean is, where the hell did the truck come from? You said there was no way back to town."

He smirks and takes one step up toward me. "No, I said you would have to walk to town...because I wasn't going to drive you. You really think I'd live up here without a truck? I would be trapped up here forever, and I wouldn't be able to do half of the tasks that need to get done around the property without a vehicle that has a big diesel engine like that."

I scowl at him.

That grin that always seems to make my stomach flip-flop makes an appearance. "You must be feeling better if you're arguing with me."

Ignoring his smug look, I focus on what's actually important. "Where's Wesley?"

He tips his head back toward the truck. "Asleep in the truck. He was conked out the entire ride down, and he slept most of the way up here for me, too."

"The motion of the car will do that."

"Mm-hmm." Wells nods and steps back down to get Wesley from the backseat. He grabs the car seat and four plastic bags and carries them in one hand. "Get back inside before you catch cold."

I scowl at him and stare up at the perfectly clear late afternoon sky. "What's all that?"

"Medicine."

Four bags full?

I'm already feeling a lot better than I was yesterday.

Whatever knocked me out so hard fled my system just as fast as it hit me.

Wells takes the two steps up, and I step back to allow him to enter the cabin, then close the door behind him as he beelines for the kitchen.

"All of that is really necessary?"

He sets Wesley's carrier on the floor and the bags on the counter and begins unloading them. "I wanted to make sure you had everything you needed. I got some children's stuff, too, just in case he develops any symptoms."

Because you're already anticipating his needs.

My chest constricts a little at his words, but I don't dare point out to Wells that what he just did without even thinking about it was act like a real father. And he seems no worse for wear after spending almost two full days alone with the baby.

"I appreciate it, but I really am feeling better. It seems like my fever broke."

He nods and returns his focus to the bags. "I checked you this morning and noticed it had broken."

Checked on me?

Something about the way he says the words makes me picture him sitting on the edge of the bed, staring down at me. "So, you were watching me while I slept?"

He freezes, one hand buried in the bag, his entire body stiffening. "No."

I approach him and lean next to him at the counter as he piles boxes and boxes upon it. "Sure sounds like you were."

"Nope, just checked on you."

I turn over one of the boxes. "A neti pot?"

"In case you got congested."

A smile pulls at my lips. "You thought of everything, huh?"

And damn if that isn't the sweetest thing ever from the man who insists he's not capable of it.

"I spoke with a friend who's a nurse, too. She said to stay hydrated and sleep as much as possible."

I release a little laugh, tipping my neck from side to side to work out some of the kinks. "Well, I've certainly been doing that. I only woke a few minutes before you pulled up."

He holds up another bag and shoves it at me. "I got you this."

I peek into the bag and almost gag at the negative memories the colored liquid brings. "I hate Gatorade. It reminds me of gym class in high school."

The corner of his mouth quirks. "You weren't athletic?"

I offer a half-shrug. "Not really. I played volleyball, but I was never very good at it. I didn't like it, either. Team sports aren't really my thing. What about you?"

He hesitates a moment before answering, instead focusing on continuing to empty the bags of boxes of various cold and flu medications I doubt I'll even need. "I played polo."

I bark out a laugh. "Of course, you did."

His head snaps around toward me, his eyes narrowed. "What the hell's that supposed to mean?"

"Seriously? Wells, you're from one of the richest families in the entire country. Playing polo is about as pretentious as you can get."

An uncomfortable silence lingers between us for a moment before he finally averts his gaze. "You think I'm pretentious?"

The hurt in his voice makes me take a little half-step back.

"No, that's not what I meant."

Wells slams a box of saltine crackers on the counter aggressively. "Sure as hell seems like it." He turns and waves an arm out absently to the living room. "Look around you. Am I living pretentiously?"

I shake my head, suddenly regretting my words. "No, definitely not, but you were two years ago."

He flinches at my words.

Shit, shouldn't have said that.

But it is relevant to what's about to come. Wells would be able to get people to support him in raising Wesley if he were back in the city, but up here, he'll truly be alone attempting what might be an impossible task.

"Why did you decide to stay up here, Wells? Was it just because you didn't want to have to interact with anyone? Why didn't you go home to your mansion, to the estate where you'd be comfortable?"

"Because I didn't want to be comfortable." His voice comes out hard and gruff, a clear indication he doesn't want to discuss this any further. "I thought you would have understood that by now."

Ouch.

Perhaps I should have seen it, the way he self-flagellates. He believes he doesn't deserve that life or that the life he had in Denver somehow contributed to Diana and his daughter's deaths. Wells stays up here so he's forced to work, day in and day out, so he *won't* be comfortable the way he would be back in the city.

I clear my throat and grab a few of the boxes and a bottle of Gatorade that I will now force myself to choke down in an attempt to alleviate some of my guilt over what I just said. "Thank you for getting all this."

Wells rests his palms on the counter and squeezes his eyes closed. "You're welcome." He lets his gaze drift over to me. "I really am glad you're feeling better. I was..." His Adam's apple bobs as he swallows thickly. "I was worried. Up here, if you had really been sick, something serious..."

Agony drips from his words, and I can only imagine the scenarios that have been racing through his head since he found me yesterday morning.

I rest my hand on his bare forearm, the same crackle of energy coursing through my fingertips that does every time we touch. He doesn't flinch away from the gesture, and I take that as an invitation to lean in slightly and rest my cheek against his shoulder.

"I'm okay, just the flu or something. Really, Wells, I'm fine."

He gives me a sharp nod, then pulls away from me quickly, grabs Wesley's car seat, and disappears into the nursery with him.

The man who wouldn't even acknowledge the baby only a few short days ago now uses him as an excuse to escape me.

Chapter Fifteen

WELLS

Wesley finishes his bottle, and I set it in the sink to wash later and gently begin to rub and pat his back as I pace the living room in what has become our normal routine over the last few days while Laurel regains her strength.

I glance toward the closed bedroom door, and the same unease I've felt since the moment I abandoned her in the rain in the clearing settles over me.

The tension between us hasn't helped anything. She wants to talk, wants to hash out whatever the hell *this* is and discuss what happened at the barn, but I'm not in any place to have that conversation mentally.

"Talk to her, Wells."

As if it's that easy.

I wouldn't have the first idea what to say about what we did, about what it means, about what my damn future looks like.

How can I plan a future when I don't even know what I'm doing one day to the next?

A horn honks somewhere outside the cabin, and I go stock still, holding Wesley against my shoulder.

Tires crunch on the gravel immediately outside in the clearing.

Shit. Who's that?

I put Wesley into his crib before I hustle toward the front door and tug it open. A black Town Car sits directly in front of the cabin, and the same old man who drove Laurel up here leans toward the passenger seat, gives me a quick wave, then motions behind him again.

It's exactly what we've been waiting for: the results of the test.

It has to be.

Yet somehow, even after all this time anticipating it, I don't feel ready. A strange sense of foreboding coils around my spine, and I take a step out into the light drizzle and make my way over to the car.

The back window rolls down, and Landry's weathered face appears, a scowl on his lips.

I lean my forearm on the roof and dip my head toward the window. "I've been waiting for you."

The corner of his lips twitches into an uncharacteristic half-grin. "I'm sure you have, and I have a bone to pick with you."

"Oh yeah? What's that?"

The man I've left in charge of Lockwood Brewing, who sat at Dad's right hand for decades and now mine for another one, has always been a straight-shooter and brutally honest with me about business *and* my personal life, which is precisely why I trusted leaving him in control.

I can only imagine what he has to say about the current situation.

He sneers, the move making his deep wrinkles appear even more cavernous. "You stole one of my attorneys. She could have gotten a lot of experience in damage control over the last week."

Of all the things Landry could complain about—bedding a woman I met at a towny bar, impregnating her, creating a possible scandal for the company—it was keeping Laurel up the mountain that set him off.

I snort and nod toward a folder on the seat next to him. "So?"

He offers me a sardonic grin. "Congratulations, Daddy."

The words I was so sure would send me into a downward spiral only a few days ago make warmth bloom in my chest and flood my veins. "Okay."

His eyes widen. "Okay? That's all you have to say?"

The rain starts to fall harder, pelting the roof of the car and soaking my clothes. These summer afternoon storms help ensure the ecosystem survives the dryer summer months, but they can be annoying as hell when I have to work outside as much as I do to keep this place running.

I incline my head toward the cabin. "Let's go inside and talk."

Landry scowls. "Just get in the backseat."

I take a step back from the car. "I have to listen for the baby."

The annoyed glare he casts at me could cut a diamond, and he grabs the folder, climbs out, and follows me through the rain into the cabin. I close the door behind us, and he hands me the folder as we make our way to the small table in the kitchen and settle into the hand-carved chairs.

"It's everything we could dig up on Candace."

"Anything I need to know?"

He shakes his head. "Not much. She was a bit of a transient. Loves to travel internationally. Dropped out of college. Bounces from boyfriend to boyfriend."

I cringe. "So having a one-night stand with me wasn't really out of character, is what you're saying."

He smirks. "No, it wasn't. I also tracked down her medical records."

I jerk my head up and narrow my eyes at him. "How the hell did you manage that?"

Leaning back, he offers a non-committal shrug. "I've been working for the company for a long time. I have a lot of friends in a lot of places. Like I said, Laurel could have been learning a lot over the last week."

I flip through the pages, scanning the words quickly. Background check. High school and college transcripts. A few newspaper articles with photos of her and interviews about visiting Belize and the Great Wall of China.

Landry inclines his head toward the rest of the papers I haven't made it to yet. "Wesley's birth records are in there, too, and the few pediatric appointments he's had. Seems to be completely healthy."

A huge weight lifts off my chest. "Good."

Shifting forward, Landry rests his forearms on the table, his entire mood shifting from friendly to business. "Now... what do you want to do about this publicly?"

"Shit." I run my hand through my hair. "Whatever it is. We probably have to do it quickly. I took him into town yesterday, and I think the rumor mill is going to be spreading exactly what we feared before we can make a statement."

He jerks back, annoyance crinkling the skin around his eyes. "Shit. What the hell, Wells?"

"Laurel was sick. I had to go get medicine."

"Is she all right?"

I nod. "Just the flu or something. She seems fine now."

The click of a door opening makes me freeze, and a second later, Laurel peers into the kitchen dressed in one of my T-shirts that hangs barely to her mid-thigh and running shorts, her hair rumpled, eyes sleepy.

She rubs at them and tries to focus on the table when her gaze lands on Landry. "Oh, shit. Mr. Landry. I...fuck."

Landry examines her with a shrewd eye, then turns back to me. "It seems like we may have more than one scandal we need to handle. You're sleeping with our employee?"

"Shit." I hold up a hand. "No, this isn't what it looks like."

Laurel's eyes widen slightly, and her bottom lip starts to tremble.

Landry's gaze bobs between us. "So, you aren't sleeping together? Then what is she doing in your T-shirt coming out of your bedroom?"

I clear my throat. "I told you. She wasn't feeling well. I let her sleep in there so she'd be more comfortable than on the couch where she has been sleeping this entire time."

None of it's a lie but withholding the part where I fucked her in the rain against the barn the other day seems appropriate in the moment. Though, the look Laurel is giving me seems to suggest otherwise.

Landry releases a deep sigh of relief. "Thank God because if I had to pay out a sexual harassment lawsuit and give her millions because you were fucking her, it would just be icing on this fucked-up cake."

I run a hand over my face and avoid looking at her.

"So, what are we doing?" Landry leans back in his chair and raises a brow. "Press release? How do you want to word it?"

I narrow my eyes at him. "We're sure Candace isn't coming back?"

He nods. "Positive. I already had papers drawn up for her to sign over sole custody to you permanently. She doesn't have any interest in raising Wesley herself, which means he's your responsibility...unless you don't want him to be."

His words hang in the air as thick and heavy as the tension between me and Laurel.

"Do you?"

"Shit." I sit up straighter, meeting his questioning gaze. "Yes. He's my son. Of course, I'm going to take care of him. He's not going into the system, and I'm not sending him off to be adopted by someone. He's a Lockwood."

Landry smacks his palms on the table. "I guess that settles it, then."

I push up from my chair. "I guess it does."

But the look Laurel's giving me tells me absolutely *nothing* has been.

Landry stands and glances between Laurel and me. "So, I'll put together the press release and send it out, stating you had a brief relationship that resulted in the birth of a child who's now solely in your care. We'll skirt the one-night stand and not-knowing-he-existed issues."

Cringing, I offer a sharp nod. "Seems wise."

He reaches out and claps me on the shoulder. "Don't worry. We can spin this. You were just keeping a low profile because of the recent deaths of your wife and daughter and didn't want the media latching onto Wesley's mother and creating any undue attention for her."

I rub my temple at the migraine forming there. "Sounds reasonable."

"You're okay with me sending it out without you seeing the final?"

That would only add another day or two to the timeline, and after what Harry witnessed yesterday, we may not have much time to get ahead of this.

I give him a sharp nod. "I trust you."

"Good." His eyes sweep over Laurel. "Laurel, are you riding back with me?"

Her gaze jumps to me, a thousand questions reflecting back in the Caribbean blue pools.

"Um, no." I walk Landry to the door. "I'd like her to stay and continue to help me with Wesley for a few more days. Once all the buzz from the press release dies down, we'll come back into town to finalize any paperwork and for me to take care of a few things at the office."

Landry shifts uncomfortably. "You haven't set foot in the office in two years."

"I know, but if I don't make an appearance after all this goes public, the shit will hit the fan even worse. I'll drop in. Say hello to the staff. Let PR take some shots to release to the media, then I'll be back up here, where I belong."

LAUREL

Wells stands with his back to me, watching Landry pull away, but long after the sound of the tires on the gravel fades, he remains at the door, unwilling or unable to turn around and face me.

My entire body vibrates with a combination of uncontrolled rage, confusion, and hurt. Every word he said to Landry was like his axe being driven into my heart, each blow knocking the wind out of me and making my knees want to buckle beneath me.

Only sheer willpower learned from years of standing my ground against people stronger than me allowed me to keep my mouth shut and my ass off the wood floor. But now Landry is gone, and Wells can't hide behind him anymore.

Finally, he takes a step back, closes the door, and turns to face me.

I point to the table they just vacated, where a file folder still sits, papers spread out across it. "What. The. Hell. Was. That?"

Wells releases a low groan and rubs at his temple. "Please, Laurel, I can't do this right now."

"When can you, Wells? Because it seems like you want to just pretend what happened the other night didn't. You want to ignore it. Act like it's some nightmare instead of reality."

His eyes open and flash with the same heat I saw in them when he pinned me against the barn. "That was anything but a nightmare, Laurel. That's the fucking problem."

"I-I don't know what you mean. Why is it a problem?"

He throws up his hands. "Are you kidding me? You heard what he said, right? You're an employee of Lockwood Brewing. I'm the fucking CEO. How the hell would it look if anyone found out you and I ever slept together?"

Slept together.

The way he says the words so dismissively, and in the

past tense like it's never going to happen again, slams into me so hard I almost stagger back.

"What is it you think we're doing here, Laurel?" He waves his hand absently around the space that has been my home for the last week. "Playing house?" He squeezes his eyes closed and shakes his head. "I can't do any of this right now, maybe ever."

I step forward and jab my finger into his chest. "Bullshit. You just don't want to."

Tears flow freely now, but I refuse to let him see me cry. I turn away from him and stalk back to the bedroom, leaving the door open behind me because if he really wanted to come in, the asshole would just break the thing down anyway.

I tug off his shirt and throw it on the bed, along with the running shorts I slept in last night. The clothes I arrived in sit on top of the dresser where he set them once he moved me into the room, and I put them back on as quickly as my shaking hands allow.

"What the hell are you doing?"

His voice comes from far closer than I expected it, and I whirl to find him standing in the doorway, jaw clenched.

"What does it look like I'm doing? I'm getting ready to leave."

"Where do you think you're going?"

"The fuck away from here." I inhale sharply, trying to keep myself in control long enough to say what I have to before I completely break down. "You have your answer. That baby's yours. Just like you and I both knew he was. So, now he's officially your responsibility, not mine. You don't have to *suffer* with my presence here any longer."

"Fuck, Laurel, you know that isn't true."

I glance over my shoulder at him as I finish buttoning my once-white shirt. "Sure as hell seems like it."

He motions vaguely in the direction of Lockwood Falls. "Where are you going to go? Landry already left, and he's probably two miles down the mountain by now."

"I'll fucking *walk*."

Athletics may not have been on the top of my activities list, but I am relatively fit, and if I have to hike twenty miles down this godforsaken mountain to get to civilization where I can call Landry to come back for me, I will do it.

Wells scoffs, crossing his arms over his large chest, making his biceps bulge against the T-shirt material. "You're serious?"

"Dead serious." I square off with him, throwing back my shoulders and crossing my arms over my chest, mirroring his stance. "I'm not going to stay up here to be a babysitter for you anymore."

His nostrils flare as we stare each other down, the anger heating my skin, making it sizzle the same way the energy does between us. "You're far more than a fucking babysitter, Laurel. You know that."

I raise my eyebrows, widening my eyes. "Do I? That's not what you just said to Landry."

He takes a harsh step toward me. "What the fuck was I supposed to tell him? That the young, pretty, brand-new attorney showed up here with my surprise baby and threw my entire world off its axis with her smart mouth and her unwillingness to back down from the way she fucking pushes me? You want me to tell him that I don't want you to leave and that scares the fuck out of me?"

His words knock me back a step, but the uncertainty still remains in his bourbon eyes. Enough that I can't believe he really means what he says. "If that's the truth, yes. That is what I want you to say to him."

"I can't, Laurel." He throws up his hands. "I'm the fucking CEO of one of the most profitable companies in the world. I can't be banging one of my employees and asking her to take care of my baby."

"Isn't that what you're *doing*?"

"That's my point. I *shouldn't* be."

He hasn't said the "M" word again, but he doesn't have to. What happened between us will never be anything but a massive mistake in his mind. A one-time loss of control he will never allow to happen again.

"Fuck you, Wells."

"Good." He moves into the room. "*Be* mad. I'd much rather have you mad at me than looking at me the way you have been the last few days."

"And how's that?"

"Like you want to stay."

Fuck, he isn't wrong about that.

The longer I'm here, the harder it's going to be to leave. That baby and this man have grown on me, worked their way so deeply into my heart that I don't know how to extricate myself from them without it hurting. I have to get out of here now, while my heart is still intact enough to try.

I move toward the door, but he steps in front of it, blocking my path with his broad chest and massive shoulders. A physical blockade similar to the one he's put up around *his* heart.

"Let me go."

He shakes his head. "I can't do that."

"Why the hell not?"

His jaw tightens as he stares down at me. The color of his eyes shifting from amber to an almost-midnight black.

"Because I don't know what the hell I will do up here without you."

"You can take care of Wesley yourself. You've proven that over the last few days. You don't need me here anymore."

"But what if *I* do?"

"If you do what?"

"Need you here." He says the words so softly that I can barely hear them.

Even though I want as much space between us as possible, I inch closer to ensure I don't mishear or misconstrue his response. "Why would you need me here, Wells, if not to take care of the baby? Because you just made it abundantly clear there's nothing going on between the two of us. So, tell me, why?"

He stares at me for a moment, like he's searching for the right thing to say. Finally, he looks away, dropping his forehead into his palm. "Christ, Laurel, you know why I want you here, and you know I'm a fucking wreck and have absolutely no right to feel this way. I have no right to want *this*, to want *you*."

His self-loathing, guilt-laden words come out so laced with anguish that I can't even get my reply out without taking a second to let them sink in.

This is really how he feels? That he doesn't deserve to have good things in his life?

"Why the fuck not, Wells?"

He lowers his hand, and his wet eyes meet mine. "I still hear my damn wife's voice in my head."

My entire body stiffens. Of all the responses he could have to my question, that was definitely not one I ever could have expected. But given how long they were together, the life they had planned, the time they spent *here*, the way he lost her, maybe it isn't so strange that he might be keeping her alive in his own mind.

I'm not sure how to respond to the confession, how one is *supposed* to when someone relays something like that, but he keeps staring at me, expecting me to say *something*. "And what does she say about all this with Wesley, with me?"

A single tear hangs from the corner of his eye, and he reaches up and swipes it away. "She says you're here to help me. She keeps saying it, over and over again."

"And I did. I helped you with Wesley, and I'm confident you can take care of him yourself now."

And if I stay, I'm going to end up getting even more hurt than I am now. He's too lost right now and doesn't want me to help him find his way back. He's too wrapped in his own guilt and drowning in his own loss to see I'm throwing him a lifeline.

"So, let me go."

A muscle tics in his clenched jaw. "No."

"No?" I raise a brow at him. "Are we back to this?"

"No." He shakes his head. "This time I'm asking you not to go, but if you really want to, I'll drive you to town myself."

Tears burn my eyes, and I fucking hate myself for it. For letting myself get attached to this man who's so wholly unavailable to me. Who fights me every fucking step of the way but also gives me glimpses of the person he can be when he's not lost in his own head.

"You're asking me to stay to do what, Wells? I need you to explain it to me. Explain what the hell is going on between us because I don't understand."

Wells shakes his head. "Neither do I, and that's the problem." His gaze softens, and he steps toward me. "But if you leave, I won't have any chance to figure it out."

Fuck.

Leave it to him to say one right thing.

He wants to figure it out.

It's more than I thought he was capable of, but I'm not sure if it's enough.

Can you really expect anything more from him right now with everything he's been through?

Can't you give him that chance?

Should you give it to him?

"Say something, Laurel."

"I don't know what to say. You heard what Landry said when he was up here. At the end of the day, you're my boss, right? Even if you and I both wanted any of this to continue, it would be a horrible idea. For you, for the business, for me. It would be way too complicated and create a whole host of potential issues."

A spark of something flashes in his eyes, and he lifts his shoulders and lets them fall. "Then...you're fired."

Chapter Sixteen

LAUREL

I recoil from his words as if he had physically slapped me. "*What?* You can't do that."

A tiny grin flickers across his lips, like my anger actually amuses him. "I just did."

Motherfucker!

Of all the ways Wells Lockwood has pissed me off over the past week, this takes the cake. He knows how important this job is to me, and he's willing to use his power over my career to get what he wants.

It's a ruthless move, one that's left me speechless.

I open and close my mouth a few times, trying to think of how to respond to his arrogance and the asshole move. "You can't fire me. I'll..."

He takes a step toward me until his chest brushes against mine. "You'll what, sue the company? Me personally? Take billions?" His head dips until his lips brush against my ear. "I'd like to see you try."

The fact that he would even suggest I would do something like that—take my personal relationship with him and use it against the company—infuriates me so much that I snarl at him, press my palms against his chest, and shove him back slightly.

"I'm leaving, *Mr. Lockwood.* Get out of my way."

Wells sneers and grips either side of the doorjamb, creating an impassable blockade I'll never get through unless he wants me to. All the time up here, doing manual labor and living alone on the mountain has turned him into a muscled Adonis, which means I don't stand a chance against him physically.

A smile plays on his lips, amusement dancing in his eyes. "I'm glad to see you're feeling better."

"Excuse me?"

Talk about a change in topic.

"This..." He looks me up and down in the pencil skirt and white blouse I arrived in. "It's a good look for you. Makes it a little easier to take you seriously."

I scoff at him. "Take me *seriously*?"

Fire burns in his lustful gaze, a renewed flame that rivals the one I saw the other night before he pinned me against the barn. "All this bravado, arguing with me and fighting me at every turn, I am glad it's back."

Retreating a step, I shake my head. "Don't look at me like that."

I intentionally repeat the same words he just said to me, hoping it will make him see what madness we've created.

One of his dark brows wings up. "Like what?"

"Like you want to forget all the reasons you just told me that this is a terrible idea."

He nods slowly, never taking his eyes off mine. "But I do. Every time I'm alone in a fucking room with you, every time you call me out on my bullshit, it's all I can think about. How damn wrong it is but how good it feels to have you here."

The tears I've somehow managed to control threaten to spill over. "Don't say things like that to me."

Wells tilts his head. "Why not?"

"Because it isn't fair." I stomp my foot and probably appear like a petulant child to the man who is fifteen years my elder, but I don't care anymore. He's pushed me to the point of not giving a damn about how I look to him. "It's not when ten seconds ago you told me that you and I can never be anything, that this will never go anywhere."

My words suck all the air from the room, and the amusement that danced in his eyes only moments ago evaporates instantly.

"I don't know anything anymore, Laurel, except that when you showed up with that baby was the first time I felt anything but agony in two years."

A vise constricts around my chest, and he pulls his hands from the doorjamb and approaches me cautiously. When I don't retreat, he wraps his arms around my waist and tugs me up against him. His hard cock presses between us, and I bite back a little moan at the way my body instantly heats in response.

He stares down at me, the sincerity of what he's about to say evident. "I wasn't sure I would ever be able to feel anything but pain and anger again."

"You were sure angry with me and Wesley."

"No"—he shakes his head—"I was never angry with him."

I raise an eyebrow. "Just me, then?"

Wells smirks. "I was angry at the situation, at it being thrown in my lap and having to deal with it on top of everything else and all the other emotions that day brings up." He squeezes me gently. "But you were just doing your job. I know that."

A heavy sigh slips from my lips, taking with it part of my anger at him.

He lifts one hand to capture my face in his rough palm. "Don't go."

Two simple words, yet they hold so much weight and mean so much more.

I really was prepared to throw on his dead wife's tennis shoes and hike however many miles I needed down that mountain into Lockwood Falls to get the hell out of here.

No matter how hard it would have been, I was willing to leave behind this man and that baby in the nursery I've grown so attached to in order to get back to my life, the one I've worked so goddamn hard for, the one I'm not willing to give up.

But standing here in his arms, staring into the fire burning in his amber eyes, something deep in my gut tells me I need to stay, at least for a little while, to give him time to figure things out. To give *us* time.

"Okay."

I release the word breathlessly, and as soon as it leaves my lips, he presses his to mine, stealing any ability I might have maintained to resist him. His hands tighten on my waist and face, angling my chin up so he can delve his tongue into my mouth to tangle with mine. Looping my arms around his neck, I tangle my fingers in his long hair, tugging on it sharply.

He groans and spins us around to walk me backward, out of the bedroom and into the small bathroom. It's tight in here with one person, but with the two of us...his already huge presence completely fills the space.

Wells kisses me as if his life depends on it, and maybe,

in this moment, it does. He was lost before Wesley and I arrived, and while he might not be found yet, he's at least on a path where that might be a possibility. It's the only reason I'm staying, letting this man ever deeper into my heart.

An insanely dangerous proposition.

I should be worried about my job, about what this will do to my future, the one I saw before Landry sent me up this mountain, but as Wells backs me toward the shower stall, my brain can only process one thing—how incredibly Wells kisses, how his touch sets my body aflame, how his passion unnerves me and sends me soaring.

He tears his mouth from mine long enough to reach in and crank on the water before he returns to press his lips to my neck and kiss his way up to my ear. His feather-light touches brush against my heated skin, sending goosebumps pebbling across my skin, and he settles his warm lips at my ear.

"I'm sorry."

I don't have the foggiest clue what he's sorry for. There are so many things he could be referencing, but if I stop to ask him, all of this ends and the dull ache between my legs doesn't get satisfied.

Everything is beyond complicated with Wells Lockwood, but I have to give him—*us*—a chance, or I know I'll regret it. He isn't someone you can walk away from easily, no matter how painful staying might be.

But I push away those thoughts and concentrate on the feel of his lips on my ear, and when he sucks the lobe into his mouth and bites down, my entire body jerks against his, my pussy throbbing.

"Fuck, Wells..."

Hands tightening at my waist, he issues a low growl. He unzips my skirt and shoves it down to the floor, fully exposing me to him. His hand immediately goes between my legs, and he nudges them open, his fingers gliding over the wetness already pooling there.

"Fucking hell, Laurel."

His entire body tenses at the merest contact of his fingertips to my cunt, and I score my nails down his neck as the room starts to fill with steam. He shifts his hand from my hip up to the top button of my shirt and jerks down on it hard, tearing the buttons free, sending them flying across the tile.

"You don't need this anymore."

Oh, God.

That shouldn't be so hot.

He just destroyed one of my favorite shirts, bought with money I really don't have for work at his damn company, but the aggressive move only ignites every nerve in my body. I kiss him eagerly, my tongue tangling with his, searching for something I'm not sure he can give me but I'll keep looking for, anyway, even if it kills me.

With one quick motion, he jerks his mouth from mine, spins me around, and pulls the ruined shirt from my shoulders, letting it fall to the floor next to the shower. He shucks his pants and T-shirt quickly and ushers me in under the double-headed spray.

The hot water pelts my skin, and I release a tiny moan at how good it feels after being in bed for the last few days. His lips find the nape of my neck, and he kisses his way across my collarbone and up to my ear.

"You're going to stay."

It isn't a question this time. It's a command. A confirmation of what I just promised from a man who always had everything he's ever wanted and asked for. A man who has never been told no by anyone for anything. A man who then lost it all in one tragic night.

Before I can issue a response, he bites down on my shoulder, and my body jerks back against his hard cock where it's nestled between my ass cheeks. I grind onto it, the slick water making it glide smoothly along my skin. Wells groans and wraps his arm around my stomach, reaching up with his other hand to grab the detachable head.

He switches the setting to an intense massage and holds it in front of us so it sprays directly on my stomach. "I know I've been a real asshole. That all I am is angry and broken, but you make me believe you might be the glue that could put me back together."

Fuck. He can't say things like that to me.

Tears pool in my eyes, and he lowers the showerhead between my legs, placing the water jet directly against my clit. My entire body twitches, his forearm pressing into my belly the only thing keeping me in place.

He moves the shower wand meticulously, hitting me in exactly the right place to make my entire body tremble.

"Oh, God."

I drop my head back against his shoulder, and he kisses my cheek until I tilt my head enough that he can get to my mouth. He groans into it, swallowing my next moan as the pressure begins to build, making my legs shake violently.

The intensity of the moment, of what he said, of what's building in my body terrifies me, and I rip my mouth away from his to tell him to stop when the orgasm hits me so fast and hard, it blackens my vision and robs me of my ability to speak.

WELLS

Laurel spasms against me, the sheer ecstasy that's coursing through her veins twisting her face into a stunning mask of perfection. I move the water slightly to hit her at a different angle, hoping to drag out the orgasm longer, make her come even harder, until the pleasure is too intense for her to take any longer.

"Please!" She thrashes in my arms, pushing at the hand holding the showerhead between her legs. "I can't." She gasps. "Stop."

I slowly pull it away and flip it back to its original setting, clipping it into place above us. Laurel sags limply against my chest, and I shift my hand to replace the showerhead at her core.

She twitches at the contact of my fingers against her drenched cunt and engorged clit, and I kiss behind her ear, sucking at the sensitive flesh there hard enough to make her bow up against my hold.

Christ, this woman...

"Do you have any idea how beautiful you are when you come, Laurel?"

To have her utterly destroyed and satiated in my arms, a blissful half-smile tilting the lips I can't get enough of kissing.

What the hell am I supposed to do with how this woman makes me feel? With the fact that she makes me feel anything at all?

It's the same question I've been grappling with since the moment she stepped out of that car and forced me to face the real world I've tried to hide from for so damn long.

And I still don't have an answer.

All I know is being with her makes me feel alive again for the first time since I lost the life I had.

Guilt starts to creep up at the edges of my mind, but I push it away in favor of relishing the reality of having her in my arms. The beauty of watching her come undone, the taste of her lips on mine.

Laurel reaches between us and wraps her hand around the base of my cock. I hiss at the contact, and she slowly strokes her palm down the length, brushing her thumb over the head. My balls seize up with that one simple touch, primed to blow already.

But I'm nowhere ready for this to end, and I have no intention of coming in her hand. Not when my cock aches to be inside her, when I crave to watch and feel her come again.

I tighten my hold on her—one hand across her stomach, the other cupping her between her legs. "You have no idea what you do to me."

She tilts her head back and looks up at me with heavy-lidded eyes. "I can feel what I do to you."

"It's so much more than that, Laurel. You are all the things I don't deserve and am too selfish to let go of. I just don't know what to do about any of it."

And that admission makes pain flash through her gaze.

Fuck.

The last thing I ever want is to hurt this woman.

She came up here to do her job and got trapped with a crazy man and a baby that isn't hers. Made to deal with my mood swings and overall ornery attitude toward life in general. She did it all without backing down from confronting me when I was in the wrong.

And fuck, have I ever been in the wrong a lot since she arrived.

It would be selfish to saddle her with all my baggage. I can't expect her to wait around for me to figure out my shit and get my head on straight.

She's in the prime of her life, starting the career she's busted her ass for, and I'd be asking her to give it all up in order to stay here with me in a place she clearly isn't meant to be.

This mountain would stifle the brilliance of someone like Laurel.

I won't do that to her.

I can't.

After this, after tonight, I have to show her why.

I have to give her the real opportunity to leave, like I should have earlier today.

I should have let her get in the car with Landry. I should have driven her down the mountain myself. There are so many things I *should* have done, and I should stop this now. I should tell her I can't let her sacrifice her future for someone whose future isn't certain. But I'm too selfish to do it right now. I need this feeling one last time in case I never experience it again.

I capture her mouth and spin her to face me. Her hand returns to grip my length, and I lift her to wrap her legs around my waist. My cock aligns along her wet seam, and she glides her hips up and down, coating me.

Fucking hell.

As much as I want her like this, pinned against the wall fast and hard, she deserves so much better, so much more. A man who can worship her properly and give her his whole heart. I don't have that capability, but I will get her off. I will make her feel good because I don't want her to regret this, though I fear she may already.

Laurel is smart enough to sense the war raging inside

me, between what I want and what I can't have. Between what's right and fair and what just feels damn good. She just isn't acknowledging it, isn't admitting she sees the struggle I'll ultimately lose. Because she cares too much already.

I walk her back to the tile and pin her to it, then drag my mouth off hers and take her face in my palm. "Tell me you want this right now."

She gives me a sharp nod, and I kiss her deeply, then slowly let her legs lower to the tiled floor.

"Turn around."

Her eyes flare, and I take a half step back, giving her room to rotate under the water.

"Put your hands above you on the tile."

She reaches up, palms flat against the wall, and I grasp her hips, dragging her ass back toward me, putting her at the perfect angle. I smooth my hand over her flawless skin, then drop my thumb between her ass cheeks. I probe gently, easing the tip of my thumb into her ass, earning me a startled gasp that echoes around the tight space.

Music to my fucking ears.

A sound I may never hear again.

Thinking about what tomorrow brings will only destroy this moment, so I grip my cock in my other hand and align it with her cunt. She wiggles her ass, begging for me to take her, and it's an invitation I can't refuse.

I plunge into her hard at the same time I slip the rest of my thumb up inside her. Her strangled groan fills my ears with the sound of her pure pleasure. My cock throbs inside her, and she tightens around me, clenching and grasping needily.

If it were possible, I would make this moment last

forever—just the two of us, locked together, our bodies becoming one and everything else just...gone.

The guilt. The rage. The memories. The dreams. The very real complications that await us outside this space.

All of it would disappear indefinitely, leaving just this exact second in time when everything feels perfect.

But nothing perfect can last, and Laurel turns her head to the side to meet my gaze, begging me with her vibrant blue eyes. I won't deny her this, can't deny myself the pleasure it will bring both of us.

I drag back my hips and plunge into her again, moving my thumb in time with my cock. She presses her left cheek against the tile. Her eyes drift closed, her mouth open, panting heavily with each harsh thrust.

"Fuck, fuck, fuck...Wells!"

Her urgency only makes me drill her relentlessly, desperate to get her to the same place I am. Ready to give in to the need for her that's been eating me alive.

Every drag of my hips, she rolls back to meet me. Our skin slapping together, echoing the thunder that rolled across the mountain the night she arrived. The storm that brought her to me fills the shower, her warmth and my ice colliding to set off a tempest neither one of us has any control over.

I grip her face and tilt her head back toward me so I can take her mouth while I fuck her into a mindless oblivion. Her legs start to shake, and I add a thrust up and roll of my hips with each drive into her. She gasps against my lips and starts to come. Her ass and her cunt both tighten on me in both places, drawing my orgasm from deep inside.

The tingle surges from my balls through my entire body, a blast of pressure that releases inside her in a heated rush.

Her pussy clasps around me, dragging it out until I gasp her name and sag against her.

Sweet mother of God...

What happened at the barn the other night was only the tip of the iceberg where Laurel Palmer is concerned. Her sass and fire only combust more when we're like this, until I'm burned to my core by the woman who has rekindled my ability to care about another human being again.

We stand, panting, hot water pelting my back, cold tile under one hand and her face still pressed against it. She issues a low groan and tightens around me one more time, and I hiss, then press my forehead to her temple.

I want to apologize again for everything. For her having to come up here. For my reluctance to believe it. For my anger at her for just doing her job. For my insistence that she stay, because let's face it, I did fucking kidnap her. For the way I've treated her as if she were a babysitter for the child I should be taking care of, as if she were an *employee.* And ultimately, for *not* treating her like one, for using my attraction to her as a way to forget my own pain for a while. Because that isn't fair to her, and it never will be.

And part of me is terrified that's all I will ever be able to give her.

Chapter Seventeen

LAUREL

The loud thwacking sound carries across the small clearing in front of the cabin so clearly. It's like a lit trail leading me directly to Wells. I weave my way through the trees, avoiding any branches, following the path he must've taken to get back here, deeper into the woods.

Even with the sun brightly shining today, the canopy above casts almost impenetrable shadows where animals rustle and move along the mossy and leaf-covered forest floor.

Mysterious flowers I might have been tempted to stop and smell or pick bloom at various spots, each one a reminder of what a moron I really was that day and how badly things could have ended.

I quickly avert my gaze from them and concentrate on the path in front of me, where the trees start to open up slightly to a larger clearing.

Thwack.

Thwack.

Thwack.

The sound reverberates off the massive trunks of the various species around me, and I remain hidden on the edge of the tree line, watching the enigmatic man swing the axe so easily, burying it deep in a massive, downed oak that lies across the open space.

He brings the axe up over his head again before slamming it into the trunk. The sound of the collision vibrates in my chest, and he breaks a chunk of wood free and rolls it to the growing pile by his side.

Given the stack he's already created, he's been at this for a while, which shouldn't surprise me. I couldn't sleep after the shower last night, so there's no way he could.

Wells moves a few steps down and sets to it again. Every swing ripples the massive muscles in his bare back and strong, broad shoulders. This man has carried so much weight on them over the last few years, has suffered more than anyone should ever have to.

Yet, he's still here. He's still alive. He still has so much left to give and to offer. He just needs to see it.

Seeing him out here, so at home in this life, it's easy to forget the other one he has waiting for him in Denver. The thousands of employees who rely on Lockwood Brewing Company for their paychecks. The friends he hasn't spoken to in years, who he pushed away when they tried to reach out to him after Diana and Maribel's deaths. Even his father, no matter how tense their relationship may be.

But it *is* all there, and at one point, he fit in there just as easily. He stood in the boardrooms at the head of the massive table and made decisions that helped further build an empire.

He seems to have forgotten that, forgotten he has so

much to offer *that* life and to me. That simple fact had me waking in tears this morning, glad he wasn't there to see them.

I watch him for a few more moments, gently bouncing to keep Wesley asleep in the Boba wrap I used to tie him to me.

Wells stops for a minute and swipes his arm over his forehead, where sweat drips down into his eyes. He turns away from the sun, and his eyes narrow on me almost immediately.

I guess I wasn't so hidden after all.

He knows this whole mountain like the back of his hand, so he likely heard me coming the entire time. I step out into the clearing, and his gaze drifts down to Wesley, asleep against my chest, then back up to mine.

"Well, that would've been handy to have while you were sick."

I smirk at him.

His eyes narrow on the wrap like he doesn't quite understand how it works. "Where'd you find it?"

I offer a little half-shrug. "One of the drawers in the nursery."

Which I have no doubt he never opened once since Diana stocked them with the things she anticipated needing for Maribel.

He nods slowly and swipes at the sweat again. It trickles down his temples and neck, over his rock-hard pecs, down his abs, and disappears at his waistline, already soaked from his exertion and the heat of the day.

Fuck, that's hot.

I chew on my bottom lip, unable to draw my eyes away from the true specimen he is. "I didn't know you were so good with an axe."

He tilts his head down to catch my eye and offers a little smirk. "It's a necessity out here."

"What are you doing?"

Wells casts a glance back at the tree. "Chopping up this big guy I knocked down the other night."

"You need more firewood?"

He shakes his head. "No. I drive into town and donate most of what I chop. I have more trees up here than I could ever possibly need to keep the cabin heated year-round. A lot of people in Lockwood Falls are struggling financially or are physically unable to cut their own, so free wood helps them tremendously." He shrugs. "This was more for...stress relief. And it's been lying here for a bit. Needed to be cut sooner rather than later."

Stress relief.

Wells doesn't say more, but he doesn't have to; I know exactly when he downed this tree—the day I arrived with Wesley. He was taking out his anguish on something else, searching for any way to release everything boiling inside him on the anniversary of the worst day of his life.

I slowly approach him, unsure whether he wants me to interrupt him when he's in lumberjack mode, but a tiny smile pulls at his lips, and he brushes his hand over Wesley's fuzzy head.

"He's out cold, huh?"

I nod. "Babies tend to do that when they're wrapped like this."

"Again, that would've been useful to know a few days ago."

This time, I smirk at him. "It's good for you to learn on your own if you're going to be up here alone with him."

Wells stiffens slightly, his muscles tightening, shoulders tensing. "You're right. There's a lot I need to learn."

You and me, both.

Law school doesn't have a class about what to do when your new boss forces you to stay at his remote cabin to help with his secret baby and you accidentally fall for him.

Maybe they should add one.

Though, I'm probably the only one stupid enough to find myself in this position—a very tenuous one. Things could change drastically tomorrow, and the double life Wells Lockwood has isn't going to wait forever. He's going to have to make a decision fast.

"You are planning to stay up here, though, with him?"

My voice breaks slightly, and he gives me his back and walks around the trunk to the other side, where he starts swinging again.

Thwack.

Thwack.

Thwack.

Over and over again, relentlessly driving into it until he finally splits a piece from the main trunk.

"You can't ignore the question forever, Wells. Are you really going to live up here with him alone? What about school? Socialization? No one to help?"

He sighs and wipes at his face, then slowly rubs at his temple, something I've seen him doing far too much. "I don't know. Even thinking about it gives me a migraine. All I do know is I'm not going back to the city. I can't."

"You can't raise a baby up here alone, either. What are you going to do when you need to come out here and chop wood or tend to the animals or hunt? Keep him in this?" I point to the wrap. "Push him along in a stroller through the woods, dodging branches and predators?"

Okay, maybe that was a bit harsh.

But necessary, given the way Wells seems incapable of

seeing the very *real* complications facing him.

He scowls at me, his jaw hardening to the point that it seems like his teeth might break. "Can we just not right now, Laurel?"

I raise a brow, rubbing my hand on his son's back. "When then?"

The brutally stubborn man doesn't want to talk about it *ever*. Even after our shower, he went on pretending like there wasn't this massive dark cloud hanging over us. That everything was normal—me being here.

And then he let me sleep alone in his bed, while he took the couch, like he still can't bear the thought of sharing his and Diana's space with another woman. If I didn't understand that at a core level, I might be deeply offended by how he acted. But I saw it for what it really was, his demons lurking again, telling him he doesn't deserve to be happy, doesn't deserve to have me.

"I don't know what you want me to say, Laurel." He shrugs. "This"—he waves a hand around—"is the only place I feel any hint of rightness, where I can find a few moments of peace. Even going to Lockwood Falls the few times I had to over the last two years...it felt...overwhelming." A pained expression crosses his face. "My chest tightened. I felt like I couldn't breathe—"

"You had a panic attack."

He glowers at me. "I don't have *panic attacks*. I handle multi-billion-dollar negotiations on a regular basis. I'm the face of the goddamn brand."

"You *were*." I put emphasis on the word in a way I know will hurt him, but it has to be said.

He has to understand that he isn't the same person he was two years ago, and maybe he never will be. That means making new decisions and changing how he sees things, even if he doesn't want to. But he also can't simply *ignore* that person he was or what's left there waiting for him.

"Yeah, I was, and I still *am*." He grabs the axe again. "At least, I still *can* be."

He takes another swing and blasts through the wood, splintering off pieces of the bark, and I take a half step back, even though we're well out of range.

"It isn't just about what you want or need anymore now that you have him. You do understand that, don't you?"

He glares and takes another swing. "Of course, I do. He might not be the child I was expecting, Laurel, but I was about to become a father. I knew what that would mean, what would have to happen, that everything I did from that moment forward was going to be for her."

Shit.

Pulling that kind of pain from him wasn't my intention.

"I didn't mean to insult you with the comment. It's just..."

He huffs and leans against the axe. "It's just what?"

"It's just, sometimes, it's hard to see past our own bull-shit and our own grief to what's really important."

He glances down at Wesley. "I know what's important, and I have everything I possibly could need, right here, right now."

WELLS

The crushing weight of what I said bears down on my shoulders, so heavy, it makes me want to collapse onto the uneven ground at my feet the longer I stare at Laurel.

I said it because it's true. I *do* have everything I need

here and now, but the woman standing in front of me needs to know every last dirty detail to truly comprehend what they mean, to understand why I can never leave here.

She has to know the truth I've drowned in for the last two years.

I release the axe and make my way over toward her slowly. The closer I move, the more trepidation seeps into her gaze, and she wraps her arms around Wesley, holding him tighter, as if she needs to protect him from something I might do or say.

It should piss me off that she would even think that, but given my track record with this kid, it wouldn't be out of the question for me to make some grave error.

I take her hand in mine and squeeze. She looks down at them clasped together, then back up at me in question. The uncertainty with which she stares at me makes a rock lodge in my throat.

That shouldn't be there. She deserves so much more than to be with a man she can't trust with her everything. If I can show her this, maybe she'll finally understand.

"Come on." I tug her across the clearing, skirting what's left of the tree and the enormous pile of wood I've created while trying to work out my frustrations and destroy my demons.

"Where are we going?"

"There's something you need to see."

She bristles slightly, pulling back on my hand until I stop. "Wells..."

"Please, Laurel, just trust me."

That's hard for me to ask after everything I've put her through the last week, but she gives me a quick nod and allows me to lead her toward the trees and the narrow path I've cut through them.

I pull her along, checking back on her every few feet as we traverse the uneven ground. I'm the only one who ever walks this path, and I certainly never thought I'd be dragging a woman and my son along for the ride.

The woods get thicker and darker, and a shiver rolls through her, making her hand vibrate against mine.

"We're almost there."

"Where are you taking me, Wells? I'm starting to get visions of horror movies."

Instead of offending me like it probably should, a laugh climbs up my throat and floats through the air, the sound unnatural out here, and I grin back at her. "I didn't even bring my axe."

She smirks at my horrible attempt at a joke, and the trees start to thin in front of us. We reach the edge of the forest, and I pull her out onto the ledge.

Her mouth drops open. "Oh, my God."

Laurel takes two steps forward and scans the horizon. From up here, on the edge of the cliff with the river running below us, you can see for hundreds of miles in either direction, nothing but vast wilderness, no signs of life except for those placed by Mother Nature.

"This is..."—she opens and closes her mouth a few times and glances at me before returning her gaze to the view —"the most beautiful thing I've ever seen."

I take her in, standing on the edge of the world, her hands protectively pressed against Wesley, where he rests in the wrap against her chest, her eyes darting all over like she wants to take it all in at once, and a vicious pain slams into my chest. Because she has no idea why this spot is the reason I can't leave.

Swallowing back the agony that threatens to drop me to my knees, I nod and try to enjoy the view the same way someone would for the first time, even though I've been looking at it basically since I was born. "It is. This is the most beautiful view on the property." I release a heavy sigh. "Up here, I feel..."

She rests a small hand on my arm, that same crackle of *something* rippling across my skin with the simple contact. "You feel what?"

"I don't know." I shake my head and rub at the growing headache. "Somehow, I feel alone, yet not alone at the same time, like I can see all the life around me, even though there's so much death."

Instinctively, my gaze drifts to the right, toward the tiny cemetery. Laurel follows my gaze and sucks in a sharp breath, pressing her hand over her mouth.

"Is that...?"

I give her a sharp nod. "It was Diana's favorite place on the property, too. We were"—I suck in a shaky breath, fighting back the tears—"we were up here when it happened."

Laurel's head snaps toward me, her mouth wide open. "What?"

"I never let the media get the full story. It was none of their fucking business, and I wasn't about to let them take my tragedy and twist it into a giant news story." So, there's no reason she would know any of this, why *anyone* would.

I pace away from her and closer to the edge of the cliff, to where I can see the falls, where the river cascades over the side of the ridge down to the pool below before it flows on down the mountain.

"She loved to sit up here and watch the water. She still had six weeks left. It was going to be our last trip up here before the birth. We didn't want to risk being stuck at the cabin if she went into labor early." My chest constricts, and

I rub at the pain there, keeping my eyes locked on the flowing water. "A storm came in that night, like the one when you arrived but worse. It knocked out my solar panels. I used to bring a satellite phone up with us, but the storm made any call out impossible. We were going to leave the next morning since we lost power, but..."

Even after all this time and everything I've trusted Laurel with, I can't say the words. I can't force them out.

Laurel closes the distance between us and loops her arm through mine, resting her head against my bicep. She doesn't say a word, just squeezes me gently and waits for me to be able to continue, offering me strength without really doing anything at all.

"We thought maybe it was Braxton-Hicks, but then she got very pale and she started bleeding. She delivered Maribel, but...there was so much blood. Too much. By the time I got Diana into the truck, I knew it was too late for her and the baby. I had to drive into town with them in the truck knowing..."

I can't even keep talking through the agony clogging my throat.

Laurel presses her lips against my skin and just stands like that for a moment before she lifts her head and looks up at me. "I'm so sorry. I understand why you don't want to leave here, why being up here with them is so important to you."

They're the words I wanted to hear from her, the ones I hoped she would be able to utter once she saw this spot, but somehow, it doesn't change the sense of dread settling over me.

I stare at the water plummeting over the cliff, remembering the last time Diana and I trekked down to the pool at the bottom before she was pregnant. The afternoon we spent in the crystal waters, likely where we conceived Maribel in the first place...

We had a beautiful house in Denver, the kind of home I always dreamed about, the one I was expected to have, but up here, alone with Diana, was my peaceful place to escape my responsibilities at the brewery for a few days. And we couldn't wait to bring the baby up here to let her experience all this.

I let my gaze drift over to Wesley.

Almost as if she can read my thoughts, Laurel offers a sad smile and looks down at Wesley. "You can show it all to him now."

I nod slowly and reach out to brush my fingers over his head. He shifts slightly and cuddles closer to her. "I will, but I'm probably going to fucking fail at it."

Her soft brow furrows. "Why do you say that?"

I pull my arm from hers and step away, needing to move, but I can't walk toward the cemetery, not during this conversation. Instead, I pace the other way, along the edge of the cliff, staring down at the river flowing so peacefully into the distance. "Because I don't know how to do this. My only experience with babies is holding them for pictures at press conferences and kissing them at parades."

Laurel smiles. "You've done just fine the last couple of days."

"Have I, though?" I scoff. "I don't have a clue what I'm doing, Laurel, but I know I can't go back, either. I can't raise him in that world, the one that drove the wedge between me and my father, the one where money and power and prestige are the most important things." I wave a hand around. "Out here, things are just simpler."

Even though staring at her holding my baby, they couldn't seem more complicated.

Chapter Eighteen

LAUREL

Staring out at the heart-stopping valley and the waterfall, it would be easy to fall into the beautiful trap of believing life is simpler up here, just as Wells seems to have.

I glance down at Wesley snuggled against me in the carrier and shake my head. "It just seems simpler, but it isn't."

Wells turns toward me, his lips twisted down. "What do you mean?"

"All this." I motion toward the panoramic view. "This place, it's stunning, and I understand that up here, you don't have to deal with the constant bombardment you do when you're down at corporate. The expectations of people, the stress of having the company on your shoulders, but..."

How do I say this without having him blow up at me?

He stares at me, waiting for me to continue, and one of his brows rises over his bourbon eyes. "But *what*?"

The hardness has returned to his gaze, like he's

prepared to fight whatever I have to say. And chances are that he will. But he's so blinded by what's happened to him that he can't see anything clearly. I have to help him, even if it means him seeing me as the bad guy.

"But this isn't real, Wells. You're not really living up here. You're just *surviving*."

He stiffens at the word, and something flashes in his eyes, almost like a recognition he hadn't had before. It melts away just as quickly, and he shakes his head as if to fully clear it, then stalks past me back toward the woods. "That's not true. This place is the only thing that's kept me alive."

I follow him, and despite expecting him to storm off like he did the night after the barn, he waits at the edge of the forest to let me walk in front of him down the dark, narrow path through the foliage.

"I believe that. I understand it, given everything that's happened, but I also see that you're using this place to hide, and you can't hide from life forever."

He stops on the path, the trees cocooning us in darkness. "Why the hell not?"

I let out a frustrated scoff. "Because you just *can't*."

Wells takes a step toward me, looming over me slightly, and if I didn't know him so well from spending the last week with him, I might actually be afraid and intimidated. "You're twenty-six years old, still a goddamn child. You've never had a family. You've never loved someone the way I did them. You have *no idea* what you're talking about."

Each word slices at me like a razor, but it isn't him talking. Not really. It's the fear that I might be right.

I get right in his face, protectively holding his son to me. "I don't? Didn't we just have this conversation where I told you everything I've been through? You may have had a difficult few years, Wells, but I had a difficult twenty-six. I might not have loved the way you have, but I've had to fight and scrape for everything I have while it was all *handed* to you."

"It sure as fuck was not *handed* to me." His immediate response makes me flinch. "I may have had the best education and never had to worry about a roof over my head. I may have had the kind of privileges other people didn't, but I worked my fucking ass off through school. I worked my ass off for my father." Rage colors his cheeks, his chest heaving as he unloads on me. "All I've done since I was fucking born is work. Work, work, work. And that caused me to lose time with Diana, time I wish I could have back. I'd give anything to spend even one more fucking day with her, but I wasted so many of them at the fucking office, in meetings, at press conferences, smiling for the media. All of it was *pointless*."

The pain in his voice makes tears well in my eyes.

"It wasn't pointless, Wells. It's your family business. It's your great-great-grandfather's legacy. You're maintaining it. You're keeping it going for future generations, so maybe one day they don't have to work as hard as you do."

"At what fucking cost?"

He turns and storms away down the path, not even looking back at me.

Shit, I didn't want this to turn into an argument.

Yet, somehow, it evolved into one all the same.

Wells is just so damn stubborn, but a lot of what he says rings true. I can't agree with all of it, not when I've lived on the other end of the spectrum. I understand what it's like not to know where my next meal is coming from, to worry about closing my eyes at night because of what might happen when I do. So, I know how important maintaining the business is for the people working there, how many rely on Lockwood Brewing for their stable lives.

But I'm not in a position to force him to do anything. All I can do is try to talk some sense into him, try to do what I can to get him to understand that he can't raise Wesley up here by himself. It wouldn't be fair to the baby or to him. And going back to Denver, where he would have a support system and be able to return to work in some capacity, would serve a greater good he might not be able to see right now.

I press a kiss to the top of Wesley's warm, soft head, and he shifts slightly, snuggling up against me and pressing his hand against my chest.

He'll be out for a little while, and while I could chase after Wells, he needs more time to think, to process everything, to cool down before we can talk like adults again.

He won't have much.

Landry will hold the press conference, probably today, and once it's out in the open, Wells will have to make an appearance. He'll have to do something other than hide up here, at least temporarily.

I slowly make my way along the path through the trees and out into the clearing between the cabin and the barn.

A loud, mechanical sound comes from the barn to my left, where Wells must have run off to in order to blow off some steam. By now, I should have learned to leave well enough alone when it comes to Wells Lockwood and his moods, but that nagging feeling in the back of my head that he shouldn't be by himself right now makes me walk in that direction instead of toward the cabin like I should.

A set of massive doors stands open, letting out the unfamiliar high-pitched mechanical sound, and I poke my head around and peer in. Pieces of half-finished furniture sit around the massive space, and he stands with his back to me, sanding a massive table with so much aggression he must be gouging giant pieces out of it. But given the parts of it I can see, something has already destroyed it. The axe leaning against it suggests it was probably Wells himself.

He stops the sander and drops his forehead to the table. "Tell me what to do, Di."

"I still hear my wife's voice in my head."

His words echo back to me like a knife twisting in my gut. No matter what I do or what I say, his heart will never be mine. It isn't available, even if he wanted it to be, which he doesn't.

The man has fought me at every turn and will continue to—both about what's happening between us and what needs to happen with Wesley.

It may be a lost cause where Wells' heart is concerned, but I have to keep trying for Wesley's sake, even if it means quitting my job—assuming I even still have one. I have to make sure they're okay, even if it's not my place. Landry put this baby in my care, and that means protecting him from everything that could hurt him, including his own father.

Wells needs to see what's best for Wesley, and it isn't living up here with a father who hates everything about the world and everyone in it.

WELLS

No amount of sanding and scraping at the table will be able to fix the damage I did. I destroyed it the same way I destroyed the family I was supposed to have.

"Tell me what to do, Di."

The words echo through the barn and off the old equipment and shatter me completely. I sag over the table, pressing my face against the abraded top and dragging my fingers through the deep grooves the axe left in it.

All the damage I did to this mirrors the way I've been destroying anything I touch recently. Everything is so fucked up, even more so than it was when I lost them, my head sitting squarely at the top of that list.

Too many thoughts. Too many decisions. Too many questions.

Wesley has to be my main priority now, but I can't see a way to move past this constant agony, the pain in my chest and my head.

What do I do with the feelings the feisty redhead brought up here with her? How do I keep her from getting hurt? How do I do any of it?

"The same way you've always done everything, Wells. One step at a time."

Diana's confidence resonates through me, and I push myself up from the table and swipe at the tears falling from my face.

"You'll carve a new top. You'll fix the legs. You'll rebuild the table just like you'll rebuild your life, like you should have been doing for the last two years."

"Don't say that." I turn and search the rafters, even though I know she won't be there. "How am I supposed to have a life without you?"

"You know how."

The statement is so crystal clear, it's as if she's standing next to me whispering the words in my ear, and she makes it sound so easy, like moving on from what I've experienced is something people do every day.

But even after two years, I can't imagine trying to do any of this with anyone else.

Going back to work...

Going back to that life of excess where I have to care about frivolous things that, in the end, don't mean a fucking thing...

Where I have to protect the family name above all else...

You've been doing a real bang-up job of that.

"Fuck!"

I stumble over to the wall and sag back against the stack of firewood, staring down at the blisters on my hands, the pain I welcome every time I wield my axe.

Of course, I could wear gloves. I could hire someone else to come do it, but I need the pain. I *thrive* on it. It's the only thing that's made me feel alive out here until Wesley and Laurel showed up.

Of all the people for Landry to send, why did it have to be her?

A feisty woman who makes me question everything...

What if it had been Landry?

If he had personally driven up here with the baby, things would be so different.

"What would you have done, Wells? Would you have sent Landry away with him? Would you have forced him to live with strangers because you couldn't get your shit together?"

I squeeze my eyes closed against Diana's accusation because it's probably true. If I hadn't had Laurel here pushing me, if she hadn't gotten sick, I might not have ever bonded with Wesley.

Would I have ever felt what I do now?

This deep connection to the boy I didn't even want to admit was mine only a week ago now lives inside me, and the thought of him not being with me is unfathomable.

Would I have continued to live alone up here until one

day I finally got what I wished for, to join Diana and Maribel, to see my family again?

"You don't want that anymore."

A burgeoning sense of hope fills what was once an empty spot my heart occupied because Di's right. I *did* want that. I wanted all of this agony to end. I wanted to leave a world that's so unfair and be in the one place where I can see them again. But now, the thought of leaving Wesley alone, the thought of him ending up somewhere like where Laurel grew up, without love, without family, hurts me just as badly.

I won't be able to give him much of a family. I don't even talk to Father anymore...

Christ, what's he going to think of all this?

Landry will tell him before he makes the announcement, and it wouldn't surprise me if a car showed up here immediately afterward carrying the old man, filled with condemnation.

He'd be right to condemn me for my actions, since I can't even clearly remember the girl.

How could you have been so stupid?

Still, I can't bring myself to regret that night. Not now that I've cradled Wesley in my arms. Felt his cries in my gut, held him while he slept.

Tears well in my eyes again, and I brush them away with the back of my hand as I stumble to my feet.

"It should have been Maribel. I should have been doing all this with *you*."

"She's here to help you, Wells."

The same mantra Diana has repeated to me endlessly since Laurel arrived hammers against the side of my skull so hard I wince and stop to rub my temples. This pain has only become more insistent over the last few months, and since Laurel's arrival, it's been almost nonstop.

Diana wants me not to just hear it but to actually feel it deep in my soul. She wants me to *act*. She wants me to do something I don't think I'm capable of.

What the fuck am I supposed to do with that?

I stagger to the open door of the barn and inhale a deep breath of the crisp, fresh air that smells like oncoming rain.

A line of dark thunderheads builds in the distance—a typical summer afternoon on the mountain. But this time, I'll welcome the rain as a way to cleanse away all the bad that's been lingering. I won't see it as simply another chance to find a way to leave this world without having to take action myself.

Such a stark change in such a short time.

And I know who I can attribute that change to—that woman and that baby back in the cabin waiting for me to stop being such a fucking wreck and return to acting like a human being.

I make my way out to the clearing and stand in the middle of it, arms spread open as the rain begins to fall. Each cool drop hitting my skin calms the part of me that made me walk away from Laurel earlier. That made me have to because being in her orbit, being so close, smelling her, feeling her, seeing her with Wesley, it's all too much.

It's starting to feel like she belongs here, but she doesn't.

She isn't mine to have, mine to keep, and this isn't her world.

Asking her to stay wouldn't be fair to either of us, but I don't know how to watch her leave, either.

Chapter Nineteen

LAUREL

I slip out of the nursery and ease the door closed behind me. The soft click makes me wince, but Wesley's a great sleeper, and now that he's down, he should be for most of the night.

After the day I've had, the thought of dropping into bed and letting the sweet bliss of sleep take me away from all the drama sounds like absolute heaven.

I release a little sigh and turn toward the living room, then freeze. Wells sits in the chair facing the fireplace, a glass of what appears to be whiskey in his hand.

He doesn't acknowledge me, just slowly lifts the glass to his lips and takes a sip.

Shit. He must have returned when I was putting Wesley down.

It was hard to let him have his space today, knowing I was letting him get in his own head the rest of the afternoon and evening. Every time he does, we seem to take a massive slide backward. I kept reminding myself that he's an adult and has been taking care of himself up here for years, but he looks so lost and so alone, entranced by the flames, that it makes that vise that seems so intent on killing me tighten around my chest again.

Any thought of staying away longer floats away, and I make my way over to him and push my fingers through his unruly hair. He issues a low groan and tilts his head into my touch. I scrape my nails along his scalp, and he purrs like a damn kitten.

"It's been a long time since anyone's touched me like that."

Fuck.

I'm an asshole.

"I'm sorry about what I said earlier. I shouldn't be talking about things I can't understand."

He slowly turns his head to look up at me, the fire illuminating the right side of his face, the other half cast in shadows, just like the man himself is all the time. "You might not have lost your wife and child like I did, but you lost a lot of other things with the life you've had. You do understand."

"Then why do I feel like every time I look at you, I can't help? There's nothing I can say or do to make any of it better for you?"

"Because you can't. Because it's not your job. You came up here for one reason." He points toward the closed nursery door. "To bring me that baby. You would've been gone in twenty minutes if I had let you. I forced you to stay here against your will." He offers a sardonic chuckle. "And somehow..."

Wells trails off, but he doesn't have to continue for me to know what he was about to say.

And somehow, we've developed this—whatever it is between us—and it's changed everything.

At least, it has for me. I don't have a clue what it's done for him.

The back and forth is enough to give me whiplash, yet I didn't take the chance he offered me to go down the mountain, to return to the job I barely got a chance to start—assuming he wasn't serious about firing me—to the life I was just starting to create for myself.

He takes another sip and holds the glass out to me. "You want some?"

I nod and take it from him. "I could probably use it."

A heavy sigh slips from his lips, and he scrubs his hands over his face. "I've really fucked things up, haven't I? All because I couldn't keep my dick in my pants."

I snort and take a sip of the fiery liquid that burns down my throat, yet the sweetness of the bourbon coats my tongue, lingering there well after the slight pain. "You talking about me or Wesley's mother?"

He glances up at me, no amusement in his eyes at all. "Both."

I hand the glass back as I step in front of him and slowly lower myself to my knees between his thighs. "Is that what this is?" I motion between the two of us. "You getting your dick wet?"

"Fuck, Laurel. No." He jerks back from me and drops his head back, closing his eyes, facing the ceiling. "*No.*"

As much as I would like to believe that, a little voice in the back of my head won't stop pushing the idea on me. I slide my hands over his thighs, waiting for him to look at me again. When he doesn't, I stare at my hands and release a heavy sigh. "Because I would understand if it was, Wells. I mean..."—I laugh—"this whole situation is anything but simple. You've been alone up here for a long time. You've only touched one other woman, one night a year ago. All this forced proximity and the stressors and the tension and—"

"Stop."

I glance up to find his eyes burning into mine, the flames behind me leaping in his amber orbs.

He grips my chin, tilting my face up toward him and holding me firmly. "This is far more than that, and you know it."

I close my eyes, unable to look at him when he stares at me with so much intensity. My bottom lip starts to tremble, and I bite it, hoping he doesn't notice.

"Please don't do that, Laurel."

"Do what?"

"Look like you're going to cry."

"I might." I release a sardonic laugh. "And you have no idea how much that pisses me off because despite how you've seen me since I arrived here, I am not normally a crier. Through everything, all the horrible stuff that has happened to me, I've kept up this wall and used my ability to compartmentalize things to get to where I am in life, to get what I want."

"What is it you want, Laurel?"

That's a loaded question.

And Wells knows it, too. He waits for me to answer, taking another sip of his drink. Part of me doesn't *want* to, though, because it means admitting some of what he said the other day is true.

I lock eyes with him and confess the shallow truth. "All the things I never had. A beautiful home where I feel safe, clothes I could never afford, stunning shoes that are more like works of art, the things a successful attorney is supposed to have." I blink away the tears threatening to fall. "But most of all, I want a family, someone to love me and who will always have my back."

He brushes his thumb over my lips. "I have more than just about anyone on this planet, Laurel, and I can tell you, it never made me happy. None of it. Being here"—he uses his free hand to motion around the cabin—"with Diana is what made me happy. When we were away from all of *that*, when we were living simply and just being together, that was when things were incredible." He shakes his head and releases a mirthless laugh. "I hated going back to the city. I hated having to slip back into a three-piece suit and stand in a boardroom."

"But I thought you loved your job, the company. I thought you wanted to expand it and make it better."

"I *did*." He sighs. "I still *do*. I just..." He offers a helpless shrug. "I don't know if it makes me happy."

"I didn't know it was possible to want something that doesn't make you happy."

Wells snorts. "Neither did I, yet..."—he waves a hand —"here I am. I can't seem to do anything right." His eyes return to the fire, and he stares into it for a moment, his hand tightening on the drink. "I never should have brought Diana up here."

"What? What are you talking about?"

Tears shimmer in his eyes, reflecting the leaping flames. "It's my fault. All of it. I thought we had enough time, that she was far enough away from her due date that we'd be safe and nothing would happen. I suggested we come up here for one last trip." He clenches his jaw. "It's my fault. If we had been in the city..."

"No." I shift forward and press my hands against his chest. "I won't let you do that. I won't let you blame yourself. It's not your fault. The same thing would've happened if you were in the city. What you described to me, it's not something either one of them would've survived even if you had been in Denver. It was a freak, tragic complication, and it wouldn't have mattered if you were up here or down there."

"You don't know that."

"And you don't know that they would've survived, yet you've locked yourself away up here and beaten yourself up over it for years, living with their ghosts."

He takes my face in his palm, the callouses scraping against my skin. "Until you showed up and brought new life to this place for the first time in two years."

"That wasn't me." I offer him a sad smile. "That was the baby."

He pushes my hair from my face and tucks it behind my ear, letting his fingers brush against my neck. "It was both of you."

That damn bottom lip that always betrays me starts quivering again, and a tear hangs from the corner of my eye, waiting to fall. He reaches up and brushes it away.

I shake my head. "You don't mean that."

He nods. "I do. If anyone else had brought that baby up here, if it had been Landry or some other random employee, do you really think I would have gotten to where I am now with him? Do you believe any of them would have pushed me the way you did? That anyone would have forced me to become a fucking father when it was the last thing I wanted to even consider?"

The corner of my mouth pulls up, picturing anyone else

dealing with the bullshit Wells has thrown at me. "I'm sure they would have tried."

"Tried and failed." He chuckles. "Because they're all 'yes' men and women. They all do exactly what they're told. Keep their mouths shut. Because I'm the boss. They would not have done what *you* did. They would not have pushed. They would not have made me *see*."

"See what?"

"That he's my son. That it may not have happened how I wanted it. Some strange, fucked-up twist of fate. But it happened all the same. And I have to deal with my own emotions about it without taking it out on him, without letting him suffer for it."

"Wow, you sound so *adult* right now."

"I'm forty-fucking-years old, Laurel. I think you forget that sometimes. I have a decade and a half on you. I've lived a lot more life."

One he seems to have forgotten is still happening around him.

"And you still have a lot more ahead of you."

WELLS

"For the first time in a really long time, I feel like that might be true." I cup her cheek in my palm and brush my thumb across it. "But I don't have the capacity to give you what you want."

Pain soaks her gaze. "What do you mean?"

"You know exactly what I mean. I can't give you what you want. What you deserve. My heart isn't mine to give."

She shakes her head and shifts even closer until our

chests brush, and she can loop her arms around my neck. "That's just not true. I'm not a fool, Wells. I understand your heart will always belong to Diana, but I've seen you give pieces of it to Wesley over the last few days. I know you're capable of it. I know you're capable of loving someone, and...maybe it isn't me. Maybe it never will be." She whispers her lips over mine. "But I can try to chisel off a little tiny piece and hold on to it for as long as I can."

Everything this woman says to me shatters me completely, makes all my reservations disappear in the moment. She stares at me with so much faith in her words that it almost makes me believe them.

I wrap my arms around her and tug her up against me fully until the heat of her body seeps into mine and we share breaths. "Fucking hell, Laurel. I definitely don't deserve you."

Brushing her trembling lips over mine again, she tightens her hold on my neck. "Yes, you do. You deserve so much more than you've allowed yourself. So much more than *this*. You deserve everything."

I don't agree with her, can't possibly get on board with the words she just uttered.

How can I with the way I've been acting, with the back and forth, push and pull I'm putting her through?

It's the juvenile bullshit I never would have accepted in any relationship, but she's still here, still in my arms, still looking at me with so much genuine emotion in her gaze that it makes it impossible to stop. I can't do what I should—walk away and lock myself in the bedroom, or better yet, go back outside where I can't be a threat to her anymore. Where she can't be one to me...

Because she is a threat. To everything I've accepted as my reality since I lost the girls. To the life I've built here for myself. To the isolation I've been content to embrace. To every damn piece of me that's barely survived on this mountain.

I warned her there were things that would hurt her up here, and I meant it. But she kept poking the bear, insisting on stepping in whenever I got lost in uncertainty and turmoil.

And now we've become the greatest threats to each other.

I crush my lips to hers, dragging her up and across my lap to devour her, to take everything she's willing to give me, even though I don't deserve any of it.

I tighten my hands on her hips, and she grinds down against my growing cock. It twitches against the confines of my pants, and I groan into her mouth. She shifts position, aligning herself perfectly to rub up and down my length, the heat of her pussy searing me even through the fabric.

Fuck.

It would be so easy to free my cock and let her ride me right here in this chair, to watch her take what she needs in the firelight, to dig my fingers into her hips and suck her breast between my lips while we did things frantically. But the two other times we've been together were heated, wild, fast, without really ensuring she was worshiped the way she should be.

I won't let that happen again.

I'd be the first to admit I'm a selfish bastard where Laurel Palmer is concerned, but I won't be tonight. Not as long as my self-control stays intact. Though, with Laurel, it never seems to last long.

I drag my mouth away from hers, panting, and she stares back at me with wide, confused eyes. Cupping her ass in my palms, I climb to my feet and stalk to the couch, taking her with another kiss, intent on showing her the way she should be cherished.

Laurel responds in kind, and when I set her down and tug on the waistband of her pants, she lifts her hips to allow me to tug them down her thighs and legs. I tear my mouth from hers long enough to pull them off and let them fall to the floor at my feet.

Sitting fully exposed to me, the arousal between her legs already glistening in the flickering light from the fireplace, the woman completely steals my breath.

"Fucking hell, Laurel. You're beautiful."

She opens her mouth to speak, but I capture her words with another searing kiss as I glide my palms up her inner thighs. Her legs quiver under my touch, and I shift my path up across her stomach, up under her shirt, and grip her breasts through the lace bra she was wearing the day she arrived.

Her nipples pucker under my thumbs, and I flick them across each taut peak, making her twitch beneath me, her hips thrusting up in search of some sort of relief.

But I won't do this hard and fast again.

I refuse, no matter how badly my body may crave that.

This woman deserves so much more than I can ever give her, but tonight, I'll ensure she gets everything I have.

I kiss her deeply one final time, then pull back and sink between her legs, letting my warm breath fan across her wet flesh. Her hips arch up toward my face as she eagerly seeks that which I'm more than willing to give her. I press on her inner thighs with my palms, spreading her open wider, and drag her legs up and over my shoulders.

She releases a tiny groan and buries her fingers in my hair. Then I drop my head and glide my tongue through her core.

"Fuck, Wells." Her grip tightens, and she tugs on the strands.

The sharp bite only spurs me on. "Fuck, you taste good, Laurel."

A flavor that is all her, that tastes of forgiveness, coats my tongue, and I glide it across her pussy, slowly, teasingly, avoiding the spot she wants the contact so badly.

I probe into her, seeking her very core, the place where she holds everything inside that she refuses to allow me to see. She may have revealed certain things, may have opened up about her childhood and her life in order to get me to do the same, but this woman holds so much in. The things she'll never tell anyone, what she's suffered with and had to carry on her shoulders the same way I have my own burden.

Tonight, she's going to release all of them. I'm going to ensure she does because she's done everything for me since the moment she stepped out of that car. She's been selfless, caring, and giving. She's gone out of her way to ensure Wesley and I are okay. Laurel has saved my life in more ways than I can even describe, and she tastes like absolute heaven.

I never want to leave this spot.

With my face buried between her thighs, I thrust my tongue into her relentlessly. Her hips arch, grinding against the scruff on my face, abrading her thighs, but she doesn't seem to care, just rolls in time with my oral ministrations.

I slide one hand up across her abdomen to pin her down and the other between her legs to slip a finger inside her. She gasps and immediately clenches around me, seeking something else. My cock throbs, wanting the exact same thing, and I curl my finger up inside her to find that perfect spot to probe, curl, and thrust, as I finally allow my tongue up to the apex of her thighs.

"Oh, God."

Her fingers twine in my hair and tug harder, and I flick my tongue rapidly back and forth across the swollen nub. She thrashes her head from side to side, and I suck her clit between my teeth, applying as much pressure as I can while I slip a second finger inside her.

Hot, hard breaths fall from her open lips, and she rolls her hips against my face, seeking her release. My cock aches, but I refuse to give in to the desire to feel her come around me.

Not this time.

This time, I want her to come down my throat. I want to feel her release against my face, taste every last drop, knowing that I was able to give her this.

Laurel presses against my head. "Oh, God, Wells, I can't. I..."

I pull my face away for a second, looking up at her lust-soaked blue pools. "Relax and just let go."

She's fighting it, fighting me, unsure what her body's going to do, but I'm about to show her. I begin the rhythmic pull and curl with my fingers that I know will utterly destroy her.

Her head drops back on a silent groan, and she undulates her hips frantically against my rapidly flicking tongue. I alternate between sucking her clit between my lips and nipping it with my teeth. Her arousal coats my fingers and hands, dripping down between us, but it's nothing compared to what's about to come.

She releases a final gasp, and her pussy contracts around my fingers so hard it feels like it might break them. And then she comes, a hot, wet rush. I swallow it down, gulping and licking to avoid missing any of it.

Fuck, yes.

Laurel is fucking stunning when she comes, and my cock leaks slightly, wanting to be inside her, wanting to feel this, yet knowing I needed this more. To take her inside me, allow her to become part of me, a part I'll carry with me forever, even if I have to let go of her, eventually.

Chapter Twenty

LAUREL

Wells looms over me while I lie back on the sofa, trying to catch my breath after whatever the hell that just was. The look in his eyes shifts from pure carnal lust to something dark and sad.

I reach up and brush the hair back from his forehead, then trace my fingertips down his cheek and over his wet lips. "Where did you just go?"

He shakes his head slightly, sending his disheveled hair flying around his face. "Nowhere. I'm here with you."

I wish I could believe his words, believe that he truly *is* here with me, but something flickers deep in his gaze that tells me otherwise. It's gone just as quickly, but I saw it before he managed to hide it away again.

He doesn't let me analyze it too much, just presses his mouth to mine, the taste of a release I didn't know I was capable of, coating his tongue and twining with my own.

I groan and arch my hips up against him. His hard cock strains against his pants, and I rub my wet core along the length. He groans and slides his hands up under my ass to lift me easily. I wrap my legs around him, and he walks us into the bedroom and sets me down on the bed.

His bed.

The bed he hasn't shared with anyone since his wife died, but he let me sleep in while I was sick, and now, he's brought me in here for *this*.

Part of me wants to stop him, doesn't want to bring up the inevitable worry about disrespect or regret he may have later, but his mouth keeps moving on mine, his hands sliding up under my shirt again, and when his fingers find my nipples and twist, I cry out, bowing against him.

He captures my cry in his mouth tenderly, kissing softly at the corner of my lips. "Be quiet. You don't want to wake Wesley."

Fuck. Hadn't even thought about that.

How the hell do I completely forget a baby is sleeping only a few feet away from us?

I'm not sure I can be quiet, not after what he just did to me, not when my body burns for him more than it ever has before. Because the way he kisses me is so different from the other times we've been together. It shares the same heat and desperation, but there's also a reverence that wasn't there before.

Maybe an acceptance of what this is.

Wishful thinking.

I told him all I wanted was for him to try, but I want so much more. I want it to be real, all of this, everything I've been feeling since the moment I got up here. I want him to be able to feel it fully, too, but that may never be possible.

He pulls back from me and tugs my shirt up and over my head, then slips a hand behind me and unhooks my bra, letting my breasts fall free. Goosebumps instantly pebble across my skin in the chillier air, and he drops his head to suck a nipple into his mouth while his hand goes to my slit.

"Fuck." I drop my head back against the mattress as he easily glides two fingers into me. My pussy contracts around them, but it wants so much more. *I* want so much more from this, from him.

I told him he would be able to look at Wesley the way he did Diana, and I want *that.* That kind of love. That kind of relationship. Where two people share a soul and a life, inextricable from each other.

It's hard to imagine that ever happening for us, but the pleasure coursing through my body helps push away that reservation.

He releases my nipple with a pop that fills the room, then shifts to the other, giving it the same attention while his hand moves between my legs. His thumb finds the hypersensitive, swollen nub, and my hips buck up toward him.

Oh, God.

I don't know if I can come again.

I don't know if I'm capable of it.

Almost as if he can read my mind, he stills his hand, steps back, and shucks his jeans, freeing his length. It juts out in front of him, and he grips it in one hand and strokes it while he returns to playing between my legs. "You have no idea how beautiful you are, spread out like this, Laurel. I could stare at you all day."

I chuckle and then groan as he curls his fingers into me. "I think Wesley might interrupt that."

The corner of his mouth quirks up as he leans down to flutter his lips over mine. "He might, which means we have to make use of the time we do have."

His tongue plunges into my mouth, warring with mine

as he pulls his hand from between my thighs and drags the head of his cock across my slick core.

I arch against him, eager to feel him filling me, and he lifts my right leg onto his shoulder and plunges deep inside me in one long, languid stroke.

"Oh, *God*." I grip his shoulders, digging my nails into the hard muscle as he bottoms out deep inside me.

"Fucking hell, Laurel. You feel so good."

I tighten around him, and he grits his teeth and draws his hips back to push back into me again. He sets a slow, lazy rhythm that has me moving in time with him. Our bodies undulate together easily, finding the perfect tempo.

He kisses his way up my neck, back to my mouth, and takes it again as he adds a sharp little swirl of his hips with every thrust in.

"Oh, oh, right there."

My gasp fills the room, and he does the move again and again until a low heat starts to spread through me again.

"Are you going to come for me again, Laurel?"

I shake my head from side to side and clamp down hard on him, fighting what is coming. Not sure if I can take what he just did to me again. "I can't."

He stills his hips, and my eyes fly open to meet his. He grips my face in his palm, his thumb at my chin, tilting it up. "You can and you will. It isn't a request."

It's a command from the man who also commands my heart. The one I shouldn't be with, the one who warned me away. Yet here I am, giving myself over to him again and again, letting myself spiral in the arms of someone who may never be available to me, who may never be able to tell me he loves me and needs me.

I've made one epically bad decision after another since the moment I set foot on this property. Yet, with him inside me, filling me completely while he stares deep into my eyes, it's impossible to regret any of it.

All of this may look different in the light of day tomorrow; *he* may look different. Everything he said to me tonight may be a lie, or he may be unable to follow through even if he wants to, but for one night, I'll get this piece of him. This piece he never thought he would be able to give anyone else, and it'll be mine to hold on to for as long as I can.

WELLS

Laurel clings to me, her hands roped around my neck so tightly that it's like she's afraid if she lets go, she'll fly off into oblivion and never return. I would love to give her that. To be the one who's able to send her there. But she's still fighting me, fighting her release, maybe because deep down, she understands that I'm not sure if I can ever give her what she really needs.

Maybe deep down, she knows that my heart still isn't mine to give, no matter how much I might want to, how much I might *try*.

If I could give it to anyone, I would give it to her.

She's fucking perfect, beautiful, smart, feisty as hell, the type of woman I need by my side in life, in business, and to help me raise my son. But I can't put that on her. I can't expect her to step into that role. I can't ask her to become a mother at twenty-six to a baby that isn't even hers.

It's bad enough I made her stay up here as long as I already have, so I'll take this last night, and I'll ensure she experiences something she never has before. Then I'll send her off to live her life without me, without all the complications and trauma I bring.

Tomorrow, I'll do what I have to do...

I grip her chin tightly and press my lips to hers. She squeezes around me, shifting her hips, seeking friction even as she struggles against the pleasure it's giving her.

She won't be able to hold out much longer. I drag my hips back and slam into her hard, and her eyes roll back in her head on a gasp.

I've kept things slow and sweet because I needed it, because she needed it, we needed it. But now she needs something else. I grind my pelvis against her clit with each thrust, and her mouth falls open. I slip my thumb into it, and she bites down hard, the sharp pain sending a jolt straight to my cock.

She clenches around me, and her entire body begins to undulate, her hips moving in time with mine, arching up to meet me. Her nails score the back of my neck and over my bare shoulders.

Each breath she draws becomes shorter until they're nothing more than pants and gasps, mixing with my own. Finally, she cries out, her pussy rippling along my cock.

I clamp my hand over her mouth, afraid she'll wake Wesley, as I pound into her again and again, drawing out her release while chasing my own.

"She's here to help you."

Fuck, of all the times for Diana to make an appearance.

My hips falter, but I push away the voice in my head and concentrate on the woman in front of me, snapping my hips in a way that will drag the head of my cock against her G-spot.

Laurel's orgasm goes on and on, draining mine from me, and I empty myself deep inside her—the hot spurts a relief and a release I so desperately needed from everything I've been holding inside me the last two years.

I finally sag down against her, my weight pressing her deep into the mattress, and bury my face against her neck. Our chests move against each other, both of us trying to catch our breath, her body twitching slightly.

Her hands fall away from my neck, and I roll to the side, taking her with me to face me, still embedded deep inside her.

She squeezes around my still-hard cock. I twitch and moan, pressing my lips to hers in a languid kiss, relishing the taste of her release still on my tongue and hers.

"That was..." Her eyes flicker open to meet mine, hooded and sated.

I lean in and press a kiss to her forehead. "It was."

There aren't any other words to say. Nothing I can, given the circumstances. Anything I could say would either be a lie or a truth I'm not willing to admit at the moment.

Too much needs to happen. Too much has to be done. Decisions, hard ones, that must be made, and I'm the only one who can make them.

I allow my eyes to drift closed and bask in the feeling of her pressed against me. She snuggles her face against my chest, her warm breath fluttering over my heated, sweaty skin.

"Are you all right?" Her question hangs in the air between us, all the things she doesn't ask floating there with it.

"No. Are you?"

She shakes her head and buries her face against me even deeper. "No."

Neither of us offers anything else—either because we

can't or we won't. Neither of us wants to ruin this moment because we might never have one like it again.

To prove the point, Wesley's cry pierces the air, and I jerk away from her slightly.

"Shit."

I quickly withdraw from inside her, the loss of her warm body cocooning my cock making me cringe. She does the same and rolls onto her back as I climb to my feet and tug my pants back on. "I'll get him."

She raises a brow, her tired, sated eyes searching mine. "You sure?"

I nod.

He's my responsibility, not hers.

My son...

And I need to figure out what his life is going to be like, fast.

The fire has started to burn down, and I throw another log on it as I pass it on my way to the nursery. I pause outside the closed door, examining the cabin, from the wall of Diana's books and my photos to the tiny table in the kitchen that should have been replaced by the much larger one a long time ago.

But that tiny table is where I sat with Laurel.

Where she fed me—both food and the truths I wasn't ready to hear.

"She's here to help you."

Another cry draws me into the nursery, and Wesley lies on his back, kicking and screaming, angry at the world in a way I can absolutely get on board with. I scoop him up and cuddle him against my chest, breathing in that sweet baby scent.

"I understand exactly how you feel, big guy."

He has to rely on me to be fed, to be clothed, to be

comforted, and I can't stay up here anymore pretending Lockwood Brewery doesn't rely on me to function.

There are thousands of employees whose livelihoods depend on the company's success. I can't act like the world ended two years ago because it didn't.

It went on without me whether I wanted it to or not. And one night, when I sought solace in the arms of a stranger, brought Wesley to me.

I look down at him and press my lips to his head as he finally starts to settle. "Everything will be okay, buddy. I promise. I'm not sure how, but you and I *are* going to be okay."

Chapter Twenty-One

WELLS

"Well, I'll be damned."

I freeze two steps into Lockwood Brewing Company's corporate office headquarters and turn slowly to my left toward the old, deep, cracking voice I would know anywhere.

Instinctively, I reach up to straighten my tie, which feels more like a noose after not wearing one for two years. "Father, what are you doing here?"

He approaches me slowly, his suit crisp and impeccable, as always. "After Landry's little announcement yesterday, I decided I was needed, since nobody's seen you here for two years, and it seems you've been *busy* elsewhere."

I wince slightly and run a hand over my hair, even though it's already slicked back, to try to hide how long and unruly I've let it get. It doesn't pass Father's scrutiny, though. He narrows his eyes on my head and lets it drift down to my shoulders, where the strands brush against my black suit jacket.

"You couldn't have gotten a haircut?"

The same judgmental tone he's always carried but that only increased after Mother's death and my stepping into the CEO role makes me bristle, and I scan the lobby and take a step toward him, lowering my head slightly so no one overhears us.

"I hadn't exactly planned on being here, Father, nor did I know I would be under *inspection.*"

He looks up at me with the same amber eyes I share with Wesley and scowls. "That's one thing you never learned. In this position, you're *always* under scrutiny and subject to *inspection.*"

Hell.

Just what I fucking need, a lecture from him, today, of all days.

I straighten and square my shoulders, running a hand over the front of my coat to ensure any wrinkles work themselves out—after hanging in my closet in the cabin for so long, I was surprised it wasn't full of moth holes or spiderwebs.

"I'm not here to argue with you, Father."

"Then why are you here?" He feigns ignorance and spreads his wrinkled hands. "Why did you decide to grace us with your presence today?"

Maybe I shouldn't have come.

Maybe I should have stayed in bed, wrapped around Laurel like I wanted to.

But I had to leave the mountain—at least temporarily. It's time to deal with things here and stop keeping my head in the sand, pretending the real world doesn't exist.

Though, I thought I would get in and get out and back up to her by dinnertime, if I'm lucky, since I left before the sun was even up. I never anticipated an ambush from the old man and being put in front of his firing squad.

"I should be asking you the same question." I raise a brow. "What are *you* doing here, Father?"

"Same as you, Son. Since you've skirted your responsibilities for the last few years, and now that I'm a *grandfather*"—his emphasis on the word makes me cringe —"I figured I would need to step in until you got your shit figured out."

"My shit *is* figured out, Father."

His white brows rise. "Is it? Splendid. Where's my grandson?" He glances behind me, knowing full well I came alone. "Have you signed the paperwork with the whore who had him?"

My hand lashes out and grips his biceps so quickly that he stumbles back a half-step, but I tighten my fingers around him, keeping him upright and dragging him close enough to say what I have to without drawing unwanted attention. "You keep your fucking mouth shut about Candace and about anything else having to do with my life and my son."

He narrows his eyes at me. "Don't talk to me like that, Wells. I gave you life, I gave you this company, and I can take both of them away."

Before, the threat might have actually hurt me. It might have made me reconsider the words I'm about to say and the action I'm about to take, but given everything that's happened, it won't today.

I tighten my grip until I'm sure it hurts him. "You may still be the owner of this company in name, Father, but I'm the CEO. I make all the decisions when it comes to what's best for Lockwood Brewing. And what's best is for you to leave the premises, immediately."

"You can't throw me out the doors of my own company."

No sooner does he say the words than the security guards from the desk on the far side of the lobby step up behind him.

"Don't make me have them escort you out."

He glances over his shoulder, his body tenses. "What the hell are you doing, Wells?"

"What I should have done years ago. You handed me the reins of the company but have done nothing but question everything I've done since then. Now, you're questioning my personal life, which is none of your fucking business."

"You left the brewery to languish while you dealt with Diana's death. You left it in Landry's hands, which I only allowed because I trust *him* implicitly. But this is *my* business. And my grandson *is* my business. You can't turn this company over to a bastard."

If there weren't people milling around, I would deck him so hard it'd knock the wind out of the old man's already-frail lungs. But I don't need to bring any more scrutiny down on Lockwood Brewing after yesterday's reveal. So, instead of punching the old coot, I suck in a deep breath and prepare to say my final words to the man who gave me life.

"He's my son. That's all that matters, and I'm going to give him everything you never gave me."

"Everything I never gave you?" His brows fly up to his receding hairline. "You must be *mad.* I gave you the world, the best schools, the best tutors, the best food, the best house, the best cars. You never wanted for anything."

"Yes, I did. I wanted a father who was actually proud of

me, who supported me in my decisions instead of questioning every single one of them. And I'm going to make sure that my son knows I love him no matter what he chooses to do in his life or with this company when I hand it over to him."

Father opens his mouth to retort again, but I look to the guards.

"Ensure my father gets out to his car safely." I release his arm and take a step back.

The guards flank him. He takes a step toward me, but one of them steps between us, effectively halting his advance.

"You'll regret this, Wells. I still have enough power to get you kicked out of the company."

"Yeah, you do, but you won't because it would be an even bigger scandal to kick a Lockwood out of Lockwood Brewing, and it would mean you have no one else to carry on the family legacy. You don't want that."

I stand back, watching security escort him from the building, then release a heavy sigh and make my way to the elevators I haven't ridden in over two years. Massive brass doors tower above me, somewhat more imposing than I remember them. I press the call button, and the doors open immediately.

Stepping in, I lean back against a wall and release a heavy sigh. The familiar smell of brass polish and cleaning solution fills my nose, so different from the fresh, clean scent of rain and the woods I'm used to now.

A migraine hammers at my brain, and I rub my palms against my temples, trying to alleviate some of it.

The change in altitude coming down from the mountain must be really fucking with me.

That and the elevator rising rapidly to the sixtieth floor.

Nausea crawls up my throat, and I swallow it back as the elevator car comes to a stop. I take a step, and the enclosed space spins slightly, darkness starting to creep into the corners of my vision.

I grip the wall and make it out into the hallway, blinking rapidly to get my eyesight to clear. It finally does, and I look up to find Landry waiting, his brow furrowed.

"Are you all right?"

I nod and wave off his concern, straightening and brushing a hand over my tie again. "I'm fine."

His shrewd gaze roves over me, but he relaxes slightly, seemingly appeased by my assurance. "I saw your confrontation with your father downstairs."

I narrow my eyes on him. "What? Were you sitting in the security office watching the video monitors?"

He offers me a half grin. "As soon as I knew your father was on campus, I had to take a peek."

Despite so many years working under Wesley Lockwood and forming a true friendship with him, Landry also understands the old man's faults—his skills as a father being at the top of that list.

"Did you hear any of it?"

He shakes his head. "Not much."

I follow him back toward my office, averting my gaze from the curious looks of various employees and ignoring the whispers. Landry opens the door and ushers me inside, but one step in, I freeze. *Nothing's changed.*

Everything I left sitting on my desk remains exactly in place—the ugly coffee mug Diana made for me during her artist phase, my favorite pen in the center of the polished wood surface, our black and white wedding photo framed on the corner.

A vise tightens around my chest, and I reach up and rub at it, then slowly walk around my desk and lower myself into the leather chair that once molded to my body so perfectly.

"Has it really been two years since I've been in here?"

Landry takes a seat opposite me and nods. "It has. You look good in that chair, though. That's where you belong."

"Is it?" I scratch at the stubble on my jaw and lean back in the chair.

"You tell me."

"I'm not sure anymore." I reach back and rest my head in my hands, letting my eyes drift closed. "I just got into a fight with my father about not turning the business over to my son when he's old enough." I open my eyes. "But I don't even know that I'll be here to do it."

Landry crosses his ankle over his knee, leaning back slightly. "You really wouldn't come back?"

"You've been doing an excellent job, even Father admitted so."

He smirks. "I know, but it isn't *my* job to do. We need you back, and now that you have Wesley, it makes more sense for you to be here in Denver. He can go to school, and you can hire a nanny to help you; you'll have friends and, dare I say, family."

I snort and shake my head, then wince at the pain that slices through it. "After that confrontation with my father, I don't think there's any chance of that."

"What about Laurel?"

Stiffening, I narrow my eyes at him. "What about her?"

He gives me a knowing look. "Is she going to be a problem if you're back?"

No, because I fired her...

I didn't really mean it, though. I'm not such a heartless

asshole that I would sabotage her career just so I could get her to sleep with me. But the complicated personal situation between us makes talking to Landry about it pretty low on the list of things I want to do today.

"She won't be a problem."

At least, not professionally.

Landry's old blue eyes soften, and he drops his foot and leans toward me. "Are you all right? You look very pale."

I nod, rubbing at my temple again. "I'm okay. Just been having a lot of headaches that seem to have gotten worse today. Probably the altitude change."

"When was the last time you saw a doctor?"

I try to think back through the endless months of misery that all seem to blend together. "Maybe seven months ago? Near the end of the year, when they came to do my physical for the insurance."

Concern furrows Landry's brow. "Then we should definitely get you checked out before you go back up the mountain. If anything happened to you up there..."

I meet his worried gaze. "Believe me, I don't need to be reminded of that."

LAUREL

It shouldn't have been a surprise, I guess, waking up to a cold, empty bed this morning. But I still lay there with my hand over the spot where he slept—or didn't sleep, so it seemed—wondering how long he'd been gone and where he went.

Unlike when he went to Lockwood Falls, he didn't bother to leave a note letting me know what was happening, just slipped away early enough in the morning for me to be passed out cold without a word.

Probably regretting what we did last night.

Touched me like he couldn't keep his hands off me. Kissed me like it provided his oxygen. How he laid me in this bed and made love to me in the way I've always dreamed about.

But no one dreams of waking up alone after a night like that.

The fact that his truck is missing from the back of the cabin suggests he went into town for something. Hell, maybe he even went all the way back to Denver, which has left me alone in the cabin today. Alone with Wesley, mulling about, dusting, cleaning—which apparently hasn't been done in two damn years—and twiddling my thumbs and wondering what the hell I'm doing getting involved with Wells Lockwood.

In the moment, what I said to him was true. There are times I truly believe he's capable of more, that his heart has room to let me into it, but leaving without a word this morning doesn't bode well for that belief. And the longer he's gone, the more my chest aches and my gut twists.

Maybe I've read it all wrong.

It's possible I've been so focused on helping him with Wesley that I've taken things that don't exist and somehow seen them as signs of something that isn't there.

The man did fire me.

Anyone might look at that and see disdain, but he did that to pave the way for us to explore whatever's happening between us.

Something he *said* he wanted.

He said he wanted to *try.*

And that's all I can ask of him when he has his hands full with this little guy.

Wesley giggles from where he lies on a play mat on the floor in the living room, kicking and shaking his rattle, completely oblivious to the emotional upheaval surrounding him.

Lucky kid.

I scoop him up and hold him up in front of me. "Hey, big man. Your daddy sure is one frustrating guy. You know that?"

Drool dribbles from his mouth, and he shoves the rattle into it and gurgles happily.

"I hope you never have to find out."

Things will come to a head—sooner rather than later—and something tells me that when Wells returns from wherever he went today, it will be with some decisions I've been pushing him to make.

For better or for worse.

It's what I wanted, what I've been praying for since I stopped hating him and started to actually *care* about the man. But waiting around for him to come back with an answer that will alter my future, one way or another, and potentially destroy my heart, makes me restless.

I prop Wesley on my hip. "Let's go get some fresh air."

This cabin is starting to feel like a prison cell again, and I can't stay cooped up in here any longer. If I do, I might drive myself crazy, considering all the potential possibilities.

If I pick something from the garden to make for dinner, it will give me something to occupy my racing mind other than waiting to hear the crunch of tires on the gravel road.

Who knows if Wells will even be back...

The thought of spending the night alone in the cabin in the dark sends a chill through me, and I clutch Wesley even closer before I open the door and descend the two steps outside. We're so remote, no one else could ever get up here without me knowing about it, but the same horror movie scenes still play through my head that did when I first saw this place.

His quip about not even bringing his axe brings a smile to my lips, and I head around the cabin to the side garden. "What should we have for dinner?"

Anything that doesn't require me to go into the cellar.

With the daylight rapidly fading, there is absolutely nothing that could get me to go down there again—and definitely not with the baby.

Wesley tugs on a strand of my hair, and I reach over and pry it from his little fingers.

"We need to work on the no hair pulling, bud."

He just continues to drool and shake his rattle, but another sound makes me stop mid-step and freeze.

Honk.

Honk.

Tires crunch on gravel, and my spine stiffens as my heart leaps.

Wells is back.

For one split second, hope starts to fill the space left empty by his disappearance, but then reality hits me.

He wouldn't honk to announce his arrival at his own home.

It must be someone else.

Acid crawls up my throat as the car turns the corner on the barely there road. A black Town Car, not Wells' truck. My eyes drift to the **LKWOOD2** license plate.

Someone from the brewery.

I swallow thickly and retreat a step, as if that will somehow prevent whatever's about to happen. Because the sense of pure dread that settles over me makes me want to run back into the cabin and hide.

The car comes to a stop in front of it, and a back door opens. Long, thin legs in perfectly tailored pants swing out, and shiny loafers settle onto the uneven ground of the clearing.

Landry climbs from the car, his face set in a hard mask, lips pressed together tightly.

I stop in my tracks, holding Wesley a little tighter. "Mr. Landry, what are you doing here?"

He motions toward the cabin. "Let's go inside. We need to talk."

Oh, God...

That unease I have been trying to keep at bay advances to full-on panic.

Why the hell would Landry come up the mountain while Wells is gone?

Only one reason I can think of, one I hadn't even considered when I woke and found him gone this morning—he sent Landry to do something he couldn't do himself.

He follows me in and shuts the door behind me. Wesley reaches out for him, but I put him back on the play mat.

"What's going on? Where's Wells...uh, Mr. Lockwood?"

A muscle in Landry's firm jaw tics. "He's still in Denver and probably will be for a while."

"What?"

Oh, my God...

Whatever I thought happened last night, I did read it all wrong. He sent Landry here to get the baby and get rid of me, to tell me it's over. "Did he send you up here to get me?"

Landry averts his gaze, glancing down at Wesley. "First, I want to assure you that Mr. Lockwood told me to ensure you maintained your job, no matter what."

"No matter what."

Because we won't be together anymore.

Because he can't do this.

I stumble back a step, my knees hitting the couch and buckling under me. Falling back on it, I look from Landry to the baby, trying to process what this will mean.

If he comes back up here, I'll never see them again, and if he comes back to work like you've been pushing him to, then you'll have to see him every single day, knowing what you could have had, what slipped through your fingers.

"Ms. Palmer?" He waits for me to look up at him. "You need to pack your things and Wesley's and come with me back to Denver."

To what?

An almost-empty apartment. An empty life with only this job to fill my time. An empty heart that will never be full again...

"Ms. Palmer? Did you hear me?"

I jerk my head back toward him, blinking away the fog that seems to be enveloping me. "Um, yes. I need to pack."

Landry scans the living room, his gaze finally landing on the photo of Wells and his father on one of the bookshelves. "How long will it take?"

"Um..." I climb to my feet, mentally trying to prepare a list of everything I have to pack. The two bags Candace left —a few remaining diapers, what's left of the formula, some bottled waters, in case he gets hungry on the drive down, the few small toys, the play mat...

What about the things in the nursery?

The thought of taking items Diana and Wells bought for Maribel out of the cabin somehow feels wrong.

Stick to the basics.

Take only what Candace sent with him.

"How long, Ms. Palmer?"

Shit.

Landry is going to think I'm a total space cadet because I can't seem to process what he says to me—Wells wants me out of here.

Fast. "Five minutes."

He offers me a tight smile. "I'll watch Wesley while you pack."

"Okay."

I manage to pull myself together enough to walk to the bedroom and grab the only things of mine present in the whole cabin—my skirt and my ruined heels.

Things have changed so much since I first stepped out of that car into the rain in this. I've changed so much.

How am I supposed to say goodbye to Wesley?

How am I supposed to walk away from Wells?

Not in these shoes, given their current state.

I return to the living room, grab one of Wesley's bags, and start packing the few things he came with. Wells probably has everything a baby could ever need in a massive, beautiful nursery at his home in Denver that he can bring back up here if he doesn't stay.

He doesn't need any of this.

Doesn't need me.

I shove my skirt and shoes into the top of the bag, then grab Wesley from the play mat and settle him into the car seat. My hands shake, trying to click the straps into place. He smiles up at me, completely clueless and so damn innocent.

Despite feeling like my heart will shatter into a million pieces, I try to force a smile. "Okay, buddy. We're going to go for a car ride."

And then my life is about to change again for the second time in only weeks.

Landry holds out his hand for the bags, and I offer another pained smile and let him take them from me while I lift the car seat and take one final look at the place that has been my home for a week and a half. Where so much happened in such a short amount of time. The only place I've ever felt even remotely like I was at home.

Chapter Twenty-Two

LAUREL

The car finally coming to a stop pulls me from deep inside my own head, and I stare up at the building.

This isn't Lockwood Brewing campus, and it sure as hell isn't Wells' Denver house, either.

A lit red cross sits above a pair of sliding glass doors, and I cast a quick glance at Wesley, sound asleep in the middle of the backseat between Landry and me, before I finally focus on the man who was sent to bring me down the mountain.

"What are we doing at a hospital?"

He offers me an apologetic look, his kind eyes crinkling at the corners. "Room 403."

"What?"

"You need to go to room 403."

I must have inadvertently dozed off during the drive back to the city and still have some lingering post-snooze haze clouding my brain because I can't seem to follow. "Why?"

Landry inclines his head toward the hospital entrance. "Just go."

"But…" I place my hand on Wesley, his tiny chest rising and falling under my palm.

Landry sets his hand next to mine in the car seat, pulling back the blanket over Wesley slightly. "I'm taking him home with me. My wife will be thrilled to have a little one in the house again."

"But…"

What the hell *is going on?*

Landry lifts his hand and rests it on mine. "Laurel, I know you only just started with Lockwood and that we don't really know each other, at all, really, but you have to trust me. Just go."

He pulls his hand from mine, and I glance at Wesley again, my stomach churning at the thought of leaving him—even with the man Wells trusts so implicitly with his business.

"He'll be fine, Ms. Palmer. I promise."

The reassurance doesn't help the trepidation seeping into my veins, but whatever is happening, it's apparently happening inside that hospital.

I slip from the car out onto the sidewalk, and Landry gives me a quick wave. Then the car pulls away, leaving me standing clueless and feeling utterly empty.

What the hell am I doing here?

No matter how hard I wrack my brain, I can't come up with a single reason for Landry to drop me off like this rather than take me home or back to the offices where I left my car when Landry sent me up to see Wells.

There's only one way to find out.

I step through the sliding doors and into unfamiliar territory. The smell of antiseptic fills my nose, and I cringe as I make my way toward the elevators, following the signs.

My hand shakes, pressing the call button, and I pace in front of the closed doors, waiting to hear the little ding. After hours of uncomfortable silence during the ride back to Denver, I thought I'd finally have answers when we arrived. Instead, I have more questions.

Ding.

The sound makes me jump even though I've been waiting for it, and I step into an open car and press "4," then lean back and chew on my bottom lip as it brings me up.

It dings on "4," and I slowly get out onto what's marked as a private floor. Double doors stand straight ahead, a nurse's desk to the right.

A woman sitting behind it glances up at me and offers a kind smile. "You must be Ms. Palmer. I'll buzz you in."

Why does she know my name?

"Um...thank you."

She presses a button on the side of the desk, and the doors swing open, revealing a short hallway with several closed doors on each side and an open one at the end.

Unlike every other hospital I have ever been in, this one is eerily still and quiet.

What the hell is going on?

403 lies directly ahead of me at the end of the corridor. Each step I take toward it ratchets up my anxiety until my palms sweat and my heart thunders loudly in my ears.

I nudge open the door fully and step through it slowly, holding my breath.

"Laurel..." Wells' familiar deep voice rolls over me like an incoming storm, and I turn toward it to find him sitting on a hospital bed, hooked up to various machines but looking as handsome as ever.

"Oh, my God, Wells, what are you doing here? What happened?"

He holds up a hand to stop my questions and motions me over to him without answering any of them. I approach slowly, scanning him from the top of his head over his gown-covered chest and to the blanket covering him from the waist down, searching for any reason he might be here since he seemed completely fine the last time I saw him.

"Landry wouldn't tell me anything. I didn't even know why the hell I was here..."

The corners of his mouth curl up into an apologetic smile. "I know. I told him not to, and I'm sorry about that. I asked him to make sure you understood you weren't being fired, so you wouldn't worry the whole ride back, but I didn't want you to have to hear any of it from him."

"Hear any of what?"

That we're over?

He motions toward the edge of the bed, and I sit down on it next to him and examine all the beeping and whirring machines he's hooked up to. But I can't figure out what any of them are doing or saying about why he might be here.

"You want to clue me in?"

He sighs and rubs a hand over the stubble on his face. "I've been having headaches off and on for the last year. I didn't think anything of it, since migraines run in the family, and I've been under a lot of stress, as you know."

Under a lot of stress is the understatement of the century.

I nod, and he reaches out but stops short of pulling my hand into his, almost like he's afraid to touch me while he continues.

His gaze darts down to where our hands lie, mere inches

from each other. "And remember I told you I've been hearing Diana's voice?"

"Yes..."

How could I forget? Not exactly what you want to hear from the man you're falling in love with.

Wells releases a little sigh and finally slips his hand over the top of mine and squeezes it gently, the callouses on his palm scratching at my skin. "I thought I was just, well"—he glances up almost sheepishly—"losing my fucking mind, but..."

He pauses and locks eyes with me, so much fear and worry swimming in their bourbon depths.

"But *what*?"

If he doesn't come out and tell me what's going on soon, I might have to storm out of here and go harass that nurse who buzzed me until *someone* gives me some damn answers.

"But Landry insisted I get checked out while I was in town because he said I didn't look good. He didn't want me going back up the mountain without at least a checkup."

"And?"

He squeezes my hand again, as if he's anticipating my reaction to whatever he's about to reveal and trying to ease it before he even says a word. "And the doctor insisted we do an MRI and a CAT scan, and they found a tumor in my brain."

A tumor in my brain...

A tumor...

It echoes through my head, and it takes a moment for me to fully process what he just said.

"A what? Oh, my God..."

Panic wells up in my throat.

"Breathe, Laurel."

The same words he said to me when I almost poisoned myself fill my ears, and he glides his hand over my arm slowly, trying to soothe me before I can let it spiral any further.

He pulls my fingers to his mouth, pressing his lips across them, giving me something else to focus on until I can finally breathe normally again. "It's been causing migraines, auditory hallucinations, and some visual disturbances I wrote off as not taking care of myself properly."

"Is it..."

I can't even say the C-word. It sits on the tip of my tongue but won't come out, no matter how hard I try.

He kisses my fingers again and squeezes my hand. "I don't know yet. Landry insisted they rush to biopsy it earlier tonight." He turns his head away from me, and a bandage on the back covers what must have been the biopsy site. "I should have the results tomorrow."

"And if it...is?"

These are the times I wish I had gone into the medical field, so I could understand anything about what's happening to him. The best I can do is sue these bastards if they fuck something up.

"I'm not entirely sure. They have to do surgery to remove it either way because of my symptoms, and if it is cancerous, then I imagine chemo or radiation."

Somehow, despite the heavy weight of the information he's giving me, Wells remains calm. Like he's relaying the weather instead of discussing something that might kill him.

Why isn't he freaking out the way I am?

"But is it..." I choke back a sob. "Are you going to..."

I can't even think about it. He just got Wesley. He just found his son, and now, he might lose him all because he was too damn stubborn to get checked out earlier.

He pulls my hand against his cheek and turns his head to press his lips to my palm. "Honestly, I don't know. They said the size and placement don't appear to be affecting any major faculties, and if it isn't cancerous, the doctor said it's unlikely to come back if they get it all. But...they won't know for sure until the biopsy comes back and they go in."

"Oh, my God."

The room starts to spin. His strong arms wrap around my waist and tug me across the bed and onto his lap. He presses his lips behind my ear. "You look like you're about to pass out."

Almost immediately, being in his arms acts like a warm blanket wrapping around me, cocooning me in the physical strength he's always had, making me feel secure and that things might actually be okay.

"This is not what I expected when Landry showed up and dragged Wesley and me out of the cabin."

"I know. I'm so sorry." He kisses my cheek. "I thought it was better you hear it from me rather than from him and have to sit through that long drive, wondering and thinking about it."

"So instead, I spent the whole time thinking about something else."

He tucks a strand of hair away from my face. "Yeah, what's that?"

"That you were trying to get rid of me."

A lazy smile spreads across his lips. "I don't think that's possible."

"What isn't?"

"Getting rid of you."

I try to smile, but a sob slips out instead. This is the time I should try to be strong for him, to hold in my emotions and pretend it doesn't feel like the world we created over the last few weeks is crumbling around us.

"Don't cry." He brushes the tears from my cheeks. "Please, I can't bear to see you so upset."

"But what if..."

He shakes his head. "No. No 'what ifs.'"

I sniffle and turn my blurry gaze to meet his. "How can you be so calm?"

Wells takes my face between his hands, a small smile pulling at his lips. "Because it all finally makes sense. Don't you see?"

"See what?"

"I told you I've been hearing Diana, and she kept saying you were here to help me." He waits for me to nod. "I thought she meant help with the baby. But now I *see*."

For some reason, I can't seem to follow what he's saying, my mind clouded by my worry and desire to rage against the world for this happening to him when he finally has a chance at a life again.

"You see what, Wells?"

The most brilliant smile he has ever given me lights up his face, his bourbon eyes warming with hope I've never witnessed from him. "That you're here for me because this was *meant* to happen."

"What was?"

Wells drags me even closer, the same woodsy scent still clinging to him even here. "This—you and me and Wesley—we were meant to be whatever it is we are." He releases a sardonic laugh. "Fuck if I know what it is, but I meant what I said last night. As long as I'm here, I'm willing to try, *really* willing to try. And maybe getting rid of this thing in my head will help me do that."

"So, it isn't over?"

Tears streak down my cheeks again as I stare at the man who was so lost when I arrived. Who was so far gone that I wasn't sure he would ever be able to find his way out of the depths of his own personal hell. But it's like this revelation has cleansed away whatever was holding him back, whatever was weighing him down.

For the first time since I met him, he looks *free.*

"When I woke up this morning and you were gone, I thought..."

I bite back another sob and try to turn away, but he forces me to keep looking at him.

"No, Laurel, it isn't over. I swear, it's just beginning."

WELLS

The darkness surrounding me dissipates slowly, light creeping into the edges of my dream. Diana and Maribel slowly fade away, replaced by a constant beeping noise, a soft hand slowly brushing over mine, and a dull ache in my head.

It takes a second for me to process what happened and where I am.

The hospital.

Surgery.

"Laurel?" My voice comes out cracked and unsteady, my throat insanely dry and scratchy.

She tightens her grip on my hand, leaning in close enough that her light floral scent surrounds me. "I'm here."

I turn toward the sound of her voice and let my eyes flutter open, then quickly close them against the brightness of the room. "Lights."

"Shit." She releases my hand for a minute, flips off the lights, then returns to the same spot, squeezing to let me know she's back. "How are you feeling?"

I take a moment to take stock of my body. The hammering in my head that has plagued me for so long has been replaced by a different kind of pain, one the surgeon assured me will go away and is totally normal after having major brain surgery. "Okay...I think."

"You don't have to lie to me, Wells."

I don't.

After all the anguish, the rage, the trials and tribulations, it feels like everything has settled. Flashes of my dream come back, of Di and Maribel happy, waving to me and blowing me a kiss.

Tears slip from my eyes before I open them and find Laurel hovering over me, her auburn hair fanned out around her face like the glowing halo of my own personal angel.

I grin at her. "I'm not lying. I feel...I don't know how to describe it. Different somehow, like a weight's been lifted off my shoulders."

Her lips twist slightly, as if she's biting back something she wants to say.

"Laurel, what is it?"

She brushes her fingers over my face softly, wiping away my tears and offering me a smile that doesn't quite reach her eyes—the same reservation I've seen there since she arrived at the hospital three days ago. "Nothing that can't wait until later."

The same answer she's given me every time I question what's causing that faraway, tormented look. I could have easily written it off as her worrying about the biopsy results, but we got them back yesterday and were assured that the tumor invading my brain was completely benign. And now that the surgery is complete, the doctor told us he has every reason to believe it won't cause me any more trouble or return.

So, she should be happy. She should be relaxed. She should finally be able to breathe again.

"No." I reach up and grab her hand. "Don't do that."

Her pale brows rise. "Don't do what?"

"I don't want to put off anything anymore. Not when it's so easy to lose it so fast."

I, of all people, have learned that sad fact all too well, and once I got my diagnosis and understood that part of why I've been feeling the way I have for the last year was likely because of the tumor, I knew it was time to stop second-guessing everything and putting off for tomorrow what can be done today.

It's something Diana always preached. I always placated her and said, "Yes, dear." I pretended I agreed with her mantra and embraced it, when really, I put off far too many things—like the chance to be a father.

Now I can see what was happening so clearly. No matter what the doctor says, her voice in my head was more than a hallucination, more than my subconscious telling me the things I knew and didn't consciously want to admit. It was *her* finding a way to ensure I would know it was okay to accept my role in Wesley's life, to embrace the one I can have in Laurel's.

Laurel offers me a sad smile and looks down at our joined hands. "I was just thinking that maybe you're right, and all of this was meant to happen." She glances up, a slight pink spreading up her neck. "You know, I had six other job offers, three of them from major law firms where I could have worked my way up and made partner, but I turned them all down to come work for Lockwood Brewing."

Having six job offers doesn't surprise me in the least.

This woman is a force to be reckoned with, one I came very close to not surviving. She will be a monster in the courtroom. I can only pray for those who have to face her when she defends the company in the future. But I don't understand why she would turn down what sound like incredible opportunities to work for a brewery.

"Why?"

She ducks her head, and the blush colors her cheeks. "Well, this is a little embarrassing, but…when I was about sixteen, I saw an interview with you on some news channel. Talking about some expansion of the brewery campus…and I always thought you were so handsome."

Well, I'll be damned.

I grin at her and waggle my eyebrows. "Did you have a crush on me?"

Her cheeks darken even more, and her lips twist in annoyance at my teasing tone.

"You did?"

She shakes her head, pointing a finger at me in that *I'm about to give you a lecture* way she always does before she's about to correct me or lay something on me I might not want to hear. "I *respected* you and what you were doing with your business."

I drag her hand to my lips and press a kiss across her knuckles. "Sure you did."

Laurel rolls her eyes at my comment. "So, what I'm saying is…" She gives me a look that says to drop it. "That maybe all this *was* supposed to happen this way. As awful and painful and horrible as it may have been for you, as it still is having to deal with losing Di and Maribel, maybe me seeing that interview is what led to me taking this job at exactly the right time to be the one sent up the mountain." A little sigh slips from her lips, and she shrugs. "Maybe you were right the other night when you said it was meant to be."

I kiss her knuckles again. "I think I am. This is the first time in two years I actually feel a sense of peace, but that could get shattered very quickly."

She narrows her eyes at me, her entire body stiffening instantly. "Why is that?"

If I hadn't just lectured her about not putting off conversations that need to happen, I might try to weasel my way out of discussing this right now. Lying in bed after major brain surgery isn't exactly the ideal place to talk about these types of things. But waiting won't change how I feel about this, and I need to make sure she is one hundred percent on board.

"Because I'm not sure what's going to happen with you and me and Wesley."

Her gaze softens. "What do you mean?"

I brush my thumb over her palm. "I meant what I said when we were out on the cliff, that I don't think *this* is my life anymore. Being out there at the cabin, it just has always felt right, even before I lost Diana and Maribel, and I don't want to give that up. But I know you were right, too, that I can't raise Wesley up there. It wouldn't be fair to him not to have access to all the things I can give him. A great education, friends."

"So, where does that leave you?" She releases a heavy sigh and leans against the bed to get closer to me, resting her head against my arm. "Where does that leave us?"

"You tell me."

All of this hinges on Laurel, on what *she* wants because

living on the mountain isn't easy, and I would never claim to her that it is.

"I don't think I can live up there, Wells. When you were gone that day and night started to descend and I was there alone, I just felt...unsafe."

I nudge her chin up until she looks at me and grin at her. "There are a lot of things lurking in the woods."

"That may be true, but I already tamed the most dangerous one, right?"

That draws a laugh from deep in my chest, and I wince at the sharp pain that causes in my head. "I wouldn't say *tamed*. Up there still feels more like home."

"So, how do we make it work?"

It's something I've been considering since I had my conversation with Landry before my world was turned upside down again by this diagnosis. And I've only been able to come to one conclusion that might actually work.

"Maybe we split our time, spend weekends up there as often as we can. I won't go back to how I was working before, but after talking with Landry and my father—"

"You talked to your father?"

Shit.

In all the worry and excitement of the hospital, I apparently forgot to mention that confrontation to her—or maybe I intentionally withheld it, knowing it might only make her more worried for me.

"It wasn't a pleasant conversation or one I need to repeat. Suffice it to say, he may be making moves to try to come back."

"Can he do that?"

I shrug. "He can try."

"And if he does?"

"That threat is precisely what made me realize I wasn't

ready to give this up entirely, either. The thought of him removing me, of the business falling into the hands of somebody who isn't a Lockwood...I just can't let that happen."

Laurel pushes up on her elbows, inching closer to me. "So, we have to find a middle ground."

I nod. "We have to find a middle ground."

"And that's doable?"

Grinning, I slip my hand under her chin and grin. "Baby steps. We get satellite internet and a phone in the cabin so I can work from there."

She returns my grin. "And what about me? Do I have a job, or does the initial firing stand?"

I smirk at her. "You have one, if you want one, but you don't have to work. You know I—"

Her icy glare cuts off what I was about to say, and she clenches her jaw, the muscles tightening in my hand. "I don't want your money, Wells. It's the last thing I want."

"Christ, Laurel, I know that."

It never crossed my mind, not even for one second, that this woman would take a fucking penny from me, even if I offered it to her on the silver platter she said I was always handed everything on.

I urge her up closer, so I can brush my lips across hers. "But you're willing to take my money in the form of a paycheck and work from the cabin?"

She smiles against my lips, then pulls back slightly. "I'll take the checks that I earn, and I'm willing to work from the cabin—sometimes—so you'll be happy." Her humor fades quickly, replaced by dread. "But don't ever leave me up there alone again."

"Did the rabbit try to come get you from the cellar?"

She scowls at me. "Don't be an asshole, Wells."

My chuckle shakes both of us on the bed. "If you

haven't already figured out I'm an asshole by now, then you're in for a very rude awakening if you stay with me."

"*If* I stay with you?"

I sigh and look away from her for a moment, the one thing still niggling at the back of my head, trying to work up anxiety again. "The doctor said—"

"I know what the doctor said. That the tumor may have been affecting your personality, that it could be more than just headaches and auditory hallucinations." Her light touch nudges my chin, and she turns my gaze back to hers. "You're worried you're going to change."

"What if I do?"

She rests her small palm on my cheek. "It doesn't matter. I saw you at your worst, right?"

I let out an incredulous laugh. "You can definitely say that."

"And I managed to keep up with you when you were like that. I wrangled you, didn't I?"

"You certainly did."

"So, if I can handle that, I can handle anything."

Blood rushes in my ears, my heart beating wildly enough to probably bring the nurses rushing back in here at any moment, but I have to ask the inevitable question. "Even being a mom?"

The corners of her lips twist up.

"He's not yours, Laurel. I would understand if you don't want to get any further involved, take on that responsibility. I would never ask that, could never ask that of you. Landry and I shouldn't have in the first place, even temporarily."

Tears shimmer in her eyes. "I've grown to love that baby, Wells, just as much as I do you, and you guys are a package deal."

I reach out and drag her up across me.

The machines beep wildly, and I'm positive at any moment, a nurse is going to come in and scream at me for having her in the bed and on top of me after major surgery.

But I need to feel her against me, need to know that this is real and not some side effects from the surgery and the drugs probably still coursing through my system.

"Did you just say you love me?"

She smiles at me and brushes her lips against mine. "I did."

"I love you, too, Laurel. You were sent to help Wesley. You were sent to help me move past my hangups and work through my grief. You were sent to help me find my heart again, and now, it's yours."

Epilogue

Three Years Later

LAUREL

The chirping birds, who decided to build their nest directly outside the bedroom window, wake me far too early. The sun isn't even up yet, darkness still greeting me when I open my eyes.

And I might be annoyed if it weren't for Wells' hard, warm body pressed against my back, holding me tightly, his light breaths fanning the back of my neck. I snuggle deeply against him, just like I do every morning, trying to get even closer, and his cock stirs to life against my ass cheeks.

He groans in my ear and presses his lips to that sweet spot right behind it that sends a little shudder through me. "If you keep doing that, we're never going to get back to sleep."

I aggressively wiggle against him again, and his arms tighten around me, one hand pressing against my stomach under his oversized T-shirt I slept in last night.

He pulls my earlobe between his lips and bites down on it gently. "You're playing with fire, Mrs. Lockwood."

I laugh and slide my hand back between us to grip his hard length, heat already spreading through my body and sizzling across my skin. "But you know how much I enjoy a nice fire, Mr. Lockwood."

My choice of words is intentional, knowing it will bring up memories of two nights ago in front of the fireplace when I gripped the mantle and he fucked me hard from behind, with one hand clamped over my mouth so my screams wouldn't wake Wesley.

Wells grinds against me hard and chuckles. "Almost as much as I enjoy it."

I stroke him in one tight, hard motion, and he groans and thrusts into my hand a few times, making my clit pulse.

"As much as I love the feel of your hand wrapped around my cock, you know there's someplace I would much rather be."

And where I would much rather have him.

Arching back against him, I alter the angle so I can align him directly with where both of us want him to be. He releases a heavy sigh, then thrusts his hips forward, sinking into me slowly, in one long, languid stroke, where I can feel every inch of him.

"Fuck, Laurel, I'll never get tired of this."

I manage to find my breath and squeeze around him. "Of what? Having sex?"

He grips my chin and twists my head back until my eyes meet his. A raging inferno burns across them, the bourbon on fire with a combination of anger and lust. "No, waking up with you in my arms, to this life that we've built together. Waking up happy."

My heart clenches, and tears start to pool in my eyes, just like they do every time he says things like that to me.

Even after three years together, the man still manages to find a way to shatter me completely in an instant.

He rolls his hips and captures my gasp with a searing kiss that makes me clench around him again. His growl of approval rumbles from his chest through my back, and he sets a lazy rhythm that has both of us slick with sweat and panting in only a few moments.

When he does this, keeps things slow and sweet, it always draws out the most cataclysmic releases, the ones that rob me of my breath and leave my heart thundering against my rib cage for hours after.

And he's pushing me closer and closer to that moment with each grind of his hips.

My entire body tenses, coiling and ready to spring with what I know he can do to me, with what he does to me every single time he touches me.

I once wanted all the passion Wells Lockwood held inside him directed at me, and now that I have it, I'm addicted, unable to break away even if I wanted to.

The head of his cock drags against exactly that right spot, and he shifts the hand across my stomach down to roll his calloused thumb over my clit.

Pleasure blasts through me, my body jerking against his as he continues to drive into me, increasing his pace slightly, just the way I like it, to drag my orgasm out longer.

"So fucking beautiful, Laurel."

He kisses me again and, a few thrusts later, empties himself inside me on a strangled groan that reverberates through my body and straight to my heart.

We lie panting for a second, enjoying the post-orgasmic haze, those damn birds chirping away right outside the window.

The bedroom door flies open. "Mommy! Daddy!"

"Fuck." Wells quickly jerks the covers up over us and pulls away, his wet cock slipping easily from inside me, so he can turn toward the door.

Wesley barrels the few short steps to the bed and leaps up on it, a giant grin on his face. "Can we make the cake now?"

Still trying to catch my breath, I roll toward them slightly, pulling the shirt down fully even though he can't see under the covers, and Wesley glances between Wells and me, his sweet little face a mask of hope.

"Can we?"

I reach over and brush his mop of sandy-brown hair from his forehead. "Sure, baby, just give Mommy and Daddy a few minutes. We're just waking up."

Wesley pouts the way that always gets him what he wants from his father.

"You know that doesn't work on me, kiddo, even if your father is a pushover."

Wells casts me an annoyed look and ruffles Wesley's hair, undoing the fix I just made. "A few minutes, buddy, then we'll be out, I promise. Go play."

He releases an annoyed sigh only a toddler can, then climbs from the bed.

"Close the door behind you." I yell the words, knowing full well he probably won't, but he surprises me this time and grabs the doorknob, tugging it closed.

As soon as the latch clicks into place, Wells falls back on the mattress and blows out a heavy sigh. "Fuck, that was close."

I bust out laughing, unable to contain it, and roll toward him, settling my cheek against his hard chest. "We have to start locking the door now that he's waking up so early."

He presses a kiss into my hair and wraps his arm around me. "I know, but that would require us actually remembering to do it when we come to bed, and typically, I have other things on my mind."

Tilting my head up, I rest my chin on him, staring at the grin that's always melted my panties straight off. "Me, too."

But the thought of getting out of bed and making the cake with Wesley sobers my mood almost instantly. I trail my fingers across the tattoo over Wells' heart, writing Diana and Maribel's names. "What time do you want to go?"

His grin slips away. "Later this morning, before it gets too hot and the storms roll in."

I nod, feeling the same sense of loss that I do every year for people I never even met.

Wells drags me up completely across his body, and I press a kiss to his lips, staring into the eyes of the man who has come so far and changed so much yet also stayed the same man he was when he forced me to stay on this mountain.

"We can go whenever you want to, whenever you're ready."

He offers me a sad smile. "I never would've been ready for any of this if it wasn't for you."

"So you keep telling me."

"And I always will." He takes my face between his rough palms and brushes his lips across mine. "I'll keep thanking you until the day I fucking die for giving me life again."

WELLS

The hot sun beats down on us as we make our way across the clearing toward the tree line, Wesley racing ahead.

I glance at Laurel next to me, balancing the cake in her hands. "Are you sure you don't want me to carry that?"

She smiles and shakes her head, her auburn hair practically glowing around her in the sunshine. "I'm good."

"Really?" I grin. "Don't say I never offered to do anything for you."

She smirks. "You do everything for me, Wells, and you know it."

Sometimes it doesn't feel like I do nearly enough for her, considering all the things she's done and continues to do for me.

I lean in and press a kiss to her cheek, swinging the picnic basket and keeping an eye on Wesley, who ducks into the trees. "Wait up, buddy."

That kid never slows down, always going a thousand miles a minute. Sometimes I wonder where he gets it from, but then I remember what I was like as a child and how Mom always said I never sat down for more than a minute at a time.

I let Laurel move in front of me to step onto the path that cuts through the trees, and she whips her head back toward me, brow furrowed.

"What's Wesley doing up there?"

Leaning around her, I finally spot him a few feet ahead, kneeling next to a clump of bright-yellow flowers.

Wesley turns and looks at us as we come to a stop next to him. "These weren't here the other day."

I squat down next to him. "Nope. They pop up pretty quick. Buttercups."

His eyes light up. "They taste like butter?"

I chuckle and shake my head. "No. They're just called that because of their yellow color. You definitely don't eat them."

"Can I bring some with us?"

My heart lightens at the innocence of his question. "Sure. These aren't poisonous."

I cast a pointed look over my shoulder at Laurel.

She scowls at me, those perfect lips twisting down. "Low blow, Wells."

I grin and push to my feet as Wesley begins plucking the flowers and clutching them in his little hand. He's learning about the mountain and everything on it the same way I did when Father and Grandfather brought me up here at his age.

When there aren't any left, Wesley holds them up proudly. "These are perfect."

I ruffle his hair and put my hand on his shoulder to guide him farther down the path, or we may never get there, given the number of distractions the forest holds. "They sure are. Let's get going."

He races ahead again, easily leaping over tree branches and roots, at home on the uneven ground, while Laurel slowly picks her way, slightly unsteady.

She glances back at me, fighting a grin. "I knew those weren't poisonous, you know."

I snicker and catch up with her to press my hand against her lower back. "You have gotten a lot better about that."

"I'm learning."

"And I appreciate not having to call poison control on you."

She rolls her eyes. "Ha. Ha."

The trees start to open up ahead, and without even

thinking about it, both of us slow our walks as we reach the tree line. Wesley has already raced off ahead and now kneels in front of Maribel and Diana's headstones, placing the flowers atop each one.

He turns back as we approach and grins. "Do you think they'd like them?"

Tears burn in my eyes, and I have to choke back the emotion threatening to knock me to my knees before I even make it to him. I take the last few steps on shaky legs, set down the picnic basket, and kneel next to him, tugging him against my side. "They'd love them, buddy."

He beams up at me. "Flowers are great birthday presents, aren't they?"

"They sure are."

Laurel sets the cake on top of the basket and stands behind us, keeping her distance like she always does, though she doesn't have to. She's the one who made all this possible, who made it a happy day when it had always been the one that destroyed me.

She turned this into a celebration of both Maribel's birth and Diana and Maribel's heavenly birth instead of a day full of death and sadness.

I reach out and trail my fingers over Maribel's name, tracing each letter reverently. "Happy birthday, baby girl."

Wesley smiles up at me and moves slightly to the right, knowing where I'm going next.

Reading Diana's name chiseled into the slab still stabs at my gut, but this isn't a day for sadness. I trail my fingers over the letters, then drop my forehead against the headstone. "Happy birthday, Diana. I hope I've been doing things right."

Her voice hasn't come back since the surgeon removed

the tumor, but every once in a while, I feel like it's still there. Like she's still talking to me, telling me I'm being a dick to Landry or one of the other employees, or that I was a little too harsh on Wesley when he does something any child would, or that I'm pushing Laurel a little too hard when it comes to spending too much time up here.

She's always there, always nudging me to do the right thing, even if I can't hear her anymore.

But I know what she'd say about the most recent addition to the family cemetery. I cast a quick glance at the newest tombstone, the one that marks where Wesley's namesake now lies. Even though the man was a shitty father and even tried to have me thrown out of Lockwood Brewing before the heart attack took him and ended the coup, he still deserved to be laid to rest with the family. Diana would be proud I did it, despite the pain seeing Wesley's name there causes.

I climb to my feet and take Wesley's hand in mine, pulling him up. "Should we have some cake and celebrate?"

His eyes widen, and he nods, clapping his hands together. "Yes."

I turn back to find Laurel with tears streaming down her cheeks. She brushes them away quickly so Wesley won't see them and gives a smile that doesn't completely convince me, even though it might him.

Releasing his hand, I take the few steps over to her and pull her against my chest, burying my face against her auburn hair and tugging her close enough to feel her heartbeat against mine.

I don't say anything because I don't have to. Even though we've only been through this a few times together, there's never anything else to say.

We both know what led us to this point, what got us to the happy little family we now have.

It meant a lot of loss, trauma, struggles, and horrible, tragic things that no one should have to live through. But she survived what life threw at her through her tenacity and refusal to back down, and I survived because of her, because of Wesley.

I pull back and tilt up her chin to ensure no more tears fall from her eyes, then press my lips to hers softly.

This time, the smile she gives me is genuine. "Let's cut the cake."

"What kind did you make?"

She hesitates for a split second, as if she's worried her choice might be wrong. "German chocolate. Diana's favorite."

Perfect.

I grin and kiss her again, blown away by how easily she slipped into this role and readily accepted how fucked up I am.

"Ew." Wesley steps between us, nudging his way with his hands at each of our stomachs. "Stop kissing. I want cake."

Three-year-olds have such one-track minds, but I can't blame him for that. His innocence is what saved me. What made me see that my life was worth saving, was worth living.

"Okay, buddy." Laurel slips out of my hold and lifts the cake so I can pull out the blanket from the picnic basket.

I spread it out closer to the trees, where we can have some shade from the hot sun. She sets down the cake while I unpack the plates, cups, and sparkling apple juice we always bring. Wesley kneels next to his mother, bouncing up and down as she slices into the cake, barely containing his excitement. He reaches out and drags his finger through the frosting, then shoves it in his mouth before either one of us can object, but neither one of us would anyway.

Not today.

We've come to appreciate these moments *every* day, but on this birthday, even more so.

It was the day that took my life from me, and the day that brought it back.

I hope you enjoyed *Billionaire Lumberjack's Baby*. Meet another all new reclusive, broken billionaire in *Billionaire Lumberjack's Bride,* the next stand-alone in the Lumberjacks In Love Series!

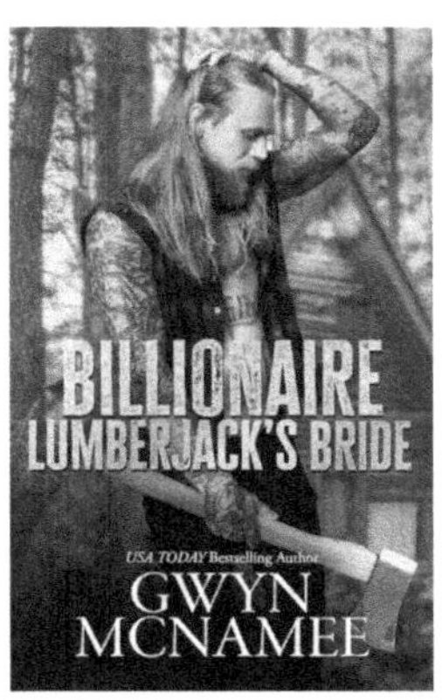

A reclusive billionaire who needs a wife. A woman with no other options. Two lost souls forced together on the mountain…

I never wanted my family's money or the trappings that came with it.

The mountain offered me refuge from it all.

A life filled with hard manual labor, fresh air, and freedom.
Until one unexpected visit from my father's lawyer changes everything.
All we've built will fall into the hands of a monster...
Unless I find a wife.
Fast.
One who can handle living in a single room cabin on a desolate mountain.
With a man who has no intention of ever touching her.
Let alone being an actual husband.
The mail-order bride service offers the perfect solution to my unusual problem.
This woman they're sending needs money.
I need to be hitched in only a handful of weeks.
Nothing but a simple business arrangement.
Once we both get what we want, we can go our separate ways.
Except the longer we share my personal space...
The more what I *want* changes and the fake relationship starts to feel very real...

Grab this steamy stand-alone about a reclusive, damaged, billionaire, the woman he pays to marry him, and what they discover when they're forced together in his cabin with deep wounds and attraction they can't deny!

AVAILABLE NOW: books2read.com/BillionaireLumberjacksBride

Meet the original *Billionaire Lumberjack* Beau in

Billionaire Lumberjack - available now at all retailers! books2read.com/BillionaireLumberjack

To stay up to date on news, releases, and sales from Gwyn, sign up for her newsletter here: www.gwynmcnamee.com/newsletter

About the Author

Gwyn McNamee is an attorney, writer, wife, and mother (to one human baby and two fur babies). Originally from the Midwest, Gwyn relocated to her husband's home town of Las Vegas in 2015 and is enjoying her respite from the cold and snow. Gwyn has been writing down her crazy stories and ideas for years and finally decided to share them with the world. She loves to write stories with a bit of suspense and action mingled with romance and heat.

When she isn't either writing or voraciously devouring any books she can get her hands on, Gwyn is busy adding to her tattoo collection, golfing, and stirring up trouble with her perfect mix of sweetness and sarcasm (usually while wearing heels).

Gwyn loves to hear from her readers. Here is where you can find her:

FB Reader Group: https://www.facebook.com/groups/1667380963540655/

Facebook: https://www.facebook.com/AuthorGwynMcNamee/

Newsletter: www.gwynmcnamee.com/newsletter

Website: http://www.gwynmcnamee.com/Twitter: https://twitter.com/GwynMcNamee

Instagram: https://www.instagram.com/gwynmcnamee

Bookbub: https://www.bookbub.com/authors/gwynmcnamee

Acknowledgments

Thank you to everyone who helped bring Wells and Laurel's story to the page! Renee, Patricia, Stephie, and Caoimhe - I could never do it without you!

OTHER WORKS BY GWYN MCNAMEE

The Hawke Family Series

***Savage Collision* (The Hawke Family - Book One)**

He's everything she didn't know she wanted. She's everything he thought he could never have.

The last thing I expect when I walk into The Hawkeye Club is to fall head over heels in lust. It's supposed to be a rescue mission. I have to get my baby sister off the pole, into some clothes, and out of the grasp of the pussy peddler who somehow manipulated her into stripping. But the moment I see Savage Hawke and verbally spar with him, my ability to remain rational flies out the window and my libido takes center stage. I've never wanted a relationship—my time is better spent focusing on taking down the scum running this city—but what I want and what I need are apparently two different things.

Danika Eriksson storms into my office in her high heels and on her high horse. Her holier-than-thou attitude and accusations should offend me, but instead, I can't get her out of my head or my heart. Her incomparable drive, take-no prisoners attitude, and blatant honesty captivate me and hold me prisoner. I should steer clear, but my self-preservation instinct is apparently dead—which is exactly what our relationship will be once she knows everything. It's only a matter of time.

The truth doesn't always set you free. Sometimes, it just royally screws you.

AVAILABLE AT ALL RETAILERS:

books2read.com/SavageCollision

***Tortured Skye* (The Hawke Family - Book Two)**

She's always been off-limits. He's always just out of reach.

Falling in love with Gabe Anderson was as easy as breathing. Fighting my feelings for my brother's best friend was agonizingly hard. I never imagined giving in to my desire for him would cause such a destructive ripple effect. That kiss was my grasp at a lifeline—something, anything to hold me steady in my crumbling life. Now, I have to suffer with the fallout while trying to convince him it's all worth the consequences.

Guilt overwhelms me—over what I've done, the lives I've taken, and more than anything, over my feelings for Skye Hawke. Craving my best friend's little sister is insanely self-destructive. It never should have happened, but since the moment she kissed me, I haven't been able to get her out of my mind. If I take what I want, I risk losing everything. If I don't, I'll lose her and a piece of myself. The raging storm threatening to rain down on the city is nothing compared to the one that will come from my decision.

Love can be torture, but sometimes, love is the only thing that can save you.

AVAILABLE AT ALL RETAILERS:

Books2read.com/Tortured-Skye

***Stone Sober* (The Hawke Family - Book Three)**

She's innocent and sweet. He's dark and depraved.

Stone Hawke is precisely the kind of man women are warned about— handsome, intelligent, arrogant, and intricately entangled with some dangerous people. I should stay away, but he manages to strip my soul bare with just a look and dominates my thoughts. Bad decisions are in my past. My life is (mostly) on track, even if it is no longer the one to medical school. I can't allow myself to cave to the fierce pull and ardent attraction I feel toward the youngest Hawke.

Nora Eriksson is off-limits, and not just because she's my brother's employee and sister-in-law. Despite the fact she's stripping at The Hawkeye Club, she has an innocent and pure heart. Normally, the only thing that appeals to me about innocence is the opportunity to taint it. But not when it comes to Nora. I can't expose her to the filth permeating my life. There are too many things I can't control, things completely out of my hands. She doesn't deserve any of it, but the power she holds over me is stronger than any addiction.

The hardest battles we fight are often with ourselves, but only through defeating our own demons can we find true peace.

AVAILABLE AT ALL RETAILERS:

books2read.com/StoneSober

Building Storm (The Hawke Family - Book Four)

She hasn't been living. He's looking for a way to forget it all.

My life went up in flames. All I'm left with is my daughter and ashes. The simple act of breathing is so excruciating, there are days I wish I could stop altogether. So I have no business being at the party, and I definitely shouldn't be in the arms of the handsome stranger. When his lips meet mine, he breathes life into me for the first time since the day the inferno disintegrated my world. But loving again isn't in the cards, and there are even greater dangers to face than trying to keep Landon McCabe out of my heart.

Running is my only option. I have to get away from Chicago and the betrayal that shattered my world. I need a new life-one without attachments. The vibrancy of New Orleans convinces me it's possible to start over. Yet in all the excitement of a new city, it's Storm Hawke's dark, sad beauty that draws me in. She isn't looking for love, and we both need a hot, sweaty release without feelings getting involved. But even the best laid plans fail, and life can leave you burned.

Love can build, and love can destroy. But in the end, love is what raises you from the ashes.

Tainted Saint (The Hawke Family - Book Five)

He's searching for absolution. She wants her happily ever after.

Solomon Clarke goes by Saint, though he's anything but. After lusting for him from afar, the masquerade party affords me the anonymity to pursue that attraction without worrying about the fall-out of hooking-up with the bouncer from the Hawkeye Club. From the second he lays his eyes and hands on me, I'm helpless to resist him. Even burying myself in a dangerous investigation can't erase the memory of our combustible connection and one night together. The only problem... he has no idea who I am.

Caroline Brooks thinks I don't see her watching me, the way her eyes rake over me with appreciation. But I've noticed, and the party is the perfect opportunity to unleash the desire I've kept reined in for so damn long. It also sets off a series of events no one sees coming. Events that leave those I love hurting because of my failures. While the guilt eats away at my soul, Caroline continues to weigh on my heart. That woman may be the death of me, but oh, what a way to go.

Life isn't always clean, and sometimes, it takes a saint to do the dirty work.

AVAILABLE AT ALL RETAILERS:

books2read.com/TaintedSaint

Steele Resolve (The Hawke Family - Book Six)

For one man, power is king. For the other, loyalty reigns.

Mob boss Luca "Steele" Abello isn't just dangerous—he's lethal. A master manipulator, liar, and user, no one should trust a word that comes out of his mouth. Yet, I can't get him out of my head. The time we spent together before I knew his true identity is seared into my brain. His touch. His voice. They haunt my every waking hour and occupy my dreams. So does my guilt. I'm literally sleeping with the enemy and betraying the only family I've ever had. When I come clean, it will be the end of me.

Byron Harris is a distraction I can't afford. I never should have let it go beyond that first night, but I couldn't stay away. Even when I learned who he was, when the *only* option was to end things, I kept going back, risking his life and mine to continue our indiscretion. The truth of what I am could get us both killed, but being with the man who's such an integral part of the Hawke family is even more terrifying. The only people I've ever cared about are on opposing sides, and I'm the rift that could end their friendship forever.

Love is a battlefield isn't just a saying. For some, it's a reality.